THE MONSTE

MW01233813

THE HORROR WRITERS ASSOCIATION PRESENTS

StokerCon®

SOUVENIR ANTHOLOGY 2023

EDITED BY

Cynthia Pelayo

Horror Writers
ASSOCIATION

StokerCon
Pittsburgh
2023

StokerCon® 2023 Souvenir Anthology: The Monsters That Made Us

Print ISBN: 978-1-957918-01-3
First Edition: June 2023

Edited by Cynthia Pelayo
Full Book Design by Todd Keisling | Dullington Design Co.
"We Are the Monsters" Mural by Todd Keisling
Art direction by Cynthia Pelayo & Todd Keisling
StokerCon 2023® Logo by Gabrielle Faust
Illustrations by Gemma Amor, Lynne Hansen, Chad Lutzke, & Ryan Mills

Published by Burial Day Books, LLC.
Chicago, Illinois
www.BurialDay.com

TABLE OF CONTENTS

WE ARE THE MONSTERS

A note from the Designer

When Cina pitched the concept to me, my immediate thought was, "*We* are the monsters, and *we* are the monster makers." This informed the overall design, turning the spotlight on us rather than our horrific creations, because what we do today paves the way for the next generation, and so on. As it has been, and as it always will be.

This mural is my attempt at representing this concept. I tried to capture as many horror creators as I could. Young and old, new and established—you'll find writers, artists, actors, and personalities who've contributed to the genre in this mural, and what follows is a row-by-row listing of who they are.

All that said, with a project of this nature, it's impossible to include everyone. Whether you're on this mural or not doesn't matter. What you're doing for the genre—and the trail you're blazing for all who choose to follow—is far more important.

And now…on with the show!

Todd Keisling

WE ARE THE MONSTERS

In Order from Left to Right
Rows from Bottom to Top

Row 1

The Tall Man (Angus Scrimm), Edgar Allan Poe, Mary Shelley, Clive Barker, David Cronenberg, George A. Romero, Daniel Kraus, Stephen King, Linda Addison, Peter Straub, Jack Ketchum (Dallas Mayr), Octavia Butler, Anne Rice, Bram Stoker, Ramsey Campbell, Tananarive Due, Sam Raimi.

Row 2

Mike Flanagan, Mary Lambert, Guillermo Del Toro, David Lynch, Laurel Hightower, Cynthia Pelayo, V. Castro, Gemma Amor, Hailey Piper, Gemma Files, Ellen Datlow, R.J. Joseph, Victor LaValle, Alma Katsu, Owl Goingback, William Peter Blatty, Dean Koontz, Robert McCammon, Red Lagoe.

Row 3

William Hope Hodgson, Arthur Machen, H.P. Lovecraft, Algernon Blackwood, Thomas Ligotti, Joseph S. Pulver, Sr., Michael Cisco, Matthew M. Bartlett, Laird Barron, John Langan, Paul Tremblay,, Stephen Graham Jones, Josh Malerman, E., Jonathan Janz, Kevin Lucia, Ronald Kelly, Bob Ford, Mary SanGiovanni, Brian Keene, J.F. Gonzalez, Caitlin Marceau.

Row 4

M.R. James, Robert Bloch, Jon Padgett, Max Booth III, D. Alexander Ward, Doug Murano, Eric LaRocca, Michael J. Seidlinger, Anthony J. Rapino, Todd Keisling, Kelli Owen, Nikki Nelson-Hicks, Mercedes M. Yardley, Alan Baxter, Adam Nevill, Matt Molgaard, Gabino Iglesias, Harlan Ellison, Wrath James White, Edward Lee, Brian Hodge.

Row 5

Don Coscarelli, Rachel Harrison, Tom Deady, Douglas Wynne, Carol Gyzander, James Chambers, Robert P. Ottone, Amanda Headlee, Tim Meyer, Kenneth W. Cain, Frank Michaels Errington, Sadie Hartmann,

Michelle Renee Lane, Bracken MacLeod, Errick Nunnally, Catherine Scully, Hillary Monahan, Joe R. Lansdale, Karl Edward Wagner, Christopher Golden, Nosferatu (Max Schreck), Lon Chaney.

Row 6

Ash Williams (Bruce Campbell), Darcy the Mail Girl, Joe Bob Briggs, Richard Laymon, Elizabeth Massie, Paula D. Ashe, Chad Lutzke, Lisa Manetti, Brian Kirk, John F.D. Taff, Briana Morgan, Kealan Patrick Burke, Shirley Jackson, Ray Bradbury, Aaron Dries, Tim Waggoner, Wes Craven, Jonathan Maberry, Rena Mason, Lee Murray, Robert W. Chambers, Conrad Veidt, John Carradine.

Row 7

Pod Person (Donald Sutherland), Rod Serling, Tobe Hooper, Richard Chizmar, Jay Wilburn, Armand Rosamilia, Kathe Koja, P.D. Cacek, Sonora Taylor, Charles Grant, Brian Lumley, Ronald Malfi, Bentley Little, Clay McLeod Chapman, John Foster, Nicholas Kaufmann, Koji Suzuki, Samantha Kolesnik, Thomas R. Clark, Stephanie M. Wytovich, Sarah Read, Nadia Bulkin, Dan O'Bannon, Adam Cesare, Dario Argento.

Row 8

Svengoolie, Tom Piccirilli, Patrick Freivald, T.C. Parker, John Palisano, Lisa Morton, John Skipp, Jessica McHugh, Scott Edelman, W.H. Pugmire, Joe Hill, Gwendolyn Kiste, Cassandra Peterson (Elvira), Somer Canon, J.C. Walsh, Lynne Hansen, Jeff Strand, John Boden, Sumiko Saulson, F. Paul Wilson, Rick Hautala, Craig Spector, Richard Thomas, Christi Nogle, Peter Cushing.

Row 9

Rob Zombie, Sara Pinborough, Brian Evenson, Tim Lebbon, Chuck Wendig, Rio Youers, Michael David Wilson, Bob Pastorella, Joe Mynhardt, Michael Burke, R.B. Wood, James Moore, Chuck Palahniuk, Ed Kurtz, doungjai gam, John Edward Lawson, Kristopher Triana, Candace Nola, Livia Llewellyn, Steve Rasnic Tem, Brennan LaFaro, Marquis De Sade, Jeff VanderMeer, Wendy M. Wagner, Neil Gaiman, Sheridan Le Fanu, Boris Karloff.

Row 10

Alice Cooper, Ann Radcliffe, P. Djèlí Clark, Caitlín R. Kiernan, Séphera Girón, S.P. Miskowski, Duncan Ralston, Johnny Compton, Maxwell Ian Gold, Damien Angelica Walters, John Horner Jacobs, Sam Lake, Michael Gray Baughan, Keiichiro Toyama, Shinji Mikami, John Carpenter, Janine Pipe, Kristi DeMeester, Paul Michael Anderson, Michael Bailey, Greg Chapman, Cassandra Khaw, Gaby Triana, Daphne du Maurier, Ambrose Bierce, Ross Jeffery, V.C. Andrews, Vincent Price.

Row 11

Papa Emeritus III, Dennis Etchison, Brian Matthews, Lawrence Watt-Evans, Gary Braunbeck, Joseph Nassise, David Niall Wilson, Deborah LeBlanc, Jacob Haddon, Katherine Silva, Billy Martin, Maurice Broaddus, Catriona Ward, Grady Hendrix, L. Marie Wood, Dr. Chesya Burke, Silvia Moreno-Garcia, Mark Miller, Alasdair Stewart, Sara Tantlinger, Garrett Haines, Lucy Snyder, Benjamin T. Rubin, S.P. Somtow, Craig Shaw Gardner, Cindy O'Quinn, Edward Gorey, Christopher Lee.

Row 12

Aleister Crowley, Trevor Henderson, Steve Stred, Usman Malik, Preston Fassel, Justin Holley, Michael Tyree, Jessica Leonard, Robert Aickman, Manly Wade Welman, Chelsea Quinn Yarbro, William "Chilly Billy" Cardille, Michael Arnzen, Jewelle Gomez, Karen Lansdale, Kevin Wetmore, C.W. Briar, Becky Spratford, Jonathan Lees, John Russo, Christa Carmen, J.A.W. McCarthy, Richard Matheson, Teri Clarke (Zin E. Rocklyn), E.V. Knight, Bridgett Nelson, Mike Thorn, Daniel Barnett, Ai Jiang, Dave Jeffery, Bela Lugosi.

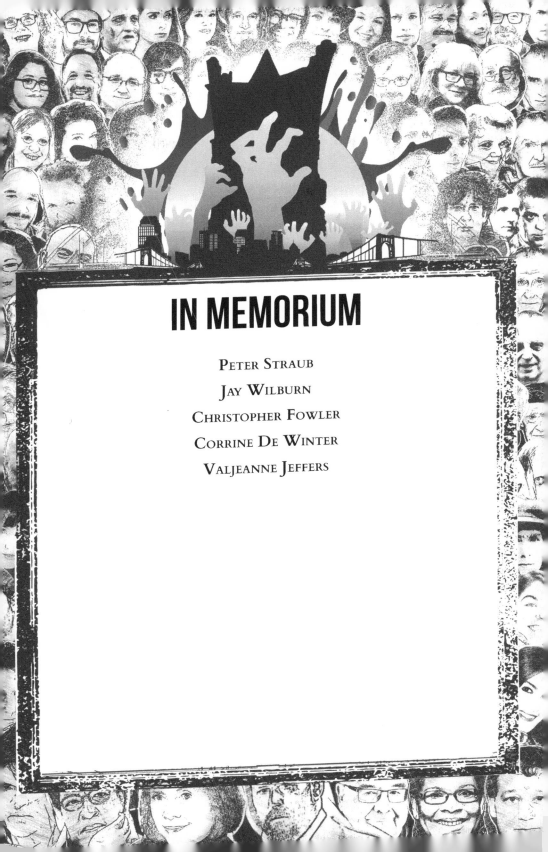

IN MEMORIUM

PETER STRAUB

JAY WILBURN

CHRISTOPHER FOWLER

CORRINE DE WINTER

VALJEANNE JEFFERS

REMEMBERING PETER STRAUB

Peter's Ghost

I miss Peter Straub. I think the last communication I had with him came about a year before he died. Via Twitter, he told me that he was feeling better than he had in a while and was looking forward to getting back to writing. A few months after this, I watched what would be his final podcast appearance, on Patrick McDonough and Brennan LaFaro's *Dead Headspace*. It was a long, generous interview, and while Peter looked as gaunt as I had ever seen him, he was in good spirits, gregarious and insightful. After that, he was supposed to appear on Neil McRobert's *Talking Scared* but had to cancel. Henry Wagner posted a picture of the two of them to social media and Peter was shrunken, though his face remained bright and lively. Somewhere in the midst of all this, I learned he had been put on a portable device designed to keep his heart pumping. I guess it shouldn't have come as a surprise when Paul Tremblay texted that Peter was gone, but it stunned me all the same. The room receded and it was as if I was looking at my phone in a dark space. Later, I told my wife the news, and she made the noise you make when a dear friend dies.

The thing is, I didn't know Peter especially well. I taught his novels, *Ghost Story* and *Shadowland*. I wrote a long review of his novel, *In the Night Room*, for the *Internet Review of Science Fiction*. I spoke with him at a number of conventions. We were on at least one panel together. I attended a couple of his readings in New York. He said very nice things about my first novel. I wrote an appreciation of his work for the Readercon souvenir book the year he was guest of honor. I visited him at his brownstone on the upper west side of Manhattan twice, the first time with Laird Barron, the second alone. I conducted a long phone interview with him for the inaugural issues of *Nightmare* magazine. He wrote very nice things about my second novel. I exchanged messages with him on a variety of social media platforms, mostly livejournal and Twitter.

I didn't spend nearly as much time with him as I would have liked. After conventions we had both attended, I would see photos he posted of late-night vigils spent in the hotel lobby, to which he had been driven by the neuropathy that burned away his sleep. If only I had known, I thought, I would have sat up with him, kept him company. When he and Susan, his fabulous wife, relocated to Brooklyn, I thought I should visit him at the new place, but I felt awkward inviting myself over, so I didn't.

While there are still video interviews of Peter available, for which I am grateful, my principal relationship with him now is through his writing, which is how I first came to know him. Stephen King had written astutely and appreciatively of *Ghost Story* in his non-fiction study, *Danse Macabre*, which led me to seek out the novel at my local library. *Ghost Story* did not have the same immediate effect on me as King's *Christine*, which in one fell swoop had made me a writer, and a horror writer, to boot, directing all my creative energy to a single end. In contrast, *Ghost Story* left me sure a great deal of what I had read had flown right over my head. But there was no resentment attached to this impression, no anger at a writer pointing out my limitations to me. Instead, I felt a kind of gratitude knowing this was a book I could and would return to in short order. I think I appreciated *Shadowland*, which I read soon after, more, in no small part because its protagonist was a teenage boy not much older than was I. But I still closed the book with the same sensation I had with *Ghost Story*, that there was a great deal going on here I had not understood. Again, though, my response to this realization was to be thankful. I'm reasonably sure these were the first times I had such reactions to literary works I knew I didn't fully understand.

And indeed, if I had to offer a sweeping generalization for what Peter achieved in his fiction, it was to write novels and stories that never finished speaking to the reader. Of course I returned to both novels. Each time I did, I understood more of what I was reading, even as I found more to understand. I had the same experience with Peter's subsequent works, with *Koko*, *The Throat*, *The Hellfire Club*, *lost boy lost girl*. He was, if you will, building enormous houses, great structures with many rooms of different sizes and configurations, full of winding hallways and secret corridors, staircases to windows with hidden views, labyrinthine basements and cavernous attics. These were spaces you could walk around in for as long as you wanted. In a few cases, Peter had used a similar frame to structure his books, but their interiors were markedly different. There were connections among many of the narratives. Some were direct passages from one book to another; others were stone pathways snaking between fictional locales. The result was less a distinct geographical region, a Yoknapatawpha or Castle Rock, than a kind of neighborhood of the soul.

It feels a little too glib, a little too pat, to say I can return to this neighborhood whenever I want: all I have to do is take one of Peter's books down from the shelf. But it's a kind of obstinacy to insist there is no consolation to be found in the work to which he devoted his life. Maybe you know Borges's line about writers becoming their books after they die; which, he says, is not a bad

afterlife. There's enough truth to the statement for me to mention it here. I still miss him, but it's past time I paid a visit to one of the grand, sprawling houses that populate Peter Straub's afterlife.

John Langan

REMEMBERING JAY WILBURN

I can't remember the first time I met Jay Wilburn, but I can remember the first time he saw me naked. It was the 71st World Science Fiction Convention, which fell on the weekend of August 19-September 2, 2013, in San Antonio, TX. My girlfriend (now wife) Lori Michelle and I launched our small press Perpetual Motion Machine Publishing (now Ghoulish Books) in the summer of 2012, and our first couple titles released in 2013—including Jay Wilburn's time-traveling cannibal novel *Time Eaters*, which was why he flew out to Worldcon that year.

At the time, I was also working the night shift at a hotel. Jay flew in early that afternoon (probably a Thursday or Friday). I came home and went to sleep, and Lori went off to pick him up from the airport. When they made it back to the house, Jay thought it would be funny if he snuck into our bedroom and woke me up himself. So that's exactly what he did. He crept up to the bed and ripped the blanket off my body.

I should mention that for *reasons* that day I had fallen asleep completely naked.

Actually, come to think about it, this might have been the first time we actually met, too.

I screamed. He screamed. Then one of us started laughing, which turned out to be contagious, because for the next nine years of our personal and professional relationship we found ourselves laughing quite often while in each other's presence.

It was also during this festival that his kidney issues started becoming a problem, which he tried to hide. I remember standing with him next to a crosswalk one afternoon during the convention. He grabbed his side and fell down. I don't think he quite understood how severe his kidney issues were yet, but he would find out soon enough. I helped pick him up to his feet and asked him if he was okay. He nodded and gave me a little hug and said, "Thanks, man."

I am writing this a decade later, and all I want to do is give him another hug and tell him the same thing.

You were a true friend, and I miss you so much.

Thanks, man.

Max Booth III

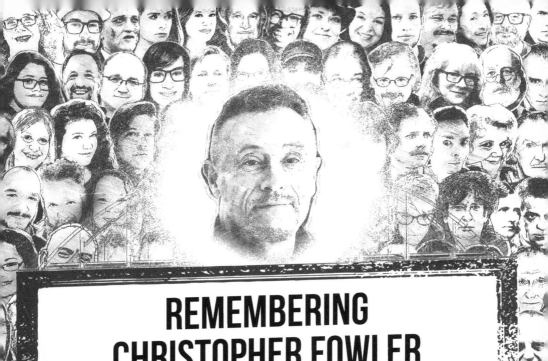

REMEMBERING CHRISTOPHER FOWLER

Saddened to hear of Christopher Fowler's passing. I hadn't seen Chris for a few years and mainly knew him from the period when I lived in London, attended Fantasycon every year and rarely missed a BFS Open Night in Holborn or London Bridge. Chris often invited me to his book launches too, with drinks afterwards at the Phoenix on the Charing Cross Road and we once did an event together in Foyles.

My fondest memory was a lock-in with him, in a pub, after an Open Night. I was a relatively new writer with one book to my name and I'd been reading Chris for years - his books were stalwarts in the horror section of Waterstones in the 90s when I lived in Brum - and I looked up to him as an established author and couldn't quite believe that I was chatting horror with him after hours in a pub.

When *Apartment 16* was published, and that was a big deal for me, Chris had read the book and came and shared some of the kindest words a veteran writer has ever said to me.

It was a real moment of confirmation that I treasure.

The last book of his I read was *Nyctophobia*, his highly atmospheric and sensory ghost story set in Spain. One of the best I read that year and I'm surprised it's not more well known.

I was always impressed with how much he wrote, the quality of his work, as well as his leading an interesting life at the same time. He was an example of how writing hard but also living a full life is not only possible but essential.

Fondly remembered and a real loss to British fantasy.

Adam Nevill

REMEMBERING CORRINE DE WINTER

I n August 2022, we lost poet and author Corrine De Winter.
I'll never forget meeting Corrine De Winter. Like movie stars, she and Lisa Mannetti rolled into the Burbank, California World Horror / Bram Stoker Awards®. Lisa was a tough-talking, chain-smoking tornado who felt like you knew her forever after talking to her for only a few minutes. Corrine had long, Raphaliette blond hair that went to her waist. They both looked like they magically appeared from the silver screen. Not only were they both charismatic, but they both also took home Bram Stoker Awards® that weekend.

Over many years, Corrine and I became good friends. She worked tirelessly at her art and craft. It was always a great day to receive her poetry chapbooks and collections. She covered some vast ground, from deep, spiritual journeys, through a collection centered around and grieving Kurt Cobain, to even darker, more challenging paths. It's on those paths where her empathy and soulfulness shined. During a rough patch in my own life, she reached out and even sent me a refrigerator magnet with a snippet of one of her pieces that I could look to. How cool and thoughtful is that? While prepping to write this, I found the last message she ever sent me, a short time before she passed. Selfless. Giving. Hopeful. 100% Corrinne.

And it wasn't just me. So many people felt touched … their lives made immeasurably better … by knowing her. She'd often call out on social media to gift people Tarot readings to help people in her unique style. She was a real blessing to many. It's said the brightest stars shine the most, and I know somewhere she's reading this and I hope she's happy and at peace.

Corrine brought her deep connection to nature and her rhythms wherever she was. Be it her poetry, storytelling, readings, or even with an email. She possessed a truly singular poetic voice. It's no wonder her resume is so vast and her collaborations and celebrations. She will be missed terribly alongside Lisa Mannetti, who predeceased Corrine almost a year to the day.

When I close my eyes I see them both––shimmering and glowing––living on in so many wonderful memories.

ABOUT CORRINE

CORRINE DE WINTER was a Bram Stoker Award®-winning poet and author who won numerous awards for her writing from the New York Quarterly, Triton College of Arts & Sciences, & The Rhysling Science Fiction Award. Such luminaries have applauded her work as William Peter Blatty, Tom Monteleone, Thomas Ligotti, Nick Cave, Stanley Wiater, James Sclavunos, Heather Graham, Harry O. Morris, and many others.

William Packard, a former editor of the New York Quarterly, was a mentor, publishing De Winter's work early on and inviting her to write "The Present State of American Poetry," a regular feature in the journal. At Packard's invitation, she read her poetry at the New School and continued a rapport with Packard until his passing. Packard was a big supporter of Charles Bukowski and De Winter published with him several times in his last years.

De Winter was known for her poetry collection *Touching The Wound-Poems in memory of Kurt Cobain*, which sold over 6,000 copies in the first year.

De Winter won the Bram Stoker Award® in 2005 for her collection *The Women At The Funeral*.

Five of her books have been Stoker Nominated.

John Palisano

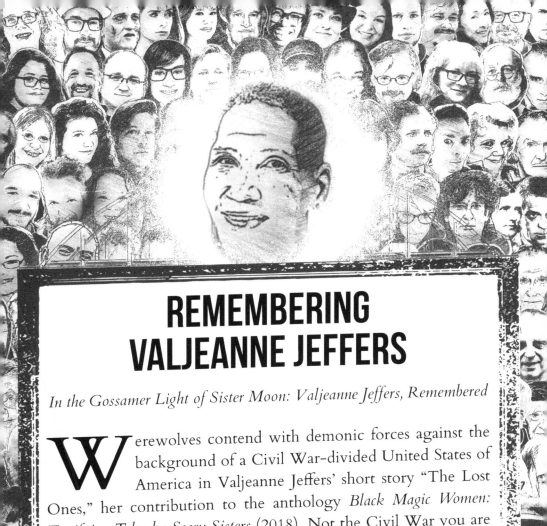

REMEMBERING VALJEANNE JEFFERS

In the Gossamer Light of Sister Moon: Valjeanne Jeffers, Remembered

Werewolves contend with demonic forces against the background of a Civil War-divided United States of America in Valjeanne Jeffers' short story "The Lost Ones," her contribution to the anthology *Black Magic Women: Terrifying Tales by Scary Sisters* (2018). Not the Civil War you are likely thinking of, but an alternate timeline where the Civil Rights movement of the fifties lead to a separation of the United States into two separate countries, North America and True America. The story takes place in the same part of the Jeffersverse as her trilogy of paranormal steamfunk novels about Mona Livelong: Paranormal Detective. An excerpt from one of her Mona stories, "The Case of the Powerless Witch," appeared in the Bram Stoker Award®-nominated anthology *Sycorax's Daughters* (2017).

Well-developed, complex worlds filled with multicultural paranormal creatures were her forte, the kind of thing one might associate with LA Banks or Charlaine Harris, worlds that exist where dark fantasy and urban fantasy meet. The other major arm of the Jeffersverse was the Immortal series, featuring time-traveling shapeshifting Lycans and sorcerers. In *The Immortals IV: Collision of Worlds* (2017), the two franchises combine.

Her books featured the art of her longtime boyfriend Quenton Veal, a poet, and artist with whom she co-edited the anthologies *Scierogenous I: An Anthology of Erotic Science Fiction and Fantasy* and its sequel *Scierogenous II.* A testament to Black Love, the two were inseparable.

Valjeanne was a weaver of worlds, but beyond her craft as an author and editor, she was one of those people who cast a loving light into the corners of the world they touch. A kind and warm person, she was well-loved by all of those she met, be it in person or online, where she was known as Sister Moon.

Thaddeus Howze, a fellow member of the Black Science Fiction Society who knew her for more than a decade, calls her this in his August 3, 2022 memorial piece, "A Name to Conjure By: Sister Moon" which ran in the *San Francisco BayView.* In the article, he lovingly recalls, "She had a way of connecting with you, no matter how you knew her, a familiarity which made you feel like family, no matter the distance between you."

Like Thaddeus, I never had the pleasure of meeting Valjeanne in person. In an alternate timeline, we would have met in person for the first time on March 27, 2020. I would have taken a plane to Atlanta, Georgia, and we would have spent three days at the beginning of spring bumping into each other on panel discussions or in the halls at The Outer Dark Symposium on The Greater Weird. No doubt, we would have had lunch together.

She lived in Talladega, Alabama. I lived all the way across the country in Oakland, California, yet from the moment we met, we got along really well and from 2014 onward, she was a part of my life, enough so that at times it seemed at times as if she lived just up the block. In mourning her loss, I was often saddened by the fact that the pandemic stole away our chances of meeting in person.

The first time I spoke to her on the phone, I remember her patiently explaining how to pronounce her name, Valjeanne. She was named after Jean Valjean from the Victor Hugo novel *Les Miserables*, and her name was pronounced the same way, the "Jeanne" is pronounced more like "Joan" than "Jean"—most accurately, like something halfway between "Joan" and "John", just like Jean-Luc Picard on *Star Trek*. Her mom was a huge fan of the play.

During those hopeful days of early 2020, none of us expected the still-distant news trickling in from overseas about a new virus to hit us hard here at home. Then, on March 4th, we got a message from the convention: it had to be postponed because of COVID-19. A couple of weeks later, the government started issuing restrictions on air travel, and some of us were asked to shelter in place and stay home.

Valjeanne and I still thought we would be meeting later that year. The news was saying the restrictions would only last for a few months. But in August, the restrictions were still in place, and The Outer Dark Symposium on The Greater Weird took place online. We didn't meet in person, but we were on a virtual panel together for Clockwork Alchemy, and several episodes of *The Erotic Storytelling Hour*. We even worked on a literary arts project to be presented at the virtual version of Burning Man in the video game *Second Life* back in 2021. We saw a lot of each other in 2020 and 2021: just not in person.

As things started to open up again in late 2021, it felt like it was inevitable: sooner or later, we'd be at the same convention, and we'd meet one another face to face.

Then, in February 2022, I was interviewing authors for the Horror Writers Association's Black Heritage Month blog series when I received the heartrending news that Valjeanne was coming toward the end of her life. She let me know that she was very ill and asked if I could interview her over the phone, rather than via email, because of her illness. I said yes, of course, and proceeded to type up her answers as she dictated them to me over the phone. Valjeanne told me at the time that she didn't think she'd be around very much longer. I asked her if there was anything I could do, and she spoke in glowing terms of her longtime boyfriend Quenton Veal checking on her regularly.

Just six months later, she was gone, taking her remarkable light from the world and leaving so many of us grieving. Valjeanne passed away on July 18, 2022, at the age of 62, due to what family members described as an extended illness. Nonetheless, her legacy lives, not just in her body of work but in the way she impacted virtually everyone with whom she came into contact.

If you haven't read any of her work, I encourage you to start here: Valjeanne's stories have appeared in many anthologies—*The Ringing Ear: Black Poets Lean South* (2007), *Steamfunk* (2013); *Griots: Sisters of the Spear* (2013); *Fitting In: Historical Accounts of Paranormal Subcultures* (2016); the Bram Stoker Award®-nominated *Sycorax's Daughters* (2017); *The City: A Cyberfunk Anthology* (2015); *Blacktastic: Blacktastic Con 2018 Anthology* (2018); *Dark Universe: The Bright Empire* (2018); *Luminescent Threads: Connections to Octavia Butler* (2017); *Blerdrotica I: Sweet, Sexy, and Special Dark* (2020); and many others. In addition to her novels, she released a short story collection in 2014, *Voyage of Dreams: A Collection of Otherwordly Stories*.

I had the pleasure of sharing a number of tables of contents with her, including the anthologies *Scierogenous II: An Anthology of Erotic Science Fiction and Fantasy* (2018), *Black Magic Women: Terrifying Tales by Scary Sisters* (2018), *Black Celebration: Amazing Articles on African American Horror* (2019), *Slay: Tales of the Vampire Noire* (Mocha Memoirs Press, 2020), and *Horror Addicts Guide to Life 2* (2022). I shared a table of contents with her for what is likely the last release of her new original work, *Blerdrotica II: Couple's*

Therapy, which was released in December 2022, half a year after she joined the ancestors.

Valjeanne was a proud member of the Carolina African American Writers' Collective (CAAWC) and the Horror Writers Association (HWA) and an uplifting presence in the horror writing community and on the speculative fiction convention circuit. Her contributions to the horror genre were many, including her werewolf series *The Immortals*. She deftly combined horror with crime noir and cyberfunk in her series *Mona Livelong: Paranormal Detective*. She was an important figure in the cyberfunk and steamfunk genres, which combine Afrofuturism and Afrosurrealism with cyberpunk and steampunk respectively. She was groundbreaking as a woman in the steamfunk genre, appearing in many key anthologies alongside names like Milton Davis and Balogun Ojetade.

Valjeanne Jeffers Thompson was 62 when she passed away on July 18, 2022, after an extended illness. She was surrounded by her family and loved ones. Valjeanne was preceded in death by her Father, Lance Jeffers Sr; Sister, Sidonie Jeffers; and Beloved Dog, Cesar Thompson. She is survived by her Mother, Dr. Trellie L Jeffers; Sister, Honoree Jeffers; Brother, Lance Jeffers, Jr; Daughter, Gabrielle Morris (and her husband Billy); Grandchildren Logan and Gracie Morris; Son, Toussaint Thompson (and his wife Kyla); Grandchildren Kody and Kyle Thompson; Beloved Cat, Cleopatra Thompson; and Special Friend, Quinton Veal.

Valjeanne attended Hillside High School in Durham, NC, and graduated from Spelman College, with a degree in Psychology. She earned a Master's Degree in Psychology from Central University in Durham. She was a certified mental health professional for many years, but her heart belonged to the literary arts.

Sumiko Saulson

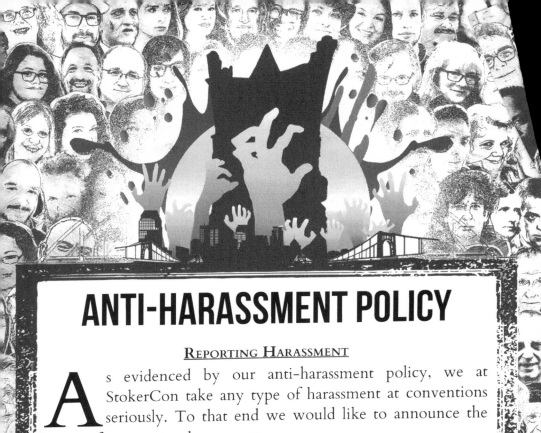

ANTI-HARASSMENT POLICY

REPORTING HARASSMENT

As evidenced by our anti-harassment policy, we at StokerCon take any type of harassment at conventions seriously. To that end we would like to announce the process for reporting harassment.

All of the StokerCon staff and volunteers will be identifiable by their specially-marked badges. Each volunteer will be briefed before the con begins on StokerCon's anti-harassment policy and on how to handle reporting. If anyone sees or experiences an instance of harassment, they can bring their complaint to a volunteer or event staff.

Additionally, we have created an email address specifically for this issue. That address is complaint@stokercon.com. Anyone who sees or experiences harassment can, if they aren't comfortable speaking to someone in person, file their complaint through that email address.

All complaints will be immediately brought to the Convention Chair(s). They will then follow-up with any needed communication or investigation. If they determine that a formal investigation is called for, they will follow the procedure outlined below.

As said, we take this topic very seriously and want to ensure that everyone who attends StokerCon has a great time free from any type of harassment.

FORMAL INVESTIGATION OF COMPLAINTS

Using guidelines set forth by the U.S. Equal Opportunity Employment Commission (at https://www.eeoc.gov/policy/docs/harassment.html) and procedures established for use by other non-profit organizations, HWA/StokerCon's procedure for investigation of harassment complaints is as follows:

1. **REPORT** – Reports of harassment that occurred at one of HWA's StokerCon events should be made to complaint@stokercon.com. The initial report should include the date and location of the incident(s), contact information for any witnesses, and as much detail as possible.

2. **CONFIDENTIALITY AND PROTECTION FROM RETALIATION** – HWA/StokerCon will protect the confidentiality of harassment allegations to the extent possible. HWA cannot guarantee complete confidentiality, since it cannot conduct an effective investigation without revealing certain information to the alleged harasser (the respondent) and potential witnesses. However, information about the allegation of harassment will be shared only with those who need to know about it. Records relating to harassment complaints will be kept confidential on the same basis. HWA/StokerCon will also work to protect complainants against retaliation.

3. **DETERMINING IF AN INVESTIGATION IS NEEDED** – As soon as HWA/StokerCon learns about alleged harassment, it will determine whether a detailed fact-finding investigation is necessary. For example, if the alleged harasser does not deny the

accusation, there would be no need to interview witnesses, and HWA/StokerCon could immediately determine appropriate corrective action.

4. INVESTIGATION PROCEDURE – If a fact-finding investigation is determined to be necessary, HWA's management or administrator will conduct the investigation as soon as possible. The investigation will objectively gather and consider the relevant facts. When detailed fact-finding is necessary, the investigator(s) will interview the complainant, the alleged harasser, and third parties who could reasonably be expected to have relevant information. Information relating to the personal lives of the parties outside the workplace would be relevant only in unusual circumstances.

5. CONDUCTING INTERVIEWS – The following are examples of questions that may be appropriate to ask the parties and potential witnesses. Any actual investigation must be tailored to the particular facts.

QUESTIONS TO ASK THE COMPLAINANT

- Who, what, when, where, and how: Who committed the alleged harassment? What exactly occurred or was said? When did it occur and is it still ongoing? Where did it occur? How often did it occur? How did it affect you?
- How did you react? What response did you make when the incident(s) occurred or afterwards?
- How did the harassment affect you? Has your career been affected in any way?
- Are there any persons who have relevant information? Was anyone present when the alleged harassment occurred? Did you tell anyone about it? Did anyone see you immediately after episodes of alleged harassment?

- Did the person who harassed you harass anyone else? Do you know whether anyone complained about harassment by that person?
- Are there any notes, physical evidence, or other documentation regarding the incident(s)?
- How would you like to see the situation resolved?
- Do you know of any other relevant information?

QUESTIONS TO ASK THE ALLEGED HARASSER

- What is your response to the allegations?
- If the harasser claims that the allegations are false, ask why the complainant might lie.
- Are there any persons who have relevant information?
- Are there any notes, physical evidence, or other documentation regarding the incident(s)?
- Do you know of any other relevant information?

QUESTIONS TO ASK THIRD PARTIES

- What did you see or hear? When did this occur? Describe the alleged harasser's behavior toward the complainant and toward others in the workplace.
- What did the complainant tell you? When did s/he tell you this?
- Do you know of any other relevant information?
- Are there other persons who have relevant information?

6. CREDIBILITY DETERMINATIONS – If there are conflicting versions of relevant events, HWA will have to weigh each party's credibility. Credibility assessments can be critical in determining whether the alleged harassment in fact occurred.

FACTORS TO CONSIDER INCLUDE:

- Inherent plausibility: Is the testimony believable on its face? Does it make sense?

- Demeanor: Did the person seem to be telling the truth or lying?
- Motive to falsify: Did the person have a reason to lie?
- Corroboration: Is there witness testimony (such as testimony by eye-witnesses, people who saw the person soon after the alleged incidents, or people who discussed the incidents with him or her at around the time that they occurred) or physical evidence (such as written documentation) that corroborates the party's testimony?
- Past record: Did the alleged harasser have a history of similar behavior in the past?

7. PREPONDERANCE OF EVIDENCE – In most civil cases/lawsuits as well as administrative hearings, a party must prove its claim or position by a preponderance, defined as a superiority in weight, force, importance, etc. In legal terms, a preponderance of evidence means that a party has shown that its version of facts, causes, damages, or fault is more likely than not the correct version, as in personal injury and breach of contract suits. This standard is the easiest to meet and applies to all civil cases unless otherwise provided by law.

8. REACHING A DETERMINATION – Once all of the evidence is in, interviews are finalized, and credibility issues are resolved, HWA's Board of Trustees will be presented with the evidence, will make a determination as to whether harassment occurred, and determine appropriate action. The parties will be informed of the determination.

9. APPEALING THE DECISION – The complainant or respondent may request a reconsideration of the case in instances where they are dissatisfied with the outcome. The appeal must be made within five (5) calendar days of the date of the written notification of the findings. An appeal must be in writing and specify the basis for the appeal. The original finding is presumed to be reasonable and appropriate based on a preponderance of the evidence. The only grounds for appeal are as follows:

- New information discovered after the investigation that could not have reasonably been available at the time of the investigation and is of a nature that could materially change the outcome;
- Procedural errors within the investigation or resolution process that may have substantially affected the fairness of the process;
- An outcome (findings or sanctions) that was manifestly contrary to the weight of the information presented (i.e., obviously unreasonable and unsupported by the great weight of information).

The HWA Board

LETTER FROM THE EDITOR

Dracula. Frankenstein's Monster. The Bride of Frankenstein. The Wolfman. The Mummy. The Invisible Man. The Creature From the Black Lagoon. The Phantom of the Opera. The Zombie! More. So many more.

To some people, these monsters are terrible things that should not be spoken about or even celebrated. To me, these monsters were my friends when I was a little girl, and today they continue to comfort and inspire me.

I grew up watching monster movies on a small black and white television my father purchased for me at a thrift store. Later on, he bought me a VCR. He walked me over to our neighborhood video rental place, BP Video, and got a membership card. I remember it was this tan, laminated card with his name and customer number printed on it. I believe we were number 13, one of the first families in the neighborhood to get one. This was before Blockbuster Video came to our area.

The horror section I remember was right in front. I'd walk in, turn left and there it was against the wall, rows of glossy boxes with all sorts of creatures staring back at me. I'd rent four or five videos every week, watch whatever horror films were being featured by Svengoolie that Saturday, and more. I'd stay up late at night watching horror movies, my monsters on my screen, because they were one of the few comforts I had.

We all love horror. That is why we are here. We all love these monsters, and I believe each and every one of us here at StokerCon has a story about how we watched a horror movie as we were feeling sadness, or grief, loss, or worry. Each of us has a story about how these monsters helped us process the world around us, to help us understand the cruelty in the world. These monsters also helped us understand who we are. These monsters made us.

In editing this StokerCon Souvenir book I thought it was fitting to celebrate all of these monsters that graced our television screens, that peered out at us from between the lines of books and that we continue to reach out to in the darkness for inspiration.

Thank you so much for joining us in Pittsburg. I also want to send a big thank you to Todd Keisling, Sara Tantlinger, Ben Rubin, Mike Arnzen, Garrett Haines and all of the contributors of this souvenir book.

Thank you,

Cynthia "Cina" Pelayo

LETTER FROM THE PRESIDENT

I've always been partial to bad guys.

If you come from a marginalized community like I do, you eventually recognize a lot of the folk heroes in your oral traditions would be considered villains by the establishment, because they are unconventional and defy the standard way of doing things.

These are certainly unconventional times during which we hold StokerCon, with many of the old standards gone for one reason or another. From the onset of artificial intelligence in the creative arts to the Writers Guild of America strike, to disruptions in the economy, and sweeping social changes like the return of book burnings and banning, we're collectively trying to find a path forward.

My father, he was fond of the Roaring Twenties. It was the decade before he was born and, the way he talked about it, it was the golden era to end all golden eras. Silly me, I was looking forward to see what our Twenties would be like after 100 years of progress, but a lot of folks consider it a dumpster fire so far.

The evolution of horror over the last century tells us a different story. What defines horror and dark fantasy and thrillers has evolved to include all people and traditions. We're increasingly finding elements of splatterpunk and supernatural horror and time-honored horror classics popping up across all the other genres in popular media. Seems like folks in other genres realized audiences are hungry for horror because it helps them make sense of real-world upheaval, giving them a chance to safely observe others navigate chaos and conflict. In that way we're shining the light in the darkness, allowing everyone else to find their way.

Fortunately, the team put in place through volunteerism and Horror Writers Association (HWA) elections is proactive. Instead of letting the general tide of interest in horror carry us until the trend fades, the HWA has been aggressively working to expand our infrastructure and community building. The new Veterans Committee was successfully launched by David Rose with the support of HWA Secretary Becky Spratford. The Mental Health Awareness Committee has expanded their initiatives to include a Notable Books Reading List. We are also recognizing those who paved the way for us by featuring our elders in the community, alongside efforts to recognize our invaluable volunteers both in person at StokerCon and online. To further break down barriers within the organization we launched our quarterly HWA Town Hall Meetings where members can interact with the Board to learn what's happening behind the scenes directly from our Officers and Trustees.

Even with all the supportive work we do the horror community is still seen by some as a place full of misfits and weirdos and—you guessed it—bad guys, because we defy expectation. The cool thing about that has been watching so many people in recent years realize they have more in common with marginalized communities than they thought, and maybe they can see why we operate outside the standard system as storytellers.

So, our Twenties decade is shaping up to be a new golden age, all right. A new golden age of horror. That path forward we're all searching for? Horror is paving the way. And one thing we know as writers is that the bad guy drives the plot, so it only makes sense that this is our time.

Thank you for helping make it happen.

John Lawson

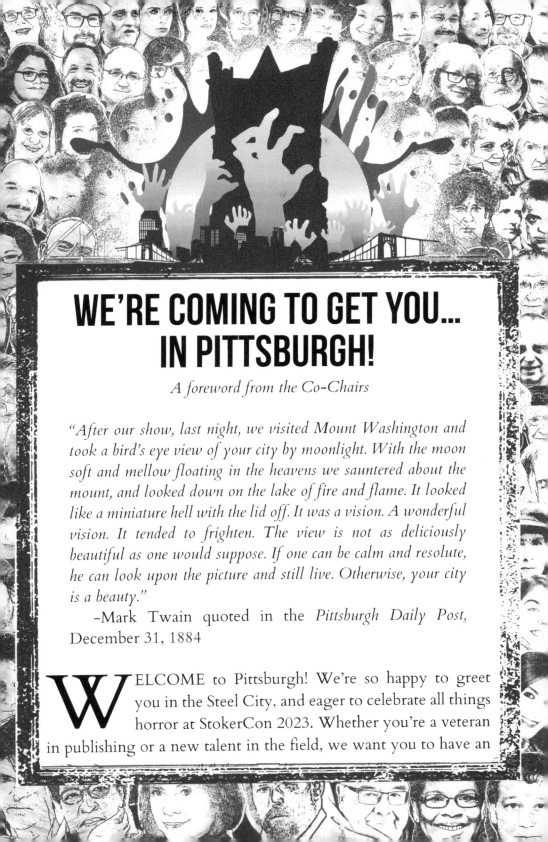

WE'RE COMING TO GET YOU... IN PITTSBURGH!

A foreword from the Co-Chairs

"After our show, last night, we visited Mount Washington and took a bird's eye view of your city by moonlight. With the moon soft and mellow floating in the heavens we sauntered about the mount, and looked down on the lake of fire and flame. It looked like a miniature hell with the lid off. It was a vision. A wonderful vision. It tended to frighten. The view is not as deliciously beautiful as one would suppose. If one can be calm and resolute, he can look upon the picture and still live. Otherwise, your city is a beauty."

-Mark Twain quoted in the *Pittsburgh Daily Post*, December 31, 1884

WELCOME to Pittsburgh! We're so happy to greet you in the Steel City, and eager to celebrate all things horror at StokerCon 2023. Whether you're a veteran in publishing or a new talent in the field, we want you to have an unforgettable experience. At StokerCon, we gather both virtually and in person to exchange ideas, tell stories, learn from the masters, party with old friends, watch movies, pitch, sell and buy books, make new friends in the industry and party some more as we applaud the best horror writing of the year in the Bram Stoker Award® ceremony.

Pittsburgh has a lot to offer; it is more education and medicine these days than forges and fires that inspired Mr. Twain's quote above, but if you can spare a moment, we hope you'll get to know the city, and possibly even explore our roots in the horror genre. We're known as the birthplace of the zombie film, as the late filmmaker George Romero famously filmed *Night of the Living Dead* at the nearby Evans City Cemetery with a cast of Pittsburgh talent, and he would go on to shoot the majority of his classic pictures in the region, from *Martin* to *Monkey Shines*. Today, his legacy lives on in the George A. Romero Archival Collection housed at the University of Pittsburgh Library System, a collection which also features the Horror Writers Association memorabilia, and papers by several of our talented authors. These collections, which are open to all researchers and fans alike, help make Pittsburgh a repository for the history of the genre and establish the city as a destination to study horror.

CableTV.com rated Pennsylvania as the #1 "Deadliest State" ... according to horror film settings, anyway, and Romero may be chiefly responsible for that. But Hannibal "the Cannibal" Lecter also famously escaped from prison here, and his colleague Buffalo Bill lived in a creepy house nearby. Even the Mothman is within driving distance. Pittsburgh's a delightfully scary place in our cinematic and literary imagination. A place of many monsters.

And as this souvenir anthology makes clear, horror is the genre of diversity, with so many monsters making up our mash. The

HWA has continued to expand over the years, amplifying the voice of marginalized communities through spotlight features in the media and in books like the inclusive *Other Terrors* anthology, and while there is always more work to be done, it is heartening to see the growth of diversity within the association. We sincerely hope the panels you see at the Pittsburgh StokerCon reflect how diversity within storytelling only makes the genre stronger and more exciting. Also, as it is June, we want to wish our LGBTQIA+ members a happy Pride Month! We're thrilled to have had so many attendees express interest in queer horror panels. We hope all panels will be a reflection of the many different voices, backgrounds, and cultures that continue to show how much depth there is to the horror genre. Your voices and contributions to the conference this year will help us make that self-evident.

StokerCon happens because of the efforts made by so many people. We want to thank all of the committees and volunteers who have helped in seeing everything come together. A special thank you to the past Con Chairs who passed us a heavy baton – Brian Matthews and Jim Chambers – for all of their work these past few years in making StokerCon such a success. Their guidance has been cherished as we took on the tasks that they made look easy. And lucky for us, they're still around, along with many past volunteers and board members, continuing to help in generous ways.

We hope you take the opportunity to participate in and attend as many programming options as possible, whether in person or over the internet. From panels and readings, to celebrating short horror films, librarians, academic papers, and of course, the Bram Stoker Awards®, our hybrid convention has everything a horror professional could want. Lift your fellow writers up and cheer on their successes. After all, despite our penchant for writing twisted

stories, the horror community is full of kind and enthusiastic people with like minds and a common bond in the darkness (and we won't ask about the bodies buried beneath your floorboards.)

Enjoy StokerCon 2023!

Mike Arnzen, Ben Rubin, and Sara Tantlinger
Co-Chairs, StokerCon 2023

A LITERARY HISTORY OF PITTSBURGH

by Ben Rubin

The Steel City, The City of Bridges, 'Hell with the Lid Off' – these monikers have generally represented Pittsburgh in the public imagination. A hardscrabble city defined by the industrial revolution, forges, and factories. It is also a Rust Belt city; one that endured collapse and despair, but also rebirth and rejuvenation as it is now shaped by education, medical research, and technological innovation. It is also a city defined by its geography—strategically nestled among the foothills at the confluence of three rivers—an essential port and gateway to the west and the Mississippi. But it has also been described as 'The Paris of Appalachia' —a cultural gem emerging from this same resource rich environ. A place that has a deep literary history if we just look a little beyond the fires and wipe away the soot and smoke for a moment. As we explore this history, I want to note that I cannot claim to provide a full literary history of Pittsburgh – but perhaps I can provide an abbreviated one here from where I know Pittsburgh best: the library and the literary archives with which I spend my days.

THE LIBRARY: FREE TO THE PEOPLE

The library, I think, holds a special place in any writer or reader's imagination. The place where one can discover the world of literature and so much more. Pittsburgh's library systems are world class and situate it as a grand repository of works across all genres.

One of the steel barons who left an indelible impression on Pittsburgh history was Andrew Carnegie. His name and influence is evident throughout the city and region. Whatever one may think about this legacy and his business practices, he also played an integral role in the expansion of the public library in America. He understood the power of the written word and the need for it to be accessible to the masses; so, he created the Carnegie Library network—a pioneering effort to build public libraries not just in Pittsburgh but across the county. The ethos of this effort is reflected in the inscription above the entryway to the main branch here in our Oakland neighborhood: Free to the People of Pittsburgh. Indeed, as he sought to build and open branches across the nation, this notion was a condition: the requirement to invest in the construction of the public library was that it must be available to all members of the community, that admission could not be limited by race or class (a condition that would unfortunately lead many municipalities in the Jim Crow South to decline his investments). Here in Allegheny County, you can still see the legacy of these efforts through the vast system of libraries that remain engaged and invested in their communities.

Our city is also home to the University of Pittsburgh Library System, among the largest public university libraries measured by volume of collections (and one of the oldest as Pitt is one of the oldest public universities). The Archives & Special Collections

Department in particular has an extensive collection of books and literary archives that document the literary history of Pittsburgh as well as the history of book collecting in the region. Since 2019, it has been home to the Horror Studies Collections. A collection that includes first and rare editions of seminal works; collections of pulps and comics; and a growing archive that includes the records of the HWA and literary papers of several of its members. This collection seeks to document the history of the genre, serve as testament of the genre's social and cultural importance, to inspire new creators and academics by illustrating the creative process, and legitimize horror as a field of study. And as is the case with the public library, these collections are open and accessible to the people, not just restricted to the academic community.

From Prose to Screen to Stage: a Diverse and Varied History

Pittsburgh's literary history cannot be summed up with one style, genre, or theme. Rather it is quite varied: from mystery to drama to horror; from prose to poetry to screen to stage. A few highlights, almost all represented in the Pitt collections, can perhaps serve as a brief introduction or teaser.

Let us start with a master who helped shape the contours of the modern mystery genre: Mary Roberts Rinehart. Her parlor murder mysteries and 'butler did it' tropes placed her as an American counterpart to Agatha Christie – two female writers molding an entire genre. A prolific writer, her works were widely enjoyed in the early 20th century and her influences can still be felt. She was also pioneering female journalist, spending time in Europe during World War I, and an avid conservationist and angler. And in her archives you can find an interesting editing quirk: she used straight pins to append edited passages to her manuscripts.

Of course, the name most synonymous with horror and Pittsburgh is George A. Romero. The godfather of the modern zombie, he stands among the most influential horror and independent filmmakers. His films are part of the American film lexicon and have been added to the national film registry for their impact. He most frequently gets credit as a director, but he was also the screenwriter for his films and indeed was a prolific writer. The establishment and opening of his archive revealed over 100 unrealized projects that he authored over an almost 40-year span. He was constantly writing and crafting stories that went beyond the zombie story, beyond horror to include science fiction, drama, and westerns. Pittsburgh was also his canvas—much like Maine for Stephen King, Pittsburgh was much more than just home to Romero; it was more than just a setting for his stories; it is a character just as important as the human or undead denizens of his movies.

No literary history of Pittsburgh could be complete without highlighting the amazing work and career of playwright August Wilson. His works, particularly his American Century Cycle, illuminated the Black experience both in Pittsburgh specifically and in the United States more broadly. His intelligent and insightful writing situates him as the most influential and impactful African American playwright in our history as well as one of the most important American playwrights period, alongside other icons Arthur Miller and Eugene O'Neill. Similar to Romero, his archive contains a multitude of unexamined writings that will be a treasure trove for fans and scholars for years to come. The public library also played a central role for Wilson: he was largely self-taught and educated, spending most of his formative years reading and learning at the public library (they even conferred upon him an honorary degree). He was also a representative of a larger scene of Black culture and arts that emanated from Pittsburgh and included fellow playwright Rob Penny and novelists Albert French and Bebe Moore Campbell.

The literary history of our city continues today. The Pittsburgh

Chapter of the HWA boasts an impressive cadre of writers, many of whom have seen their works be nominated and win Stokers and other awards. Mike Arnzen, Doug Gwilym, Gwendolyn Kiste, Michelle Lane, Sara Tantlinger, and Stephanie Wytovich are just a few such authors that call western Pennsylvania and the PGH Chapter home.

Lastly, StokerCon 2023 itself marks the most recent entry into Pittsburgh's literary history. We will make this one together and I look forward to how we will be able to reflect back on it and its impact. Further, I hope that you will take the time while in the Steel City to explore the histories noted above, meet local writers and chapter members, and uncover the many other names that could not be included here.

BEN RUBIN is the Horror Studies Collection Coordinator for Archives & Special Collections at the University of Pittsburgh Library System. He is responsible for building, managing, and curating archival and rare book resources related to horror studies including the George A. Romero Archival Collection, the records of the HWA, and literary papers of several of its members. He also works with students, faculty, and researchers to facilitate access to these resources. Book nerd and lifelong horror fan, the gorier the better.

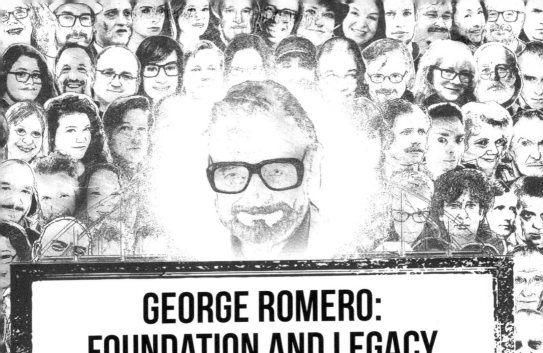

GEORGE ROMERO: FOUNDATION AND LEGACY

A conversation with Suz Romero, Ben Rubin, and Daniel Kraus

We will never have another George A. Romero. His singular vision and muscular output in cinema ranks him among the most unique auteurs of the America he often portrayed in peril. Thankfully, his legacy lives on through the George A. Romero Foundation, a supportive avenue for burgeoning filmmakers, and the George A. Romero Archival Collection, hosted at the University of Pittsburgh.

The Final Frame Horror Short Film Competition is honored to have the Foundation be the premier sponsor this year to support our finalist filmmakers. To learn more about these institutions and the legacy of Romero himself, I hosted a conversation with Suz Romero (Founder/President, GARF), Benjamin Rubin (Curator, The George A. Romero Archival Collection), and Daniel Kraus (NYT Bestselling author of *Whalefall* and Co-Author of Romero's novel, *The Living Dead*) to explore his art, independence, and drive to create compelling narratives that we cherish to this day.

JONATHAN LEES: Like the undead, fans of George Romero's films are legion, but let's talk about what the Romero archive is doing to expand upon that legacy and let people know a little bit more about George as a creative outside of the "dead" space?

BEN RUBIN: I think that was probably the most surprising aspect. A *Resident Evil* script and maybe one other actually had zombies in it. Of over a hundred unproduced projects that he wrote, treatments, scripts, none of them have zombies. There's a lot of sci-fi type scripts, a western, there's dramas. What came through the clearest is that he was a child of the space race and early science fiction, so, you can see those influences and also just how character driven all of his material is.

SUZ ROMERO: Like Ben said, he had such diverse interests. He loved swashbuckler movies, monster movies, romcoms and, of course, the old classics! He spent a lot of time writing or "noodling" as he would say. He loved the fact that he could be in his own bubble and do his own creative work, without any outside interference. So, I think he became a writer, as opposed to, initially just really wanting to be a director of films. Write it, shoot it and produce it… that was his jam!

DANIEL KRAUS: When I first started working on completing *The Living Dead* book and I met with Suz, I asked her to give me as much biographical information about George as she could and she provided me a list of all of his favorite works of film and music. It was a reminder that his experiences and what was affecting him was really outside the genre.

In the manuscript for *The Living Dead,* the parts that he wrote that really came to life had nothing to do with the zombies. It was really the scenes between the characters and their backstories that you could tell where his interest really lied.

I think it's what made him ultimately possibly the greatest kind of filmmaker ever is that he wasn't always saturated in the genre. He was like, "How can I tell the stories I want to tell through the horror filter? Because that's the only one being offered to me." Whether it's an unfinished novel or these unproduced scripts that Ben's talking about, that's where you can really feel the love... He's writing things purely for him, and not for what's being anticipated from him.

JL: I think some of my favorite films of his don't have much to do with the undead. How much have you all learned, whether from the archive, or for Suz, in speaking with him, on how he approached collaboration?

SUZ ROMERO: George was always a collaborative guy. He loved to work with a family of craftsman and he was willing to teach young people who showed passion. If he saw a glint in their eyes, he would mentor them. He definitely ran a democratic space, but he still would get the final word. He knew where he wanted to go and he was not going to deviate from that lane, but he was more than happy to have people come in and give their ideas. He welcomed it.

DANIEL KRAUS: My contribution with him was posthumously, unfortunately. I was going on cues, whether it was interviews with Suz or an exhaustive study of his writings and interviews and commentary tracks. Again, almost the most key thing was really in immersing myself in the art that he loved and trying to figure out what inspired him from that art and how I could draw from that. To take the most obvious example, he was obsessed with *The Tales of Hoffmann*. So I watched that a bunch of times and just tried to figure out what was he responding to. I can't speak of his in-person collaboration, but I hope that I continued on in the spirit of it.

BEN RUBIN: Certainly I've talked to lots of people in Pittsburgh that worked with him in some way or another. Every single one of them was like, oh yeah, if he showed up on the set, George would listen to you. You learned how to do something on set by just showing up and talking to him.

Also, in the archive itself, I think you see some of this collaboration either through the scripts and the author attribution or through some of the correspondence. I think it's fairly well known he worked a lot with Stephen King. While *Creepshow* and *The Dark Half* are the only films that came from that, they worked on several other projects together and clearly they were friends. *Apartment Living* and *Before I Wake* both originated with other authors and then they collaborated on a final script. You see it with *Black Mariah.* He worked with [Whitley] Streiber on a project. He was sent early adaptations of *The Light at the End* by Skipp and Spector. There are documents where he was writing back and forth with Guillermo del Toro in 1993, letters with the Wachowskis in 1999, within months of the Matrix coming out. He was always very encouraging even if he couldn't specifically work with them.

SUZ ROMERO: The style of his art changed because initially it was a bunch of merry men with a camera and then they shot a movie called *Night of the Living Dead*…and then as his career progressed he starts to have union sets where he can't be the cinematographer, he can't be the grip, he can't be any of those things. He has to rely now on department heads. It ended where he couldn't even talk to the zombies, for instance. He had to have his assistant director say to that guy in the red shirt "a little too much on the zombie thing". So it really is quite interesting how, you know, as a collaborator and as an independent filmmaker, his role changed. as it became much more "official." *Knightriders* would've been a very different set than *Land of the Dead*.

JL: Distribution of duties is one of the hardest things to achieve as a director. Especially for someone who came from that space where they were not only doing everything, but understanding each element that it takes to make a production.

SUZ ROMERO: He knew each role, he could *do* each role, but then as it got more sophisticated, he was not allowed to do them. He became less of a teacher/mentor towards the end because he was running with professionals. He liked to collaborate with other writers, but at the end of the day, George really wanted to do his own stuff, You know? He wanted have complete control over his art as much as possible. That was the number one thing, is that he wanted sovereignty over his work. Such a rarity. The more money a filmmaker has to work with, the less control you have.

JL: Do you have a favorite piece of George's outside of the dead films? Is there a piece within the filmography that you feel gets overlooked all too often?

BEN RUBIN: My favorite film of his is *Creepshow.* I think one that gets overlooked are *Two Evil Eyes*, an [Edgar Allan] Poe adaptation that he updated and made his own in a really interesting way, but is also a fairly obscure Poe story, probably his most gruesome.

Land of the Dead really was a rich film to come back to the Dead series with. I think the way he wrote that and, particularly the film that we saw versus the original script, showed a maturity in how the franchise developed into the new millennium.

I've seen his unproduced stuff. There are definitely scripts that are very serious versus ones that seemed kind of goofball scripts. My favorites are *Nuns from Outer Space and Monster MASH* that reads like a *X-Files* / Monster of the Week episode. They had still that social commentary that he was known for, but, it felt like he was just actually having fun writing those. They were projects he typed out on one weekend and never revisited it but they're super fun to read and a different side of who he was creatively.

JL: Suz, I know I have read that you weren't even a fan of *Dawn of the Dead*, and I'm wondering… over the years of getting to know George and eventually watching a lot of the films, what did you connect with most?

SUZ ROMERO: I had never seen any of his films. I had heard of *Night of the Living Dead* but that's it! So three months after we started dating, he said, "Well, I guess we ought to see my movies." So we spent the weekend doing a Romero film festival and then we watched them in sequence. I really loved *Night* [*of the Living Dead*]. It's just an astonishing film. To this day, I get the creeps. I think it's one of the best endings of any film ever.

I didn't like *Dawn* [*of the Dead*] because I thought it was cheesy. He laughed because he thought I was probably the only human being on the planet who didn't like this movie. You know, we never saw horror films together. He wanted me to see *Citizen Kane*. He wanted me to see every John Ford film. He wanted me to see [Roman] Polanski, William Wyler and David Lean So, I went to George Romero cinema school. It took me six years to graduate. (*Laughs*) And, what an education. It was fantastic.

DANIEL KRAUS: I mean, George never made a bad movie. That's one of the rare things about his filmography. They're all good. The film I would pick that gets overlooked is *Survival of the Dead*, his final film. The whole vibe of it works for me. It's a really smart film that underplays everything and I think that's what throws off hardcore horror fans. It's so subtle and deft in what it's doing. It has an oddly gentle feel, this slower pace, sort of like the westerns on which it was based.

Then I'll say *The Amusement Park*, which I absolutely love. I think it and *Night of the Living Dead* are really the two movies he made that were meant to terrify. I think it is an incredibly disturbing movie and one of the few he made where he was really able to indulge in his more experimental side, which was clearly something, especially in his early films, that he was always excited to do.

JL: Whether in-person or not, you all gained insights from being around his work for so long. Do you feel there's something else you can take away that you feel just applies to the way he did things, the way he created… anything that feels very aspirational or inspirational for you or other people.

DANIEL KRAUS: I mean, his movies changed the trajectory of my life wildly from when I first saw [*Night of the*] *Living Dead* at age five or six. I think attaching myself to Romero and Rod Serling at that young of an age, I couldn't have picked two better people because all their work had other things going on. It wasn't exploitation or shock, which, you know, has its place in the genre. They were both artists who were working heavily in metaphor, which taught me how genre can be used as a mask for deeper ideas.

I live my artistic life very much modeled on how I think Romero lived his. I'm a horror fan, but it's only one segment of what I'm interested in. What can create a smarter horror artist is when you're not caught in the horror feedback loop, you're consuming other things and being inspired by international writing and cinema of every genre. I also have always been inspired by his interest in working with friends. I think that probably, professionally, was counterproductive for him. I'm guessing he sometimes said no to projects that might have been financially beneficial, but he wanted to maintain certain controls and standards. I've certainly followed the same path, for better or for worse. I don't want to one day look back on years wasted on projects I didn't care about.

JL: That's beautiful. I think he'd be really proud of *The Living Dead* novel and also what you've done outside of that collaboration.

Suz Romero: I know more about his work now than I did when I was with him. My relationship with George was, you know, he was my friend, my guy, we had so many common interests... so it was only after his death I jumped into his career in depth.

I think he really blossomed as a human being because we concentrated on other interests. Now, I'm very focused in his work and his legacy. My role has changed 100%. I'm still learning about George Romero, the worker, the artist. Every day somebody tells me something I didn't know.

JL: Daniel, you've continued a legacy and are bringing it to the world in various ways, how are you and Suz connecting now on future projects or during the writing of the book?

Suz Romero: We have high respect for each other. We both love George Romero, so it's a no-brainer, you know?

Daniel Kraus: It's hard to say with Suz sitting right here, but it's really been one of the best, if not *the* best, working relationships of my life.

The trust has been so humbling, that I've been trusted to handle these manuscripts. I've tried to pay that back with a hard work ethic. It's a dream relationship to me. Again, I don't know how Suz will take this, but I lost my mom at an early age and there's something about Suz that I have a connection to, and quite frankly, I just love her.

Suz Romero: It's hard enough to write for your own, but to write for somebody else...with a name like George Romero. It was a task that not all people could do and he did it beautifully.

JL: Daunting.

Suz Romero: Seriously daunting. I was so afraid that I wasn't gonna like it but then I just fell in love with the book and I could see George and I could see Dan in there and it was just a beautiful read, an emotional experience.

JL: It must be so bizarre for you to feel your husband's presence come through someone else's lens but also touching as well.

Suz Romero: Yeah, it really was. He's a beautiful writer. Different than George, for sure. I think George's style is really sort of, everyman, you know, he was very able to write characters that were very real. The way they spoke, they're real people.

JL: Almost like what Daniel did, you're filtering George's essence to connect to a new generation of people that are interested in furthering their own careers in film. What is the goal right now for the foundation, for the archive? What are you most excited for?

Suz Romero: Well, I would love a horror study center. It would be a dream come true for me if it ever happened. A mecca where people can come and study horror, study the genre, because it's important. The genre has been around for centuries and it doesn't really get the respect it deserves.

JL: Daniel, have you had a chance to sift through the archive or attend anything at the foundation?

Daniel Kraus: I was, I think, the first civilian to go through the archive.

Suz Romero: He sure was!

DANIEL KRAUS: It was just like opening an Egyptian vault to me. It was like realizing that everything that we knew about George's work was just the tip of the iceberg. And there was this huge chest full of other ideas and half-finished scripts and flights of fancy. It was just really, really cool.

SUZ ROMERO: And, you know, Dan Kraus is in the archive, his body of work is there. That's so thrilling for me because it's another artist who's put themselves in this space where people can study and sift through Dan's treasures. The whole archive is growing all the time.

JL: Ben, is there anything you can tell us about *The Latent Image* [Romero's early production company] and what you do have in the collection from that formative period?

BEN RUBIN: So, we have some of the kind of promotional type materials that they made to establish themselves as a production house. We have some of their brochures that they were clearly being given out as a way to fundraise. That includes even a promotional booklet for what they had hoped to have been their first film, *Whine of the Fawn*, that, ultimately, was not made. There are similar booklets for what became known as *There's Always Vanilla* and *Night of the Living Dead*, these semi-professional looking booklets to give out to get money. All of it sort of called attention to the fact that they were actually making industrials and commercials and doing real work in Pittsburgh.

JL: I cannot wait to see what the foundation does and the archive uncovers. It's a huge undertaking, so congratulations to getting that done and furthering the work and the studies. I love the idea of a horror center. I really appreciate the time and all of your perspectives on George's work.

Suz Romero: I'm so "stoked" about StokerCon. We're now part of the Horror Writers Association. I can't wait to be in that room, to be honest, with all these great writers and I've got so many ideas, so many hopes for collaboration. I'm hoping people there are going to be keen on helping funnel some of their artistic work to the foundation. I think it's synergy. I think together it could be a beautiful thing.

The George A. Romero Foundation (GARF) is a nonprofit organization dedicated to preserving and promoting Romero's legacy. The GARF's mission is to advance the causes for which George Romero was a champion—creativity within the horror genre and independent filmmaking in general—as well as preserving and documenting the history of the genre in all forms and contributing to its future by encouraging new generations of filmmakers, artists, and creators.

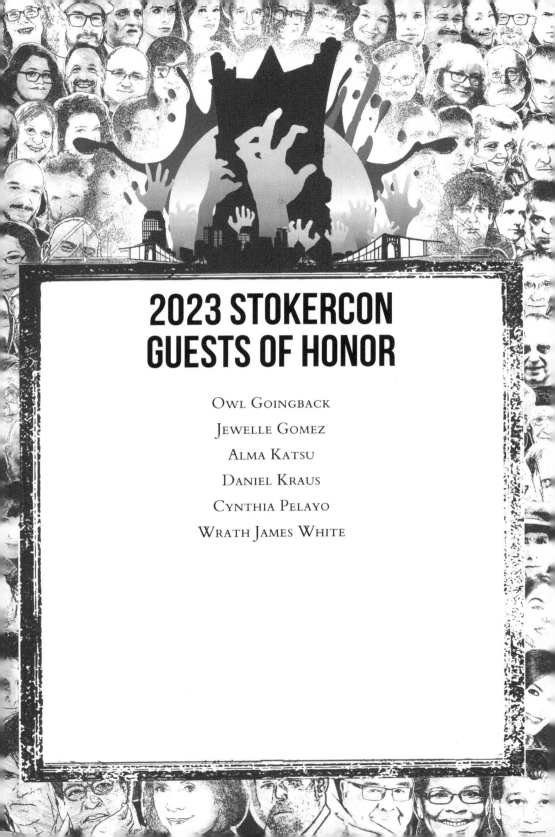

2023 STOKERCON GUESTS OF HONOR

Owl Goingback

Jewelle Gomez

Alma Katsu

Daniel Kraus

Cynthia Pelayo

Wrath James White

OWL GOINGBACK

Owl Goingback was conceived in Oklahoma, born in St. Louis, and grew up surrounded by forests and farmland in the rural Midwest. It was a lonely existence, and he often turned to novels, monster magazines, horror comics, and long treks in the wilderness to keep boredom at bay.

Not wanting to spend his life in the middle of nowhere, and wanting to see more of the world, he enlisted in the United States Air Force at the age of seventeen, spending most of his military years in Europe and the Middle East.

Owl left the military at the age of twenty-one, having earned the rank of sergeant, to open a bar/restaurant in central Georgia. Late at night, after the bar closed for the evening, he would hone his literary skills by writing self-defense articles for martial arts magazines, and short fiction for anthologies. He sold the business six years later, moving to Florida to become a full-time writer.

He has been writing professionally for over thirty years, and is the author of numerous published novels, children's books, short stories, screenplays, magazine articles, poems, and comics. He is a two-time Bram Stoker Award® Winner, a Nebula Award

Nominee, and the recipient of an HWA Lifetime Achievement Award. His books include *Crota*, *Darker Than Night*, *Evil Whispers*, *Breed*, *Shaman Moon*, *Coyote Rage*, *Eagle Feathers*, *The Gift*, and *Tribal Screams*.

In addition to writing under his own name, Owl has ghostwritten for Hollywood celebrities. He has also lectured across the cou ntry on the customs and folklore of the American Indians, and worked as a caretaker in a haunted cemetery. He is a member of the Authors Guild, Science Fiction and Fantasy Writers Association, and the Horror Writers Association.

Owl lives in central Florida with his wife, Nancy, not far from several theme parks, a space port, and the shark bite capital of the world. When not writing, he can be found exploring historic places, researching reports of hauntings and strange encounters, dancing at powwows, or just waiting for the mother ship to come back and take him away.

JEWELLE GOMEZ

JEWELLE GOMEZ (Cape Verde/Iowa/Wampanoag; she/her) is a writer and activist and author of eight books including the double Lambda Literary Award-winning, Black Lesbian vampire novel, The Gilda Stories. Her adaptation of the novel for the stage, "Bones & Ash: A Gilda Story," was performed by the Urban Bush Women company in 13 U.S. cities. In print for more than 30 years, the novel was recently optioned by Cheryl Dunye to develop a TV miniseries. Her newest collection of poetry is Still Water. Her new novel, Gilda: Blood Relations, is forthcoming.

Her writing has appeared in such anthologies are Dark Matter: A Century of Speculative Fiction from the African Diaspora, Reading Black Reading Feminist, Stories for Chip: A Tribute to Samuel R. Delany, Blood Sisters, Heiresses of Russ, Red Indian Road West, and Luminescent Threads: Connections to Octavia E. Butler.

Her last two plays, "Waiting for Giovanni" and "Leaving the Blues," premiered in San Francisco and New York City. "Unpacking in P'town" will premiere in Spring of 2024.

Formerly the executive director of the Poetry Center and the

American Poetry Archives at San Francisco State University she is also the former director of the Literature Program at the New York State Council on the Arts and director of Cultural Equity Grants for the San Francisco Arts Commission.

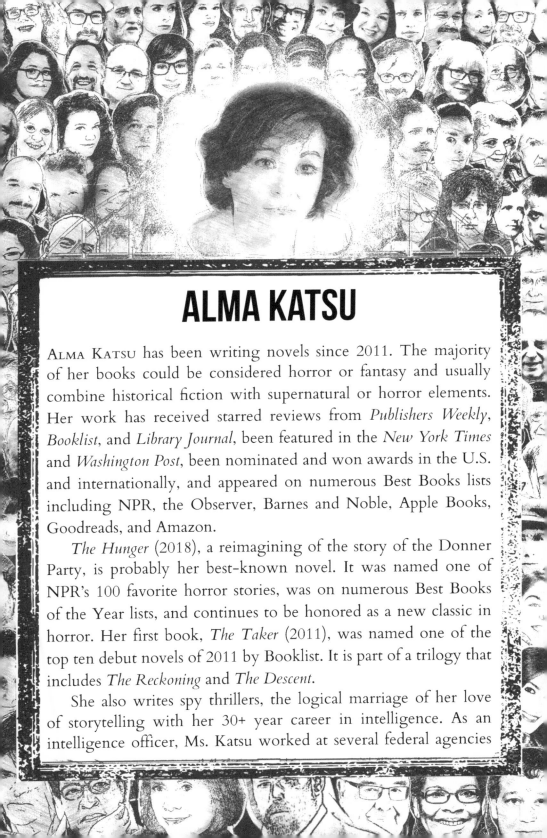

ALMA KATSU

ALMA KATSU has been writing novels since 2011. The majority of her books could be considered horror or fantasy and usually combine historical fiction with supernatural or horror elements. Her work has received starred reviews from *Publishers Weekly*, *Booklist*, and *Library Journal*, been featured in the *New York Times* and *Washington Post*, been nominated and won awards in the U.S. and internationally, and appeared on numerous Best Books lists including NPR, the Observer, Barnes and Noble, Apple Books, Goodreads, and Amazon.

The Hunger (2018), a reimagining of the story of the Donner Party, is probably her best-known novel. It was named one of NPR's 100 favorite horror stories, was on numerous Best Books of the Year lists, and continues to be honored as a new classic in horror. Her first book, *The Taker* (2011), was named one of the top ten debut novels of 2011 by Booklist. It is part of a trilogy that includes *The Reckoning* and *The Descent*.

She also writes spy thrillers, the logical marriage of her love of storytelling with her 30+ year career in intelligence. As an intelligence officer, Ms. Katsu worked at several federal agencies and at the RAND Corporation as a senior analyst. *Red Widow* (2021), her first spy novel, was a *New York Times* Editor's Choice, nominated for International Thriller Writers' Best Novel, and widely praised for its authenticity. The second book in the series, *Red London*, was published March 2023. She also wrote a serialized graphic novel for Porsche called *The Spy Collector*.

Ms. Katsu has relocated from the Washington, DC area to the mountains of West Virginia, where she lives with her musician husband Bruce and their two dogs, Nick and Ash. She did not sell her first book until she was 50 and so has a relatively short list of publications. You can find links to stories published in anthologies and everything else you'd like to know about her work at www. almakatsubooks.com

DANIEL KRAUS

DANIEL KRAUS is a *New York Times* bestselling author. His collaboration with legendary filmmaker George A. Romero, *The Living Dead*, was acclaimed by *The New York Times* and *The Washington Post*.

With Guillermo del Toro, he co-authored *The Shape of Water*, based on the same idea the two created for the Oscar-winning film. Also with del Toro, Kraus co-authored *Trollhunters*, which was adapted into the Emmy-winning Netflix series. Kraus's *The Death and Life of Zebulon Finch* was named one of *Entertainment Weekly*'s Top 10 Books of the Year. Kraus has won a Scribe Award, two Odyssey Awards (for both *Rotters* and *Scowler*) and has been a Library Guild selection, YALSA Best Fiction for Young Adults, multiple Bram Stoker finalist, and more.

Kraus's work has been translated into over 20 languages. He lives with his wife in Chicago. Visit him at danielkraus.com.

CYNTHIA PELAYO

Cynthia Pelayo is an International Latino Book Award winning poet and author.

She is the author of *Loteria, Santa Muerte, The Missing, Poems of My Night, Into the Forest and All the Way Through, Children of Chicago*, Crime Scene, *The Shoemaker's Magician*, as well as dozens of standalone short stories and poems.

Loteria, which was her MFA in Writing thesis at The School of the Art Institute of Chicago, was re-released to praise with *Esquire* calling it one of the 'Best Horror Books of 2023.' *Santa Muerte* and *The Missing*, her young adult horror novels were each nominated for International Latino Book Awards. *Poems of My Night* was nominated for an Elgin Award. *Into the Forest and All the Way Through* was nominated for an Elgin Award and was also nominated for a Bram Stoker Award® for Superior Achievement in a Poetry Collection. *Children of Chicago* was nominated for a Bram Stoker Award in Superior Achievement in a Novel and won an International Latino Book Award for Best Mystery. *Crime Scene* was nominated for a Bram Stoker Award® for Superior Achievement in a Poetry Collection. *The Shoemaker's Magician* has been released to praise with *Library Journal* awarding it a starred review.

Her forthcoming novel, *The Forgotten Sisters*, will be released by Thomas and Mercer in 2024 and is an adaptation of Hans Christian Andersen's "The Little Mermaid."

Pelayo studied journalism at Columbia College in Chicago. She received a Master of Science at Roosevelt University. Later she received a Master of Fine Arts in Writing at The School of the Art Institute of Chicago. She is a also doctoral candidate at The Chicago School of Professional Psychology.

Pelayo was born in Puerto Rico but was raised in inner city Chicago where she still lives today with her husband and children.

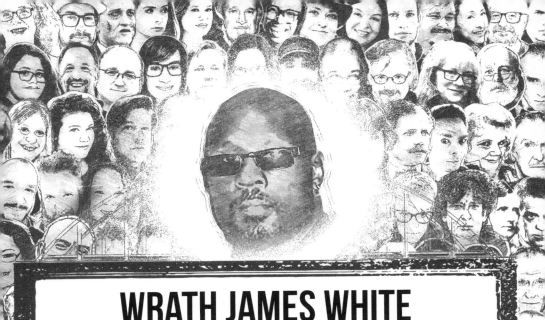

WRATH JAMES WHITE

WRATH JAMES WHITE is a former World Class Heavyweight Kickboxer, a professional Kickboxing and Mixed Martial Arts trainer, distance runner, performance artist, and former street brawler, who is now known for creating some of the most disturbing works of fiction in print.

Wrath is the author of such extreme horror classics as *The Resurrectionist* (now a major motion picture titled "Come Back To Me") *Succulent Prey*, and its sequel *Prey Drive, Yaccub's Curse, 400 Days Of Oppression, Sacrifice, Voracious, To The Death, The Reaper, Skinzz, Everyone Dies Famous In A Small Town, The Book Of A Thousand Sins, His Pain, Population Zero, If You Died Tomorrow I Would Eat Your Corpse, Hardcore Kelli*, and many others. He is the co-author of *Teratologist* co-written with the king of extreme horror, Edward Lee, *Something Terrible* co-written with his son Sultan Z. White, *Orgy Of Souls* co-written with Maurice Broaddus, *Hero* and *The Killings* both co-written with J.F. Gonzalez, *Poisoning Eros* co-written with Monica J. O'Rourke, *Master Of Pain* co-written with Kristopher Rufty, and *Boy's Night* co-written with Matt Shaw among others.

Wrath lives and works in Austin, TX.

OWL GOINGBACK

DOUGLAS FORD: First things first: you once used to own and drive around a hearse. How did that come about, and what sort of reactions did that earn you?

OWL GOINGBACK: Being a devoted lover of all things strange, bizarre, and spooky, I've wanted to own a Cadillac hearse ever since I was old enough to drive. I love the way they look, especially the landau models, and you couldn't ask for a smoother ride. Add in the creep factor of owning something that once hauled dead bodies and they are everything I dreamed of in a vehicle. Forget Porsche, Mercedes, and other high-end luxury cars; if you want to turn heads while driving get yourself a hearse.

Of course, a hearse is the perfect ride for a horror writer. Plenty of room to carry books, and victims, in the back. And why settle for that new car smell when you can enjoy an old dead smell? Not that there really was a smell in my hearse, but that didn't stop me from hanging a zombie shaped air freshener on the rearview mirror.

And I didn't buy just any hearse; I purchased one from a funeral home I did business with while working as a cemetery caretaker.

The vehicle and I already had a history because I helped unload bodies from it on several occasions. I even found a toe tag under the front seat that had been tied to the casket of a woman I buried.

Most hearse owners customize their rides to fit their personality; I was no exception. I had the hood and rear door wrapped with a mural of the Grim Reaper leading an army of skeletons, had stickers of a zombie family on the back window, and a license tag that read CU NEXT. I also had the word BONEPICKER emblazoned in vinyl letters across the top of the windshield.

Bone picker was a title my ancestors (Choctaw, Cherokee) gave to the men, and sometimes women, who prepared the dead for burial. Bodies were placed on scaffolds and left to the elements. Later, the bone pickers would peel the remaining dried flesh from the skeletons prior to placing them in the ground.

My wife, Nancy, loved the hearse as much as I did. She used to laugh when other vehicles inched forward at stoplights, the occupants trying to get a peek at who was driving the creepy car. It was even funnier when I had a fake skeleton riding in the front seat between us.

All good things eventually come to an end, and I sold Bonepicker to a friend who is a horror photographer. I was only kidding about wanting to sell it, but he was serious about buying my hearse and I knew it would be going to a good home. Maybe someday I will buy another one.

DOUGLAS FORD: Many writers have held down some unusual jobs. Is that true for you? And what is the best "day job" for a horror author?

OWL GOINGBACK: I've had a lot of different occupations over the years. I bucked hay bales for two cents a bale, owned a bar/restaurant, worked in a bookstore, and for a newspaper, even turned wrenches on fighter aircraft and nuclear bombers in the Air Force.

Crawling under the back end of an F-4 Phantom II Fighter on a trim pad, with both engines running in full afterburner, is a head rush, and an experience I will never forget. So is working on a B-52 Bomber when it has a bomb bay filled with doomsday weapons. In both of those situations, you really want to focus on what you are doing and not slip with a wrench. Definitely not a job for the nervous.

Probably my most unusual job, and sometimes the creepiest, was serving as a full-time caretaker for historic Greenwood Cemetery in Orlando. The cemetery covers a little over one hundred acres, dates back to the late 1800s, and contains approximately eighty thousand burials.

Greenwood is also considered to be the most haunted place in central Florida, and has been the subject of numerous paranormal investigations and ghost tours. And yes, I have had a few encounters with the unexplained while working there.

In the seven-and-a-half years I worked at Greenwood, I buried thousands of bodies. I also dug up quite a few for relocation. With some of the removals, the wooden caskets had disintegrated and we were forced to wrap the bodies in plastic sheeting, lifting them out of the grave with ropes. It gave me a unique opportunity to get up close and personal with the dead, in various stages of decomposition. I was never bothered by the sight of a rotting corpse, but the smell was sometimes strong enough to make me glad I had skipped breakfast.

Working at the cemetery provided lots of ideas for future horror stories. As a matter of fact, I used Greenwood for one of the settings in my novel *Coyote Rage*.

The best job for a horror writer is one that sparks the imagination, or gives fodder for future stories, something that lets you experience people, places, and things. A writer needs to experience life in order to write about it. Sit in your home office all day and you're eventually going to go stale.

DOUGLAS FORD: You collection of horror memorabilia is legendary. Tell us about some of the prized items in your collection.

OWL GOINGBACK: I wouldn't call my collection legendary, but my home is filled with creepy artwork, autographed photos of horror actors, signed movie posters, statues, funeral items, life-size figures, Halloween collectables, animal skulls, and dead things in jars. That comes from attending horror conventions for thirty years, and having friends who work in the movie industry.

One of my favorite items is also the biggest. It's a Batesville oak casket given to me by a funeral director after he saw my hearse. The casket is a rental, which means there have been dead bodies in it (it has a new liner, so no smell or disgusting stains).

Rental caskets are used when the deceased is going to be cremated, but the family still wants a viewing. After the viewing, a panel is opened at the foot of the casket, body and liner are slid out, and a new liner installed for the next funeral.

My casket was featured in the music video "Beautiful Corpse" by The Bloody Jug Band, featuring actor J Larose, of Saw III, and LeeAnne Vamp. It now sits in the parlor, where I often entertain guests, and has an animated zombie in it. Definitely a conversation piece.

A couple of other goodies I'm proud of came from the Ripley's Believe It or Not! vault, which is located here in Orlando. One is a duplicate plaster cast of a Sasquatch footprint, the original acquired in the state of Washington in 1973. The other is a limited casting of the Vincent Price wax mask made by Katherine Stuburgh for the 1953 horror film *House of War*. It sits on a shelf in my office, next to a life-cast bust of Mr. Price from *Edward Scissorhands*.

DOUGLAS FORD: Your work has been celebrated with many honors and awards, including multiple Stokers. Which one makes you feel the most proud?

OWL GOINGBACK: My favorite genre has always been horror, dating back to 1968 when I bought issue #51 of *Famous Monsters of Filmland*. I was only nine years old when I discovered the magazine on a rack at the Rexall Drug Store in my hometown—a town so small there were no bookstores, or comic shops, and only one four-way stop sign.

Famous Monsters turned me into a dedicated horror lover, and monster kid, quickly isolating me from "normal" people. I bought every scary magazine and comic I could get my hands on, put together model kits of Frankenstein, Dracula, and all the other Universal monsters, spent hours at the local library searching for horror novels to read, and watched Creature Features on the portable black-and-white television in my bedroom.

With horror being my favorite genre, and having such a profound impact on my youth, winning a Bram Stoker Award® means more to me than all my other accolades. Never in my wildest dreams did I imagine I would one day be allowed in the same room with horror influencers, let alone sharing the stage with them at the Stoker Awards in New York City.

Winning a Bram Stoker Award® for my first novel, *Crota*, came as something of a shock, but receiving the award twice more since then completely boggles my mind. Not only have I been allowed in the same room with horror writers whose work I admire, but someone actually set a place for me at the table. And for that I will be eternally grateful.

DOUGLAS FORD: What is a typical writing session like for you?

OWL GOINGBACK: I've been a chronic pain sufferer since the age of twenty-three, when a chiropractor screwed up my back after a martial arts class, so every moment I spend in front of the computer is a sheer test of determination and willpower.

On those nights when I can get enough caffeine and Tylenol in my system to push back the pain, I will turn on the old laptop, put in the earphones, and crank up the music. I listen mostly to rock and roll, in all of its various subgenres, with an occasional Native American artist thrown in for variety. Can't tell you how many pages I've written while listening to Alice Cooper, but I handed him one of my novels as a thank you.

For me, when working on the first draft of a short story, or novel, it's all about getting words on paper. They don't even have to be great words, just something on paper that propels the story forward and forces my mind to work. I never back up on the first draft, don't worry about spelling, sentence structure, formatting, or plot twists. That is something I will address in future drafts. I'm just trying to get the insanity out of my mind and down on paper, mentally hemorrhaging onto the keyboard.

I love it when the writing takes me late into the night, or even early morning; when I'm jazzed on enough caffeine that the walls are moving, and I'm seeing imaginary ghosts out the corners of my eyes. During those incredible moments I'm less of a writer, and more of a witness, strapping in as my characters seize control of the story and take me on a wild ride.

I think one day my wife will find me dead at my keyboard, music still playing, and smoke coming out of my ears. The computer screen will be filled with horrific passages worthy of Cthulhu, and there will be a ghastly, big grin upon my face. And truthfully, I cannot think of a better way to go.

DOUGLAS FORD: In recent years, your repertoire has come to include writing for comics. How does writing for that industry compare to writing prose?

OWL GOINGBACK: With prose I can pretty much sit back and let the story flow, but with comic scripts I have to stay focused on the formatting and structure. Only so many panels are allowed per page, only so much dialogue or narration per panel, and each page has to end with some kind of page turner. I also have to allow the artist to show off their talent by putting in a splash page, or at least a few larger panels.

In addition, the editing process can be a lot tougher. If a change is needed on one page, it often means I have to make adjustments on the pages before and after to make it work. It can be a little frustrating, but the finished product is very rewarding.

DOUGLAS FORD: I've seen you perform live readings in which your work has a profound effect on people in attendance. Do you find yourself similarly affected during these readings? Is it easy to find an emotional connection with your audience?

OWL GOINGBACK: I really enjoy connecting with the audience when I do a reading, and the best way to do that is to make them laugh, or cry. It's cruel to make people cry, I know, but pulling at heartstrings, or, better yet, ripping the beating hearts from their chests can be a lot of fun.

My favorite story for turning on the waterworks in a room full of strangers is "Grass Dancer." It's a Vietnam/powwow story about the love between two Kiowa brothers, and a Nebula Award Nominee. I've read it so many times in public I know the exact place in the story, down to the paragraph, when people will start tearing up.

The only problem about reading "Grass Dancer" in public is making sure I stay detached from the story during the performance so I don't get emotional myself (not saying I teared up when I wrote it, that's just an ugly rumor started by my wife). I usually accomplish this by picking out four or five members of the audience, on opposite sides of the room, and focusing on them while reading.

Focusing on select individuals has always kept me from being drawn into the story. Except my little trick failed me when I read the story at the World Fantasy Convention in Montreal. During that particular performance I was wearing new reading glasses, and when I looked up everything was a blur. Unable to focus on members of the audience, I felt myself starting to choke up at the familiar point in the story where I had yanked the heartstrings of so many others. I barely made it through the reading, and the audience had a good laugh at my discomfort.

DOUGLAS FORD: I have to ask since we both live in the same state: Is Florida scary?

OWL GOINGBACK: Florida is definitely scary. We have backwater swamps, hungry alligators, crazy rednecks, Skunk apes, crotchety old people, serial killers, deadly hurricanes, angry tourists, and palmetto bugs the size of alley cats. We lead the nation in shark attacks, lightning strikes, and highway fatalities (along the infamous I-4 Dead Zone). Ruthless conquistadors, pirates, and frontier soldiers put their mark on the land, decimating and enslaving native populations, and leaving behind a territory steeped in blood. Everywhere you go there are stories about ghosts, hauntings, and cryptids, with warnings to beware of things lurking in the dark. Add in all the Florida Man stories and the Sunshine State can be a pretty scary place. If that wasn't already enough to give you the shivers, we have Ron DeSantis as governor.

I have often considered moving somewhere a little less insane. But every time such thoughts enter my mind I discover another legend, a bit of folklore, or a forgotten news report that reminds me just how weird and spooky this state can be, and makes the horror writer in me love it even more.

DOUGLAS FORD: There is a resurgence of interest in your earlier work, including a beautiful new edition of *Evil Whispers* coming soon from Cemetery Dance. In your experience, how has the world of publishing changed since then?

OWL GOINGBACK: When I first started out it was very difficult for a new writer to get their foot in the door. There were very few small press publishers, or open anthologies, leaving only the big houses in New York. Those publishers wouldn't even talk to you without an agent, and to get an agent you needed to already have a few sales under your belt.

It was also harder for people from different social or ethnic backgrounds to break into the writing game. Diversity was not a word used very often back then, and the publishing industry wasn't too interested in producing books showcasing other cultures, or told from a different perspective. My first novel, *Crota*, was turned down by dozens of publishers before finally being bought by Donald I. Fines books.

Writing can still be a very frustrating career choice, but I do think it's easier today to make those first few, all-important, sales. There are numerous small publishers willing to take a chance on new writers, and a lot more anthologies open to submissions. You can also make money, and get your name out, by going the self-publishing route provided you are willing to do the necessary work.

DOUGLAS FORD: Your work has been the subject of academic scholarship and, according to at least one account, been taught in prisons. Can you comment on the wide appeal your writing has? Has it surprised you? I imagine you've received some interesting correspondence from readers.

OWL GOINGBACK: I've gotten lots of letters over the years from people saying their spouse, friends, kids, etc., don't normally like to read but enjoy my books. Maybe it's because I don't use big words in my stories, making them easy to read. Heck, I don't even know any big words. Whatever the reason, I seem to appeal to a wide audience. I have ten-year-olds and grandparents reading my horror novels.

I had a deputy sheriff write to me years ago saying he had used my novel *Crota* to teach himself to read. And because we were both from the same small town, he had been inspired to do something with his life and became a law enforcement officer.

I also had several U.S. soldiers write me during the war in Iraq, saying how much my novels helped relieve the boredom on the days they weren't being shot at. Sadly, one of the soldiers who wrote came home in a flag covered box.

Finding out my books are being used in schools and universities always comes as a surprise, and a real honor. Being able to reach young people makes me happy. Just the other day, I was taking a walk and had a teacher stop me to say she still uses my children's books every year in her elementary class.

In addition to institutes of formal education, my novels seem to be very popular with people behind bars (talk about a captive audience). Four of my novels are used in a course for youthful offenders at the Orange County Correctional Facility, in Orlando, Florida. The inmates enjoy the books because of the horror elements, and the instructors like them for the traditional teachings I weave between the lines. Those who pass the course are rewarded with a home cooked meal, brought into the jail by their family members.

DOUGLAS FORD: What is next for Owl Goingback?

OWL GOINGBACK: Death. I mean, none of us are getting off this planet alive, despite the promises of Elon Musk, and I have been living on borrowed time for many years. But what is death but another adventure, and a chance to explore unknown worlds. I just hope the hereafter is one gigantic library, or a well-stocked con suite, and I get to sit around and swap stories with Poe, Lovecraft, Bradbury, and the other greats who have gone before me.

But until my timecard is punched, I will continue to take readers on strange trips through the shadow world of my mind, perhaps touching a few hearts along the way. If I can spin a few more tales, tickle or terrify a few more readers, then I will die a happy camper.

PROFESSOR DOUGLAS FORD teaches horror literature at State College of Florida.

JEWELLE GOMEZ

Jewelle Gomez is a poet, playwright, educator, political activist, the self-described "foremother of Afrofuturism," and the author of seven books, including her double Lambda Literary Award-winning novel, *The Gilda Stories* (Firebrand Books, 1991). This groundbreaking novel subverted traditional vampire narratives by reimagining these classic monsters from a lesbian feminist perspective and gives voice to an escaped slave who comes of age over the span of two hundred years. Gomez's debut novel tackled often unexplored territories of identity and created a backdoor into the horror genre that bypassed its traditional gatekeepers.

This book provided the nourishment many writers of color (like me) were starving for in the form of vampires who were Black, brown, indigenous, female, queer, and most importantly, powerful. *The Gilda Stories* allowed me to see myself in the narratives I loved, where Anne Rice's Vampire Chronicles left me feeling invisible. Even Akasha, the African mother of all vampires, is described as having skin that appears to be made of alabaster (read white) after centuries of being hidden from the world in *Queen of the Damned*.

Gomez adapted *The Gilda Stories* for the stage. "Bones and Ash," a play that began touring in 1996 was performed by the Urban Bush Women Company in 13 U.S. cities. Her other plays include "Waiting for Giovanni," a tribute to the work of James Baldwin (2010) and "Leaving the Blues," about singer Alberta Hunter (2017).

Her other books include *Don't Explain*, a collection of short fiction; *43 Septembers*, a collection of personal/political essays; and *Oral Tradition: Selected Poems Old and New*. Her fiction and poetry is included in more than one hundred anthologies, including the first anthology of Black speculative fiction, *Dark Matter: A Century of Speculative Fiction from the African Diaspora* (2000), edited by Sheree R. Thomas; *Home Girls: A Black Feminist Anthology* from Kitchen Table: Women of Color Press, *Daughters of Africa,* edited by Margaret Busby (1992), and *Best American Poetry of 2001*, edited by Robert Hass. Her graphic novel, *Televised*, recounts the lives of survivors of the Black Nationalist movement, which was excerpted in the 2002 anthology *Gumbo*, edited by Marita Golden and E. Lynn Harris.

Gomez's literary and film criticism has been featured in *The Village Voice*, the *San Francisco Chronicle*, *Ms. Magazine*, and *The Black Scholar*. Her work as an activist, which has heavily influenced her writing (and perhaps vice versa), has garnered the attention of LGBTQ publications like *The Advocate*, the *Journal of Lesbian Studies*, and she appeared in the 1999 documentary, *After Stonewall*.

Gomez's activism exists at the intersections of race and gender in America. She was on the original staff of *Say Brother* (now *Basic Black*), one of the first weekly Black television shows (WGBH-TV Boston, 1968), and was on the founding board of the Gay and Lesbian Alliance Against Defamation (GLAAD) in 1984. She has served on the boards and been a founding member of several political action groups including the Astraea Lesbian Foundation and the Open Meadows Foundation, both devoted to funding women's organizations and activities, the Cornell University Human Sexuality Archives, and the advisory board of the James Hormel LGBT Center of the main San Francisco Public Library. She was a member of 100 Lesbians and Our Friends, which was co-founded by Andrea Gillespie and Diane Sabin, and designed to educate lesbians who were culturally miseducated—as women—about the use of money and benefits of philanthropy.

She and her partner, Dr. Diane Sabin, were among the litigants against the state of California suing for the right to legal marriage. The case was brought to the courts by the City Attorney of San Francisco, the National Center for Lesbian Rights (NCLR) and the American Civil Liberties Union (ACLU). Gomez has written extensively about gay rights since the 1980s, including articles on equal marriage in *Ms. Magazine* and was quoted extensively during the court case. In May 2008 the Supreme Court ruled in favor of the litigants, allowing marriage between same-sex couples in the state of California.

She is the former executive director of the Poetry Center and American Poetry Archives at San Francisco State University, the former director of Cultural Equity Grants at the San Francisco Arts Commission and the former director of the Literature Program for the New York State Council on the Arts. She is currently the Director of Grants and Community Initiatives for Horizons Foundation, the oldest lesbian, gay, bisexual, and transgender foundation in the US. And, she formerly served as the President of the San Francisco Public Library Commission.

Beyond her work as an activist and writer, she has taught at numerous institutions of higher learning including San Francisco State University, Hunter College, Rutgers University, New

College of California, Grinnell College, San Diego City College, Ohio State University, and the University of Washington (Seattle).

MICHELLE RENEE LANE: Before we get started, I just wanted to say how thrilled I am to be chatting with you again. This obviously isn't the first time we've met and spoken with each other, but I am still a little awestruck about being in conversation with someone who has been such a powerful source of encouragement and inspiration to me as a writer. When I first reached out to you back in 2019 to ask if you'd be willing to blurb my novel, *Invisible Chains*, I took a risk not knowing if you'd respond. One of the mantras that drives me to keep taking risks is: if you don't ask, the answer will always be "no". What risks have you taken as a writer, and what advice would you give new writers about taking risks to create their most authentic work?

JEWELLE GOMEZ: I have a quote over my desk, I can't remember where I found it but it says: "If you can imagine it you can do it."

MICHELLE RENEE LANE: Taking risks means batting your inner critic. Standing up to the voices that say, "you can't do that." Many writers struggle with imposter syndrome. Has imposter syndrome ever kept you from reaching your personal goals, and what weapons have you used to do battle with it? Are there skills you've developed over time to combat it when it gets in the way of your writing?

JEWELLE GOMEZ: I feel I lost about five years early in my career because I didn't think I had anything to say that was of interest to the world; even though I'd wanted to be a writer since I learned to read. Then I saw Ntozake Shange's "For Colored Girls..." (1975) about five times on stage and I needed to write about myself and women I knew and loved. Suddenly the path cleared and I haven't stopped writing since then.

MICHELLE RENEE LANE: *The Gilda Stories* was your debut novel. I think it's interesting that as BIPOC women writers, we both chose to write vampire novels that deal with slavery and its effect on the American psyche. Your novel and Toni Morrison's *Beloved* were inspirations to me. What inspired you to write *The Gilda Stories*? Where did this narrative come from and why did you decide to make it a vampire novel?

JEWELLE GOMEZ: The original story grew out of a moment on the street when two drunk men were harassing me as I was talking on a public phone—so you know how long ago that was! For some reason I didn't just ignore them as we women usually do. And even ignoring them causes us damage. I just flipped out and challenged them and cursed them until they became afraid. They thought I was crazy and ran away. When I got home the adrenaline was still coursing through me and I sat down to write a story of an attacker who gets a shock when his prey turns the tables. Vampires were always my favorite horror movies so it seemed natural she'd have the strength and power of a vampire.

MICHELLE RENEE LANE: It's been over 30 years since *The Gilda Stories* was published. It has been adapted for film and the stage, and it celebrated a 25-year anniversary with an expanded volume. I've slowly been working the sequel to *Invisible Chains*, which was published four years ago, and I agonize over making sure the next book will meet the expectations of readers. What has the process been like for you to write the sequel to *The Gilda Stories*? What stopped you from writing the book sooner? What advice would give writers who want to write a sequel to a published work that has had a positive response?

JEWELLE GOMEZ: I did several chapters of the sequel (now called *GILDA: Blood Relations*) just as I did the original. I picked a decade and place and constructed a story around the circumstances of that moment. Then I rethought the arc and what Gilda was searching for and decided to do it all in the first person. Making a decision about what your character wants and how it might be different from the first book is crucial to creating a sequel. Time passed very quickly so I didn't notice it was 30 years! I was doing readings of GILDA all the time on college campuses and at conferences. And writing my plays—one based on GILDA took 3 years. And the previous 10 years I was playwright in residence at New Conservatory Theatre Center in San Francisco.

MICHELLE RENEE LANE: Your work has been adapted for the stage and I believe you in the process of adapting *The Gilda Stories* for television. We've all seen examples of how a writer's work is adapted to the screen and thought, "the book was better." As a reader, I often think of books I love as sacred texts, so I can't imagine what it would be like to have my writing adapted by people who might interpret it in ways I didn't intend. What has that process been like for you? How much input do you have as a writer in creating these new interpretations of your work?

JEWELLE GOMEZ: Cheryl Dunye, (*Watermelon Woman*, *Lovecraft Country*) who is doing the mini series is one of my favorite filmmakers and a friend. I trust her vision and integrity so this is a very exciting process for me. We have extraordinary meetings about what the show could look like; how it might be structured, etc. and I feel like she and her team honor the character and the principles behind it. At the same time the mini series is Cheryl's vision. So it's like raising children: give them the best you have then let them go.

MICHELLE RENEE LANE: You have accomplished a lot in your career(s) as an academic, as a writer and as an activist. Which of your accomplishments are you most proud of, and what accomplishments do you still have your sights set on for the future?

JEWELLE GOMEZ: When someone comes up to me at a conference as happened at the Saints & Sinners Lit Fest in New Orleans recently and says GILDA changed my life or GILDA showed me the courage I needed I feel I've done my best work. I'm very pleased with my play about James Baldwin "Waiting for Giovanni" which was kind of ahead of the curve in the renaissance of interest in Baldwin. I have a speculative fiction novella I'm hoping to get published soon then who knows?

MICHELLE RENEE LANE: Aside from the fact that you wrote one of my favorite vampire novels of all time, I think the one thing that stood out to me the most in your bio is that you were on the staff of the television show "The Electric Company." Growing up, I loved that show more than "Sesame Street" and wondered what your role was in creating one of the coolest, most diverse shows on Public Television.

JEWELLE GOMEZ: I was just out of undergraduate school when I moved to NYC to be a production assistant on "The Electric Company." I was really not prepared for the pace and more technical requirements of a NY show so I got fired! But I treasure the chance I got to watch some of my icons work: Morgan Freeman was a gentleman of the highest order and a lot of fun. Rita Moreno taught me how to take off my make up! And dear Irene Cara was a musical delight.

MICHELLE RENEE LANE: A few years ago, we were interviewed in conversation with each other for the Women in Horror Series hosted by University of Pittsburgh Library System Horror Studies program. In that conversation, you talked about your relationships with Audre Lorde and Toni Morrison, two of the most influential writers of the 20th century. You told some memorable stories about your time together. Can you talk a little bit about how they influenced your work as a writer and helped shaped your evolving identity as a BIPOC woman in activism and academia?

JEWELLE GOMEZ: I only had the pleasure of meeting Toni Morrison once but her work had a lasting effect on me. Her elegant style and ability to wrestle with topics like skin color and slavery encouraged me. And her quintessential ghost story, *Beloved*, made me know Black people can really write horror!

I had the joy of becoming friends with Audre after I audited one of her poetry classes at Hunter College in NYC. She had a wicked sense of humor and was a delightful flirt and took her writing and the writing of other women very seriously. I loved that Audre always insisted on being introduced with all her identities: poet, lesbian, feminist, warrior, mother! It helped me keep all of myself in focus as I write.

MICHELLE RENEE LANE: To continue that idea of BIPOC women supporting each other, what are your thoughts on the importance of community among BIPOC women in creative circles. What advice do you have for building and maintaining communities that support the lives and work of BIPOC women? Why does that matter right now in the world we live in?

JEWELLE GOMEZ: I think it's been difficult with the pandemic lockdown to hold on to a sense of community. The internet and the various things like Instagram (which I love) and Facebook give the impression that we're communicating and connecting. But it's only in a superficial way. We know after experiencing the 'George Floyd Summer' that we can come together for important political action. It's important for us to find ways to meet in person to keep the energy and intention going. Whether it's a regular book club or a volunteer activity you do with friends we need that in-person and continual contact to keep a movement going. For writers to connect with other writers and their work is key. If workshops aren't your jam, then maybe one on one.

MICHELLE RENEE LANE: I feel like it has taken a long time for writers like yourself and Toni Morrison to be recognized for your contributions to the horror genre. You write about race, gender, queerness, and other intersectionalities of identity politics, and let's not forget, vampires. Slavery alone provides a wealth of inspiration for horror stories. To paraphrase Tananarive Due, Black history is Black horror. What would you say to those who believe that Black women and their stories don't have a place within the horror cannon? Why are they wrong?

JEWELLE GOMEZ: Tananarive Due said it all. When I started writing GILDA some were afraid vampires were too negative to connect with Black people or women. Now we've evolved and see that the horror was always there and we benefit from bringing it to the surface. Women of color have always been in the vanguard around exploring the things most painful in our history.

MICHELLE RENEE LANE: What's the next book on the top of your TBR pile? Are there any writers we should be paying closer attention to in horror or any of the other speculative fiction genres?

JEWELLE GOMEZ: I want to read NK Jemisin's work. I know I'm behind but I'm catching up! Then I've got on my stack *A Strange and Stubborn Endurance* by Fox Meadows and *The Wicked and The Willing* by Lianyu Tan.

MICHELLE RENEE LANE: What's next for you? Any new writing projects or other projects we should know about?

JEWELLE GOMEZ: I'm finishing a new play for New Conservatory to premier in the spring of 2024. And my goal is to finish the new GILDA by then too. After that...?

MICHELLE RENEE LANE writes dark speculative fiction about identity politics and women of color battling their inner demons while falling in love with monsters. Her work includes elements of fantasy, horror, romance, and occasionally erotica. Her short fiction appears in several anthologies. Her Bram Stoker Award® nominated debut novel, *Invisible Chains* (2019), is available from Haverhill House Publishing. The Spanish language translation, *Cadenas Invisibles* (2022), is available from Dilatando Mentes Editorial.

Born and raised in the middle of nowhere Pennsylvania, Michelle spent countless hours of her youth obsessed with the occult and consumed by vampire fiction. She climbed into strangers' cars, explored abandoned buildings seeking secret passageways to hidden worlds, taught herself to read Tarot cards, and consulted the dead with a Ouija board. Michelle's first and subsequent heartbreaks have given her much material for her cautionary tales about the perils of falling in love with monsters. She holds an MFA in Writing Popular Fiction from Seton Hill University.

ALMA KATSU

I first met Alma when we were co-readers at the venerable KGB bar reading series, hosted by Ellen Datlow and Matt Kressel, in September of 2012. At that point, the first two volumes of her *The Taker Trilogy* had recently been published. She was and is very nice, humble, down to earth, and easy to talk to. My main memory from that evening, aside from it being one million degrees inside the bar so the windows were open, was when it was Alma's turn to read, some sort of school marching band decided to set up practice on the street below the open window directly behind the lectern from which we read. Alma was a trooper though, and with grace and wit, powered through her reading with the backing of the band. Hmm, KGB, window…now I'm wondering if her spy thriller *Red Widow* was originally called *Red Window*. Anyway, fast forward to the spring of 2018 and Alma dropped *The Hunger* on us unsuspecting cretins. The novel is an utterly gripping, expert blend of horror and historical fiction, that in retrospect reads like a mission statement and a preview of the wonderful books and stories to come.

PAUL TREMBLAY: Anyway, hi, Alma, I'm honored to be here to ask the pointed, difficult questions.

ALMA KATSU: I remember that night. I remember thinking I could see how people become snipers. I adore your work and I'm honored to be interviewed by you.

PAUL TREMBLAY: Aw, go on with ya. Since I brought it up, was the KGB reading your first exposure (and I use that term purposefully, like being exposed to a virus) to a section of the horror writing and reading community?

ALMA KATSU: Yes, and it was a scary experience. I wasn't sure if I belonged to the horror community. My first book, which eventually became a trilogy, was more in the fantasy/paranormal romance realm though—and I can't stress this strongly enough—*The Taker* is not romance. There's no happily ever after; it's dark and violent and abusive (of both the characters and readers). My sense at the time was that the horror community wasn't fond of the paranormal romance crowd, so I have no idea what I thought I'd accomplish by barging my way into the KBG Bar. I think I was trying to make inroads into whichever community would have me.

PAUL TREMBLAY: Let's go back to the beginning. You spent much of your childhood in Concord, Massachusetts. You've spoken about living in that area informing both your love of history and horror, and um, I'm going to ask you to speak about it again.

ALMA KATSU: I call that area Colonial Ground Zero. Everything you are surrounded by is old: farmhouses, barns, the commons, cemeteries. That's where I got my deep-seated love of the Gothic. My whole world was spooky and dark. Everything in New England, it seemed, was haunted.

At the same time, everything was drenched in history. I didn't appreciate until later that I was surrounded by things that had been around for centuries. When you're a kid, you walk into houses that are centuries old and don't think of the history in those timbers. You're just in your friend's stupid decaying house with the dirt cellar and the giant fireplace. I didn't realize how much I'd internalized the history until I was writing *The Taker*.

PAUL TREMBLAY: This might be a dumb question, but did those dual interests feel dichotomous initially or had it always seemed like there was natural overlap?

ALMA KATSU: I was blind to it. It literally wasn't until the book was on its way to the printer that I realized I'd been drawing on my entire childhood in writing that book. [Slaps forehead. D'oh!] I think our first books are usually therapy. We wrestle with our subconscious. We just don't realize it at the time.

PAUL TREMBLAY: You got your degrees in literature and writing (even studying with John Irving if Wikipedia is to be believed) and then you ended up with a 34-year career working for government intelligence—and you don't have to tell us how that happened if you don't want to, as I assume you'd have to then kill us—but I'm curious if you were writing fiction during your time working in intelligence. Or, when did the itch to write your first novel, *The Taker*, become an undeniable one? Was that a scary leap to make?

ALMA KATSU: I'd been writing fiction since I was a teenager. I wanted to become a novelist but in those days, the process was a complete mystery. No internet! I knew no novelists (John Irving not withstanding. I did study with him briefly but it was like sitting at the feet of a god, the air too thin). I pursued the only way I could see to make money writing: newspaper work. I was a stringer for several papers when I got the opportunity to interview with the National Security Agency. I thought the interview process alone would make for an interesting experience and had no expectations past that. They ended up offering me a job, which meant I could move away from my family and start to have those grown-up adventures writers are told they need to have something to write about. It was all in service to, one day, being a novelist.

I thought I'd stay five years and ended up having an entire career. I wasn't a national security nerd or loved foreign affairs. I was a writer and they just happened to need people with writing skills. Back in those days, that was enough. It was a great career. I spent time at CIA, the Office of the Secretary of Defense. I was in the West Wing! So many stories. But it was also tough, demanding, very competitive. I learned a lot about human nature, our predilection (some might say addiction) for conflict and pain. So many lessons.

I'd had to quit journalism shortly after I joined NSA. I wrote about the music scene in DC, but the subject didn't matter. At that time, they didn't want you to do any outside writing. So, I decided to give up all writing, including the little bit of fiction I was producing at the time. I didn't write creatively for about 15 years. But then I developed a serious illness and while we were sorting it out, I started writing fiction to take my mind off things. I really enjoyed it even though my writing sucked. Writing even a mother couldn't love! I told myself if we could get the illness under control, I'd take up writing again.

So that's what happened. It took about a year to get better enough to get back to work and write in the evenings. I went to grad school for fiction. I started writing *The Taker* then, but it would take 10 years in total to get the story in a position where it was salable.

PAUL TREMBLAY: How did your husband and coworkers react when you said, hey, I'm going to write books now?

ALMA KATSU: The husband wasn't surprised but my coworkers were. When they heard I'd sold a book, they thought it was a scholarly book on my area of expertise. Imagine their surprise when I told them it was full of magic and love.

PAUL TREMBLAY: There was a four-year gap between *The Taker Trilogy* and *The Hunger*. While the latter novel features the supernatural, it's grounded in a retelling of a gritty historical event. Which, from a distance, seems like a real shift in writerly gears. Was that shift purposeful? Was writing the history aspect of *The Hunger* a challenge or a natural fit or somewhere between? Where did *The Hunger* come from anyway?

ALMA KATSU: *The Hunger* came from two places. One, I'd always been curious about the Donner Party. I'd written a little screenplay in grad school, an exercise, but the Donner Party was mentioned in it. So, it was on my radar.

But the idea for *The Hunger* was pitched to me by Glasstown Entertainment. They hadn't done adult fiction at that point and asked if I'd be interested. I thought it would be interesting to work with other writers, accomplished writers. I'd had a negative experience with the *Taker Trilogy* and came out of it feeling shaky. I thought it would be good to see what I could learn from someone else.

Historical horror is a good fit for me in that my life as an analyst is, basically, research, so a big research project doesn't frighten me. If anything, I probably prefer to have the handrails of history to lean on. *The Hunger* ended up being a great learning experience, figuring out where the story is—a new story, a different one—from one that already exists and which many people think they know (but do they, really?). Like everything in life, the experience wasn't exactly what I thought it would be, but we produced some good books together (including *The Deep* and *The Fervor*) and I learned a lot in the process. But it wasn't all cupcakes and puppy dogs.

PAUL TREMBLAY: One of the things I greatly admire about your historical horror work is that the stories are relevant to our now (the feminism of *The Deep*, the xenophobia and AAPI racism in *The Fervor*, the ascendency of Nazism in "The Werhwulf"), despite being set decades or over a century ago. Was the now-relevance something you actively baked into the stories, or was there a more organic approach to the storytelling?

ALMA KATSU: Well, thank you. I'm fond of this, though I wonder if it costs me readers. I get a lot of reviews that groan about having lessons shoved at them. I think it's something I can't help after decades of being an intelligence analyst. Your job is to find the relevance of all these little pieces of information: you put them all together, and what does it mean? What's the "so what?" And yet, when writing fiction, the goal is the opposite. The "so what" is often so subtle that it's almost invisible. It's something you feel in your gut but maybe can't express. That's graceful and beautiful. That's art.

I was able to do this once with a short story, "The Familiar's Assistant" (Dark Stars anthology). That was probably my subtlest story to date.

The Fervor and "The Wehrwolf" are at the other end of the spectrum. These stories were designed to teach a lesson, based on actual history. In both cases, it's because I have a little inside knowledge that outrages me and makes me think a story has to be written. In the case of "The Wehrwolf," for instance, I worked on civil conflicts that led to genocides and mass atrocities. I saw the same behaviors we'd seen in Bosnia and Rwanda and yes, Nazi Germany, playing out in America and the fact that Americans just accepted this blew my mind. Was it ignorance? I want to think my little werewolf story maybe changed a few minds but that's probably just hubris.

PAUL TREMBLAY: If you lose those kinds of readers they were and are lost anyway. Perhaps, if we're being hopeful, your stories will linger and win some of those damaged hearts and minds.

The Fervor, especially with the passionate, call-to-arms essay at its conclusion, certainly reads like a pointed, purposeful response to our now. What was the kernel that inspired this novel? Is there a personal/familial connection to the internment camps that you drew upon?

ALMA KATSU: *The Fervor* is probably my favorite of all the novels I've written. I'm half-Japanese, but my mother is from the old country so I didn't know anything about the internment until I married. My husband's entire family had been interned. I learned about it watching documentaries and reading books, and of course hearing personal stories. I didn't have to do much research at all for that book: it was all baked into my brain, but with stories from inside the barbed wire fence.

The Japanese at the time were told by their elders to cooperate with this pretty outrageous demand from the government to show America that they were, actually, good Americans and that their neighbors were wrong about them. After the war, studies show there were ZERO cases of Japanese committing espionage against the U.S. In other words, there was no basis for locking 120,00 people in camps (of which 70,000 were U.S. citizens). It was done out of irrational fear and blind belief in lies. Now, fast forward decades and we're still seeing discrimination and prejudice against Asians—witness the violence against Asians because of the way the pandemic was politicized. And you wonder why we can't learn from the past.

You grow up reading and admiring books like *Fahrenheit 451* and *The Handmaid's Tale*, political books, and you think this is why we write books: to make people think. You think maybe you could do something remotely similar and do some good. You think this is why you become a writer.

PAUL TREMBLAY: Very well said. Writing is a political act.

I feel like our careers have some similarities insofar as our first novels were not horror, and we had a good chunk of time between those books and our break-out horror novels. Did you feel pressure writing *The Deep* (which is a haunting, beautiful book) to reproduce/replicate the reader/reviewer response that *The Hunger* received? How did you deal with that pressure?

ALMA KATSU: I did feel pressure to come up with another *Hunger*, and I think you can see some similarities between the books. But it had a lot more elements to it—the Titanic being many people's favorite disaster (don't fuck it up!), the many moving parts. Plus the stories are developed in partnership with Glasstown and for this one in particular, they wanted a lot of elements in it that were difficult to reconcile. I feel like writing these books must be a lot like writing a TV show, very collaborative. As an aside, I'm in the process of writing my first horror novel without collaborators, nor is it historical, and it's somewhat daunting.

PAUL TREMBLAY: You've recently published a spy novel to great acclaim, with the following up *Red London* coming in March, both of which clearly draw upon your intelligence work experience. I wonder how that experience has informed your historical horror novels as well.

ALMA KATSU: Thanks for mentioning the spy stories; I do love them. I've come to see that I write the kind of novels I do—lots and lots of sub-plots and characters and moving pieces that get woven together—because of the analysis work. That's what it's like: every day, you get confronted with a hundred (or thousands) of tiny pieces of information, and you have to figure out how it all goes together. And you do it again the next day, and over the course of days or weeks you start to understand what it all means. My writing gets described as "twisty" a lot, and I think that's why. It's intrinsically complicated. I probably can't write a straight-forward story to save my life.

PAUL TREMBLAY: Is switching hats between genres difficult? Is it more like a battery-charging relief kind of thing, like 'oh, now I get to take a break from this to write that?'

ALMA KATSU: Writing spy stories is much easier for me. The ideas just flow. But it makes the difficulty of writing good horror more apparent to me. I feel less sure of the ground under my feet there.

PAUL TREMBLAY: Who are your primary writing influences? Who are some of your favorite contemporary writers?

ALMA KATSU: Well, you for one, though I know you're not fishing for compliments.

PAUL TREMBLAY: I'm always fishing for compliments! And I'm honored.

ALMA KATSU: I like writers who try something different, particularly those who like to experiment with form. I tend not to follow individual writers now and am drawn more to books that sound interesting. Kelly Link has a new story collection coming out that I'm really looking forward to. I've been more interested in short stories than novels lately, too.

PAUL TREMBLAY: Speaking of short stories, you've been writing more of them as of late. What has the experience been like shifting from novels to short stories, which is the opposite experience for so many of us who started writing short fiction?

ALMA KATSU: Like most, I wrote short stories in grad school though I transitioned to a novel for my thesis. I liked writing stories, but it was scary, like what do you do if you can't make it work? Whereas with novels, you have lots of real estate to make things come together.

Writing short stories has been liberating. It's a different kind of challenge, which feels good. It's nice to get in and get out and not to need worry about doing so much work. On the other hand, the challenge is making something artful happen quickly. It seems like a magic trick. I'm afraid I like it a little too much—I seem to come up with a lot of short story ideas lately.

PAUL TREMBLAY: What's next?

ALMA KATSU: As the Magic Eight Ball would say, 'reply hazy, try again.' My next novel will be contemporary horror, scheduled for fall 2024.Its tentative title is *The Coffin Club*. I've also got another Amazon Original Story coming out summer 2023, "Black Vault," which is an X-Files-esque spy thriller. After that, it's uncertain. It's really, really hard to write in two genres, mostly for marketing purposes, and I have a feeling I'll have to make a choice soon.

PAUL TREMBLAY: Well even if you leave horror for a bit, you'll be back. It's like a curse. One last question is the dreaded writerly advice question. Dreaded, because I dread it when I'm asked, but I look forward to your answer.

ALMA KATSU: I have nothing new, I'm afraid. Reading out of your genre is my favorite. Read broadly: I find it renewing.

PAUL TREMBLAY: You made it through my poorly worded, fumbly questions, Alma! You're the best.

ALMA KATSU: Not poorly worded at all. One thing about you that's always impressed me is your eloquence. You're a great speaker for a mathematician.

PAUL TREMBLAY: The calculus test is coming in the mail. Keep an eye out for it.

ALMA KATSU: This is like one of those recurring nightmares where it's time for the final and you haven't studied.

PAUL TREMBLAY has won the Bram Stoker, British Fantasy, and Massachusetts Book awards and is the author of *Survivor Song*, *The Cabin at the End of the World*, *Disappearance at Devil's Rock*, *A Head Full of Ghosts*, the crime novels *The Little Sleep* and *No Sleep Till Wonderland*, and the short story collection, *Growing Things and Other Stories*.

His essays and short fiction have appeared in the *Los Angeles Times*, *New York Times*, *Entertainment Weekly* online, and numerous year's-best anthologies. He has a master's degree in mathematics and lives outside Boston with his family.

DANIEL KRAUS

KATHE KOJA: Daniel Kraus, I am delighted and honored to be doing this interview with you today, and my only regret is that we are not doing it in the halls of the Romero Collection. But he was very much present as I was putting together my questions. And my questions are reflections on themes and preoccupations that are coming up in pretty much everything of yours. All of these books touch on three themes over and over again in different permutations. The three hearts of everything you do or everything is in this book, are family, monsters, and dissolution that occurs again and again and again and I found that fascinating.

DANIEL KRAUS: Yeah, that sounds accurate.

KATHE KOJA: Let's start with *The Living Dead*. In the very moving afterward, you talk about George Romero almost as a family member. Talk about the family in the *Living Dead*.

DANIEL KRAUS: The family in the *Living Dead* reflects my favorite kind of family, which is not the one you're born but the ones you pick up along the way. An apocalypse is a good way to force that. The family units that exist at the beginning of *The Living Dead* all disintegrate pretty fast and the ones that don't, there's a reason for that. Everyone has to then naturally connect to whatever the strongest family is going to be at that moment. And for some of them, it is people they already know, and for some of them it's people they know but aren't supposed to like, and for others it's people they haven't yet met. There's one character who dislikes all the versions of all the families that she's been offered in her life and prefers to live alone. The book does give me a chance, particularly in the last act, to posit what the ideal family and the ideal society would be.

KATHE KOJA: *Scowler*, obviously, has family, too, at the core. Talk about monsters and *Scowler*.

DANIEL KRAUS: For quite a while in my career, I didn't write really anything supernatural. My first four or five books, they're all horror novels but none of them had anything beyond the human realm. It was people driven to various kinds of monstrosity and the idea that the things that *look* monstrous weren't the things that *were* monstrous. Ultimately, I started to edge into more fantastical materials sort of mid-career.

KATHE KOJA: Was it a ramping choice or did that evolve organically?

DANIEL KRAUS: I don't think it was really until *The Shape of Water* that I started writing distinctly about a more classic type of monster. And obviously, that was a monster who was quite beautiful. Up until then, my mission that I'd given myself in my career was to write beautifully about ugly things. I really wanted to dissect things in a beautiful way. So, yeah, monsters more overtly show up, although, really, I still have a preponderance of human monsters. Obviously, yes, I'm very interested in monstrosity and how it relates to the eye of the beholder.

KATHE KOJA: The triangle is the most interesting shape because if the pressure on any side is uneven, the whole thing falls apart. *The Autumnal* is very balanced, almost a perfect triangle.

DANIEL KRAUS: That's interesting because *The Autumnal* features the most effective family unit I've ever written. I know when I was writing it, it felt notable: a mother and a daughter who had their problems but were basically functioning. It did feel like a bit of optimism that I hadn't allowed myself up until then.

KATHE KOJA: I thought the family in *Scowler* was successful. Even though they were hampered and broken, they were still moving toward wholeness.

DANIEL KRAUS: I guess why I don't think about that for *Scowler* is that because they were so broken by the father, to begin with. Whereas I think, despite their economic situation, the mom and daughter in *The Autumnal* start on really good terms and only then receive the challenge.

KATHE KOJA: But there's also the inherent challenge from the grandma in *The Autumnal*, which starts the engine of the story going.

DANIEL KRAUS: In my work, family tends to be a weight that's chained to your ankle. It usually isn't something that you can return to as a well of strength.

KATHE KOJA: And it becomes, or can become, an antagonist almost.

DANIEL KRAUS: Oh, yeah.

KATHE KOJA: The character has to push against, or elude, or figure out how am I going to navigate this.

DANIEL KRAUS: I've built up quite a bit of ambiguous feelings and even suspicion about traditional family units that trace back to growing up in a small town in Iowa. There's this popular sense of the heartland having all these sturdy families, but that wasn't what I saw at all. I saw families holding family members back and re-establishing bad patterns, and tradition acting as roadblocks to growth and development.

KATHE KOJA: Well, then let's look at the third point of the triangle, which is rot and dissolution—or, as you just said, growth and development. Where does all this rot come from? There is a powerful lot of it and you are very, very skillful and poetic about bringing in that gore and the goo. There's a lot of goo.

DANIEL KRAUS: That started with *Rotters* which, of course, is about grave robbing. I wanted to write realistically about corpses. And so I did a lot of research on what corpses would really look like as opposed to what you see in movies when people pop open a coffin. It was a visceral training. It is a wet, runny disgusting soup that we all turn into if we're buried.

KATHE KOJA: There are so many great passages in *Rotters* about the smell, and the power of that smell, and it's not a smell you forget.

DANIEL KRAUS: There was something about the physicality of what we are when we die that felt really at odds with the ceremony *around* dying. You know that people dress up in these nice suits. We put people in a nice coffin. Then we have a nice minister who says some nice words, and then we put the person underground like that does something or safeguards us in some way.

KATHE KOJA: And then caskets are locked too, right?

DANIEL KRAUS: Yeah, caskets are locked and have cement casing around them.

KATHE KOJA: I don't want to smell that.

DANIEL KRAUS: The funeral industry felt duplicitous to me. It felt predatory. It began to form in my mind as a metaphor for a lot of modern society. We're fed or advertised things that supposedly matter but none of them do. When you open up the box it isn't someone in a beautiful robe being welcomed into heaven, it's a stew of melted flesh, and describing those bodies felt like not turning away from reality.

KATHE KOJA: There's the rot at the core of institutions, or at the core of the false vision of the family, or the false definition of what a monster is. But there's a great deal of love in these books too. There's a great deal of frustrated love and accepting love and very honest and clear love. There's not a lot of false emotion.

DANIEL KRAUS: There's little romance in my books. Because there can't be. There can't be when you know how things are really going to end and you're honest about death and decomposition and all these things. It intrinsically removes a lot of the safety valves we have when you don't have a belief that we're all going to end up in some heaven, or the feeling that family is more important than anything. These beliefs are largely self-centered.

KATHE KOJA: We have death, but death is the gateway to eternal life in our cosmology.

DANIEL KRAUS: IF you can be honest about death, that leads you to be honest about everything. The love that pops up in these books has to acknowledge everyone's failures and weaknesses and dark sides. I've often said how I have very little interest in good versus evil, but I have a lot of interest in bad versus worse.

KATHE KOJA: And that makes the character's victories and losses so much more effective. I don't believe in saving the town from the monster either, I don't think it can be done. It's intrinsic to the fabric of the time, you're never going to get rid of the monsters the same way, you're never going to get rid of the rot.

DANIEL KRAUS: That's exactly right. It doesn't take much. It's going to get all of us.

KATHE KOJA: A book like *Rotters*—or *The Autumnal*, which I thought was so beautifully spare and is almost a distillation of these themes and tropes—it's really trying to keep bringing that truth down, like cook it down. With ingredients that are part of the horror cookbook let's say, but the way that you're combining them makes your work very different.

DANIEL KRAUS: I think what I've tried to do with my books does mirror what George Romero tried to do with his movies. He was not in a lot of ways a horror filmmaker. He made one horror movie and it became popular enough that he bracketed into the genre. But his interests were rarely to scare you. He only made, by my account, two movies that were meant to scare you. My interests are not primarily to scare you, although I like when I do it. But I also like when I make you cry. I give those things equal weight. I'm not ever going to look at my books and say, well, I haven't done a werewolf book yet, so I guess I'll do a werewolf book. That checklist approach has no interest for me.

KATHE KOJA: I think that's very wise what you're saying about fear because there are no jump scares in these books. But the cumulative weight of sorrow and grief is very dense. Each of these books has this kernel of grief close to the center.

DANIEL KRAUS: I don't know exactly where that comes from. I know that I want to power the books with emotional engines.

KATHE KOJA: I think what you're saying is that you're not necessarily going out with the emotion shovel to say, "I'm going to make you feel like this." You're creating these conditions and these people will have to wade through things they might never have considered.

DANIEL KRAUS: I'm interested much more in dread than I am with horror. The kind of pits that we dig ourselves into, and maybe that's why *Rotters* has been such a lodestar for me in my bibliography. It's such a perfect metaphor. We dig ourselves into these holes in our lives and what's scary is that we're going to be stuck in our respective holes forever.

KATHE KOJA: It's literally digging your own grave, right?

DANIEL KRAUS: We all are. We're all digging our own graves.

KATHE KOJA: That has to be the natural title for this interview, "We're all digging our own graves."

DANIEL KRAUS: All right.

KATHE KOJA: Even in a book which I love a lot, *Blood Sugar,* the family, the rot, and the monster are the trinity. That's an extremely poignant book, which, when you first get into it, that's not your immediate reaction. But it's a constructive family again, right?

DANIEL KRAUS: Generally when people try to connect my books, they talk about father and son relationships. But I like how you're framing it, that it really is about the uses and misuses of family and value. I see it all over American society. Whether it's the *Fast and Furious* movies or TV commercials, the Republican party, you see this constant emphasis on the family. And I just don't agree with that at all. Biological families are things you land into, you have no choice in it, and you make the best situation you can. But anything you don't challenge isn't worth anything. If you don't think critically about your family and what your family is doing, or what beliefs they're foisting upon you, you're not living a life well lived.

KATHE KOJA: That narrow definition of family, it flies in the face of what most of us know. I mean that's kind of a living death as well, right? This coffin of expectations saying this is what a family is this is how we all need to live. Not only are you digging your own grave, but now you're digging a grave for me, right? And you're digging a grave for my possibility as a kid or as a spouse or as a whatever. No way forward for me.

DANIEL KRAUS: I think you stumbled upon it. I so fortuitous that I ended up working with Romero on a book called *The Living Dead*. A big theme of my books is living death. People who are stuck in terrible relationships or terrible jobs or just some sort of unalterable situation that perpetuates. They're alive but not really.

KATHE KOJA: Either a thing is growing or it's rotten. So if my family unit is not a living, growing unit, it's rotting. It's rotting in place and pretty soon you're going to smell it.

DANIEL KRAUS: In my *Zebulon Finch* duology, the main character is an undead 17-year-old. He lives for a hundred years. But he's not really a zombie or a vampire. He's a very erudite, intelligent person. Essentially, it's taking him 100 years to rot away. But his goal of those years, whether he realizes it or not, is one of redemption. To redeem himself for all the terrible things he did when he was alive, to make amends before his body falls apart. It's visceral for him because his body's literally rotting in front of him—but really that's happening to all of us.

KATHE KOJA: That really talks about the human condition, right? It's like if you're privileged to live long enough, to be able to reflect and say, boy, I really wish I could fix some of the things that I've done or I wish I could experience life differently, or whatever, before my parts fall off, or before I get hit by a bus whatever—there's not a fear of death in any of these books.

DANIEL KRAUS: From the author's standpoint there's not. Obviously, the characters can fear death.

KATHE KOJA: But I mean from you, I don't feel any of that. I don't feel like the feeling you get from Poe, like, boy, does this guy not want to die!

DANIEL KRAUS: Right.

KATHE KOJA: He'll die.

DANIEL KRAUS: I can't say that I don't fear death. We all do to some extent. But you can make peace with your own irrelevance, and I think that's what so many people are unable to do, Americans particularly.

KATHE KOJA: Your life is still important and valuable but it's not precious.

DANIEL KRAUS: I think we would all be better off if we could accept our irrelevance. I think if we can be good to one other and not feel that we're all so special, that's a means of pulling together that would actually be good for the planet, and good for the species.

KATHE KOJA: It helps some people in the face of the vastness that really doesn't care about us to think Jesus wants me for some reason. I think irrelevance is one of the constituent powers of rot, right?

DANIEL KRAUS: Rot is not death. Rot itself is life. The things that are rotting you are living microbes, and that's why it's not good to pack a corpse into a box. Your body parts will be well used by the Earth.

KATHE KOJA: That's what I mean, that is a form of dissolution that you would think we could look forward to with peace, right? That would be so great to think of all my molecules becoming parts of the soil and helping other organisms. If you want eternal life, baby, that's it.

DANIEL KRAUS: Exactly.

KATHE KOJA: Being put a concrete envelope is sort of the opposite of that.

DANIEL KRAUS: Injecting your body with embalming fluids and sealing it inside cement is the direct opposite of everlasting life.

KATHE KOJA: And the best part is, you're still going to rot but it is going to be much worse and much less pleasant.

DANIEL KRAUS: Exactly.

KATHE KOJA: There is a lot of unexpected humor in your books.

It's not funny in the sense of hahaha, but it's very much a part of the life. It gives the books growth and pleasure, and even in the saddest of them there are moments of hilarity, sometimes a very quiet kind. *Blood Sugar* is very funny.

DANIEL KRAUS: I don't think anyone has ever asked me about humor in my books, so this is a new one. I'm always conscious of that. In most of my books, you have to scrape away the horror to find the humor. *Blood Sugar* leads with humor and then, because the narrator is so bouncy and optimistic and funny, you almost have to look past the jokes to see the horror! It almost creeps up on you.

KATHE KOJA: *Blood Sugar* was very sad too.

DANIEL KRAUS: Yeah, *Blood Sugar* is very dire and very sad. It's sort of like the sad clown, right? Like someone who's always cracking jokes. That friend of yours who's always being funny is probably the saddest and that's what *Blood Sugar* is. Laughing to cover up the pain. One could make an argument that *Blood Sugar* is among my very darkest.

KATHE KOJA: *The Ghost that Ate Us* is also pretty funny. I love the format of it. It's black humor and there are moments in there that are just cringe-worthy funny.

DANIEL KRAUS: I wanted to play with the idea of something that's so intrinsically funny to people that it clouds the reality of it. The book begins by talking about how the humor of the situation blinded people to how tragic it was. The subtitle of the book is *The Tragic True Story of the Burger City Poltergeist*.

KATHE KOJA: It's like a punch line but there's not really a joke.

DANIEL KRAUS: I was experimenting in that book b peeling away the humor until at the end there was no humor at all. You feel yourself getting tricked into something that's really quite scary.

KATHE KOJA: And overwhelmingly there's also a lot of effluvia and grease. More so than *Rotters* in some ways. It's an icky book.

DANIEL KRAUS: It's a book about meat in a lot of ways. Like the qualities of carnivorous activities. One of my favorite parts of that book is a fast-food worker's theory that the poltergeist is all the slaughtered animals that were used to make the fast-food menu are coming back to haunt the eaters.

KATHE KOJA: That's why we call it beef and not a dead cow.

DANIEL KRAUS: That's right.

KATHE KOJA: That's why we call it veal and not little dead calf.

DANIEL KRAUS: Or even better, that's why we call it Big Macs.

KATHE KOJA: That's back to the rot, right? You're eating a piece of a dead thing when you're eating your burger.

DANIEL KRAUS: What *The Ghost That Ate Us* is saying, and what all the books are saying, is be aware of what you're doing. Be honest with yourself, whether it's how you eat, or how you behave, or how you worship, or whatever. Stop hiding behind facades, whether that facade is a fancy church, or a mascot on a fast-food menu. The festooning of society makes it easy for us to not look piercingly at what we're doing.

KATHE KOJA: They're all very truthful books. Let's end by saying these are books about family, and monsters, and rot, that are very truthful and very funny, and they're here to help you if you will take them in the spirit in which they were constructed. So, thank you, Daniel Kraus, for this interview.

DANIEL KRAUS: Hey, it was absolutely my honor.

KATHE KOJA is a writer, director and independent producer. Her immersive work combines and plays with genres, from YA to contemporary to historical to horror. Her novels - including *The Cipher, Velocities, Buddha Boy, Talk,* and the *Under the Poppy* trilogy—have won awards, been multiply translated, and optioned for film and performance.

CYNTHIA PELAYO

MICHAEL J. SEIDLINGER: Horror, what scares you? I mean I feel like we're horror writers, we find something in the actual act of exploring something that quote-unquote frightens the reader and I'm really curious. What scares you?

CYNTHIA PELAYO: People scare me and losing people scares me now even more so. I also think it's the coldness with which some people treat one another. They treat one another not like a fellow human being. They treat one another like a product that can be used and discarded.

MICHAEL J. SEIDLINGER: Was being scared of the possibility of bad people out there, was that always something—like a constant fear throughout your life?

CYNTHIA PELAYO: My Dad loved to watch the news. He was always connected to the news and to the newspapers, and both of my parents experienced, not directly, but had known people that really awful things happened to them. My parents would just tell me these things. I kind of stay away from the news today because it gives me so much anxiety.

MICHAEL J. SEIDLINGER: I feel a lot of parents they try to protect their kids by sheltering them from these cruelties that are literally just down the street, around the corner. Sometimes right in front of us. Like specifically now in our technologically, socially driven world. Do you feel like it was your parents' way of not wanting to hide it from you?

CYNTHIA PELAYO: They didn't want to filter it. From a very young age they wanted me to recognize that there are horrible people out there. That they will take me and they will do awful things to me and no one will ever see me again. My mom would always say that, 'They will take you and they will do bad things to you and no one will ever see you again.'

MICHAEL J. SEIDLINGER: It makes sense that they were raising you to be hyper aware. It informs one's childhood and then, of course, one's own adulthood and in your writing. We've talked about this a lot, like you're explorations, your studies with psychology and how your characters are reflections of their own dire worldview. Can you just talk a little bit about what attracted you to psychology in general and how you've embedded that in your characters?

CYNTHIA PELAYO: I reached a point where I accepted that I could just never truly understand the logic that other people apply. They're people that I've seen that have a very strange moral code, they have a very strange compass. They're driven by very strange things that I will never understand.

I know I can't understand fully and truly why people do some of the things that they do. In writing, I thought, how can I get close? I'm fascinated with the role of the detective in fiction because your job isn't just to analyze a crime scene, your job is also to put your thoughts into potentially committing this crime. What would you have done? How would you have executed that? So, I've always been really fascinated by somebody that can dance that line and there's something almost sinister about them in a way, right? Because you could project your thoughts into somebody that would commit this heinous crime and then you'll be able to solve it. So, what does that say about some people? That there's some people that can think these things through and they don't execute those actions but there are people that think these things through and then execute those actions. Why?

MICHAEL J. SEIDLINGER: Have we lost touch with what even was the definition of humanity? Like are we so lost in the spiral of our daily discourse and whatnot that we as a society we're kind of losing? Or, is it that we just can't even really answer these questions because we don't even have our foundation?

CYNTHIA PELAYO: I think we always want to look towards a distance past and think it was better. I think social media has created a situation where we no longer know how to interact with one another in certain situations.

And with the online world, well, I feel like we've lost a lot of what it means to be physically connected with one another, what it is to be empathetic with one another, and sympathetic with one another and because of that we disregard one another's emotions and we just don't care. We move along our life barreling through people, barreling through their emotions and causing a lot of harm and trauma.

MICHAEL J. SEIDLINGER: It's like so much of it we get lost in the proverbial weeds and like how can you be in touch with anyone and like connect with anyone if you can't even really connect with yourself?

CYNTHIA PELAYO: How can you live in the present if you're fixated on some words on a screen typed out by someone you've never even met in the physical world, and may never ever meet?

How can you live in the present if you're having anxiety about a potential job promotion that really wouldn't move the dial much in terms of quality of life?

We don't look at things in the present anymore. I love documenting things but I also make it a point to live in the present moment and I just see people not enjoying their day-to-day moments.

Because of that I want to write about human connection. I feel like I've gone a little bit more into that area, just being really fascinated of what it is to write about individuals that work toward keeping their relationship intact while everything around them is falling apart. Because I feel like we're losing a grasp on things at times.

MICHAEL J. SEIDLINGER: We are, yeah. Do you want to can you talk a little bit more about how it's informed? How you've explored that in recent projects, how it's informed your characters and the things that direct to them through their conflicts and their own issues?

CYNTHIA PELAYO: Well, *Loteria*, is definitely more light-hearted. I always think of that like as a fun series of B movies that you're just gonna sit and watch. I don't think I really started, I mean maybe my YA novels, where I started exploring some of these things. Where like in *Santa Muerte* and *The Missing* where I talked a little bit about the drug cartels and femicide that we've seen throughout the Americas.

I think where I showed that meanness was in *Children of*

Chicago where I wrote about a character who was charged with taking care of people, but we saw she wasn't really taking care of anyone, not even herself. She had a very distorted worldview and a very distorted moral compass and a moral code.

I'm fascinated when people create their own rules and how they need to interact. It's just very strange to me. And so, I started exploring that there.

I think my poetry serves a different function. In *Into the Forest and All The Way Through* I wrote about missing and murdered women because I wanted to explore these crimes from their perspective. I wrote it because I was completely disgusted by the celebration of all things true crime, and there was a release of several Ted Bundy films at the time, which I thought was very poor taste, that and programs that highlight serial killers, like Jeffrey Dahmer, are the consumption of cruelty.

I think *Crime Scene* does its own exploration on what a crime scene looks like without writing about a specific individual. But I feel like I've stepped back, and my interests now are how individuals interact with one another and how they process grief and how are they processing cruelty around them while losing everything around them.

So, like grief, mourning, I've been exploring that more and maybe my writing now isn't so mean, like *Children of Chicago*.

The Shoemaker's Magician, that's where I'm going with my writing. That's what I want to write, and keep writing. I want to write beautiful things, that are thoughtful, that explore themes around processing the trauma of life. I don't need or want to write anything mean. The world is mean enough. I want to write about hope after horror.

MICHAEL J. SEIDLINGER: You talk a lot about lore. Fables and dark fantasies. Historically, weren't they written sort of to teach kids lessons or teach people lessons?

CYNTHIA PELAYO: For the most part. I mean many of them were written as little warnings.

Strangers and cruel parents and avoiding the less traveled path. And so, I mean those were the very first stories that were told to me and I remember my mother telling me "Little Red Riding Hood" but in Spanish which I remember just being terrified. I was like why are you telling me this story mom? Even children's rhymes, "There was an old lady who lived in his shoe, she had so many children, she didn't know what to do." And so, that always stuck with me, these wicked little tales. That's why now I essentially have an MFA in fairy tales Edgar Allan Poe and Jorge Borges because those were the things that I was most fascinated with, oh, and Agatha Christie too and I just kind of like mushed all those things together.

MICHAEL J. SEIDLINGER: We should pivot to something less dark for a minute and get all nerdy on craft. Let's talk about what kind of writer are you. A quota writer, daily writer. I feel like any writer anywhere all the time always is inherently curious about how one goes about but not only just finishing a project, right? What is your usual process to finish a project, getting through it on a daily basis like is it number of words, is it just a duration of time, is it every day, is it whenever you can find time, or any and all that?

CYNTHIA PELAYO: It's every day, I have to write every day. In terms of like word count, I don't really think I go off of word count or even time so much as it just feels right that this is my end point.

But when I am on deadline, which I've been on deadline for quite some time my last few projects, then there is a word count that I'm working off of, and that I need to like tick off just to make sure that I'm getting there. And I get there regardless. It doesn't have to be fully edited. It just needs to go.

I outline and I have a very strict way of outlining. It's in Excel.

I break it down by chapter, and by scene, what characters appear in those scenes, how does that chapter propel the plot forward, what elements of the theme are represented in that chapter, and so on. I do a lot of pre-planning but then as I'm writing I'm also in that map updating it at the end of the day just to see where I've adapted.

MICHAEL J. SEIDLINGER: Has it always been this process or has it evolved over time?

CYNTHIA PELAYO: It's I think *The Shoemaker's Magician* is when I got it down finally where I'm like yes I can write a novel I'm happy with in three months.

MICHAEL J. SEIDLINGER: What are your writer goals?

CYNTHIA PELAYO: I just want to keep doing this every day. This is why I'm here and as long as I have this, as long as I have writing to hold onto, then I have myself.

In terms of like concrete writing goals, I want to be seen as a writer. It's always been very important for me that I'm not labeled or categorized. I've always said that horror is my basis and that from there things will emerge, but it's important for me to be seen as a writer.

I never want people to think that well my success is because of this or my successes is because of that. No. I want to stand firm that I'm successful because my writing is good. And that's it.

It's always been very important to me, and maybe that comes from my dad being like 'I don't want you to be perceived as this or that' because you're good and that's it.

I do want to explore historical novels at one point in my lifetime but I think for now the next four to six books that I have planned are more are speculative, and when I say that it's important that people also know that I write genre blends. I like to incorporate horror and mystery and detective, more. And some of my writing has become more fantastical with time and I've been looking to fantasy to see how I can weave that in. I don't like when it goes too far fantastical, but I just like the hint of it. I think that's really pretty.

MICHAEL J. SEIDLINGER: I mean writing is life. It's therapy. It is where we come alive on the page for sure. I mean same, 100%. Also yeah, historical going into historical fiction, not only can I see that happening, but I mean you know me, like I'm gonna cheer you on, like encouraging you to do that.

I know you just put out *Loteria* and *Shoemaker's Magician* but there is *The Forgotten Sisters* on the way and we'll blink and it'll be here. Can we talk a little bit about that?

CYNTHIA PELAYO: *The Forgotten Sisters* is my first novel with Thomas and Mercer. It'll be published March of 2024 and then there will be one right after that. *The Forgotten Sisters* takes place in, shock, it takes place in Chicago.

It deals with a lot of the things that I've explored with the city of Chicago in my fiction, and how we haven't addressed some of the tragic events that have happened. It also deals with my fascination of people when they're forgotten.

Like what does that mean? What does it mean when somebody dies? Like what is the ripple effect throughout space and time and I wanted to explore that. Like how does a single death impact the trajectory of somebody else's life? How does the death of an entire family, like what kind of holes does that leave, what kind of wound does that leave? And so, I explored that. It's also a retelling of "The Little Mermaid" and it's a detective novel as well, and I think that's all I can say.

MICHAEL J. SEIDLINGER: Yeah, that's great. I think we're good.

CYNTHIA PELAYO: Yeah.

MICHAEL J. SEIDLINGER: And that's it.

MICHAEL J. SEIDLINGER is a Filipino American author of *Anybody Home?*, *Scream* (Bloomsbury's Object Lessons), and other books. He has written for, among others, *Wired*, *Buzzfeed*, *Thrillist*, *Goodreads*, *The Observer*, *Polygon*, *The Believer*, and *Publisher's Weekly*. He teaches at Portland State University and has led workshops at Catapult, Kettle Pond Writer's Conference, and Sarah Lawrence. He is represented by Lane Heymont at The Tobias Literary Agency. You can find him at michaeljseidlinger.com

WRATH JAMES WHITE

BRIAN KEENE: Growing up in Philadelphia, your mother was a big influence on your love of reading, and horror fiction. Talk a bit about that environment and how it shaped you.

WRATH JAMES WHITE: I used to watch *Creature Double Feature* and *Doctor Shock* with my mom and my sister on Saturday mornings, lying across the foot of my mom's bed. Those are my best memories from my childhood. I watched all the old Bela Lugosi and Lon Chaney movies, all that stuff Hammer films was putting out.

My mother had me when she was only nineteen, so my sister and I were her best friends. When she read a book, she was excited about, she would pass it to us to read so we could discuss it, and back then she read mostly horror. I read *Pin* by Andrew Neiderman when I was eight. I read *The Entity* and *The Amityville Horror* when I was nine and ten years old. I didn't think it was unusual at all.

BRIAN KEENE: Same here. My parents never censored my reading, so I was discovering *The Amityville Horror* and *Salem's Lot* and *The Keep* at around that age.

Speaking of 'back in the day', I was doing some math when Mary and I sent out wedding invitations. You and I have known each other almost twenty-five years now. I remember when you and I first met. Back then, you were transitioning from professional fighting to being a writer. And I recall your approach to it. In some ways, you went after this career just like you were going into the ring against an opponent. But were you ever secretly apprehensive or anxious or uncertain about whether you had what it took to be successful?

WRATH JAMES WHITE: The hardest thing about that transition was my sense of identity. When I was fighting, I was a fighter. You get me?

BRIAN KEENE: Yeah.

WRATH JAMES WHITE: If you asked me what I was, I would answer that I was a kickboxer. Fighting wasn't just what I did, it was who I was, my entire identity, but I didn't feel comfortable calling myself a writer yet. It took a long time to grow into that. I think that's part of the reason I took writing as seriously as I did. I thought if I treated it like I was training for a fight, then I would feel like I earned that title.

BRIAN KEENE: You were trained by some of the best. You got mentored by folks like Edward Lee and Jack Ketchum. And you met other people who were in training, too – writers like J. F. (Jesus) Gonzalez and Maurice Broaddus, who became some of your dearest friends.

When you sit back and reflect on the last two decades, is it fair to say writing professionally has fundamentally changed your life? Ever wonder what your life would be like if you hadn't written that first novel?

WRATH JAMES WHITE: I do wonder. Ex-fighters have a terrible history of descending into drugs, alcohol, and domestic violence. We train ourselves for years, decades, to be weapons and then we are expected to let all that go and become regular citizens. It's a lot like what war veterans go through, I suppose. A lot of guys really struggle with that. I think the writing saved me from all of that.

BRIAN KEENE: The reading public and many of our peers think of you only as an extreme horror writer. And sure, granted, we founded the Splatterpunk Awards to recognize works of merit within the Splatterpunk and Extreme subgenres. And sure, a lot of your more popular works are classified as extreme horror. But you've also written mainstream fare, as well as erotica and poetry.

Edward Lee has often tried to write things other than extreme horror – *The Death of the Cold War Kings*, *The Stickmen*, his middle-grade novel *Monster Lake*, and some of his Lovecraft pastiches, for example. But he's found that what his readers want – what sells the best – is his extreme horror. Do you find the same is true with your audience? Or do they embrace your non-extreme stuff, as well?

WRATH JAMES WHITE: It's a little of both. My erotica is dark enough that it satisfies my extreme horror fans. One reviewer even noted that *Fight For Me* had a higher body count than most horror novels. Same with my poetry. But the more extreme stuff definitely generates more hype.

Skinzz wasn't terribly extreme, but it has a pretty strong fan base due to its sentimentality, and the controversial nature of the subject matter. Likewise books like *Everyone Dies Famous In A Small Town*, and *The Reaper*. But *Succulent Prey* and *The Resurrectionist* were just so popular they tend to overshadow everything else.

I remember when Jesus and I collaborated on *Hero*. Everyone was expecting an all-out Wrath James White and J. F. Gonzalez extreme bloodbath or gross-out like when I collaborated with Edward Lee on *The Teratologist*. But, that's not really what either of us do.

Yes, Jesus's novel *Survivor* was pretty extreme and so was *Succulent Prey*, but they both had serious stories behind them, and they are far more extreme than most of the stuff Jesus and I had written at that time.

Hero wound up being a deeply emotional story, gut-wrenching in a different way. My other books like *400 Days of Oppression* and *Yaccub's Curse* all have extreme horror elements, but the stories themselves, the plots were what made them so intense. I don't really write much gross-out stuff. Violent, visceral, even pornographic, but not vomit and feces type stuff.

BRIAN KEENE: Let's talk about *Hero* a bit more, because – given that it was the first novel-length work by two writers of color – it's an important book in our field. And then I want to talk about the second novel you guys did together.

I know how you write, and obviously, given that I'm his literary executor and cowrote five books with him, I know Jesus's creative process intimately. I suspect that in writing *Hero*, both of you were more focused on the story, rather than being conscious of the historical footnote that novel would occupy in horror fiction.

But your second novel together, *The Killings*, which focused on the real-life serial killings of Black Atlantans in 1911 and the 1980s, was a very different animal. Was that a harder book for the two of you to write?

WRATH JAMES WHITE: *Hero* was harder emotionally. Torturing a sweet old lady who we consciously modeled after Rosa Parks, was hard. I found myself holding back. Luckily, Jesus had no such qualms.

With *The Killings* maintaining continuity was the hardest part. Switching back and forth between the 1700s, the 1980s, and the 2000s was hard. It was also very research intensive. I read an entire book on the Atlanta Ripper and another on the Atlanta Child Murders before we even began writing.

I was a kid when the child murders were going on in Atlanta. Even in Philadelphia we were terrified. We didn't know if it was the KKK doing it and it was going to spread across the entire country. That was the rumor going around at the time. Writing about it brought back all those memories.

BRIAN KEENE: Well, let's switch back to good memories then. We've mentioned Maurice and Jesus in this discussion. Now, Jesus got started a few years before you and Maurice, but when you first came on the scene, you could probably count horror fiction's writers of color on two hands. Hell, you and I have living memories of the very first 'Black Horror' panel, held back in 2001.

Enormous strides have been made since then, and many times, your steps were the longest of anyone leading the way. But I know that it has not been an easy walk for you, by any means. I've watched you push back against racism and adversity, both hidden and overt, for twenty-five years now. Perhaps the most widely known case of this was when a UK-based editor publicly decried your inclusion in the programming for the 2007 World Horror Convention. Most horror writers and readers who were around back then remember that. But what the general public doesn't know is that you've received death threats and other bullshit.

On the flip side, there's amazing newer authors like R. J. Joseph and others who credit you as being a direct influence. And I dare say that UK-based editor wouldn't publicly grouse about you being included in convention programming anymore.

When you look back on how things were then, versus how they are now, does it give you any sense of personal satisfaction to know that you are at least partially responsible for many of the things that have changed for the better? Or does it just frustrate you that there's still so much work to be done, in that regard?

WRATH JAMES WHITE: Maurice and I discussed this very thing last year at KillerCon. It definitely fills me with pride when young POC writers tell me I inspired them to write, or that seeing me at a convention helped them feel more comfortable.

But, the number of POC authors represented in anthologies, magazines, awards, and even as guests of honor at convention is still not representative of our presence in horror. It still galls me that we continue to be overlooked by major award juries when it comes to their top awards. Twenty years ago, I didn't think we would still be discussing how no Black authors have ever won a Stoker for Best Novel. That's a tragedy.

BRIAN KEENE: It is indeed, and – perhaps naively on my part – it's something I thought we'd see in our time. But we're getting older, Wrath. You and I have talked privately about that this past year – about getting older, and how being in our mid-fifties impacts our daily lives in ways we never imagined.

Do you find that age is impacting or changing your creative process and the way you write? Is it impacting your thoughts or views on our field and the genre?

WRATH JAMES WHITE: I used to treat writing like a job and I went about it the same way I went about training for a fight. If I had a fight coming up, I wasn't going to skip a day of roadwork, or bagwork, sparring, rain or shine. I did the same with my writing. I woke up and wrote every morning and I wrote again every night. I wrote while bouncing my newborn daughter on my lap. I wrote in the middle of a New Year's Eve party once. You used to see me writing sitting in a hallway at a convention.

BRIAN KEENE: (laughs) I vividly remember seeing you sitting in the hallway at a horror convention in New York, head down and just writing like a man possessed. Meanwhile, Maurice and I were sitting in that same hallway playing *Magic: The Gathering*.

WRATH JAMES WHITE: (laughs) I was supremely disciplined. Now, I write when I feel like it. I want it to remain something I love and not another chore. I still have five or six entire novels floating around in my head at all times, but I don't feel like I have to get them out of there as soon as possible anymore. I know a new idea will just pop up to take its place. I take time to enjoy more of what the rest of life has to offer instead of being constantly chained to my laptop.

BRIAN KEENE: I think that's a great outlook and approach.

Okay, brother... I know we're getting close to the space they allotted us, so we need to wrap this up. Any final thoughts? Anything you want folks to know about?

WRATH JAMES WHITE: Yes, please! My new collection, *The Agony of Ecstasy*, is debuting here this weekend at StokerCon.

BRIAN KEENE: *The Agony of Ecstasy*? That sounds almost autobiographical, Wrath.

WRATH JAMES WHITE: (winks)

BRIAN KEENE writes novels, comic books, short stories, and nonfiction. He is the author of over fifty books, mostly in the horror, crime, fantasy, and non-fiction genres. They have been translated into over a dozen different languages and have won numerous awards. The father of two sons and the stepfather to one daughter, Keene lives in rural Pennsylvania with his wife, author Mary SanGiovanni.

BREED

(Excerpt –Chapter 6)
by Owl Goingback

Kevin Bess sat at a quiet little bar on Cordova Street, slowly nursing a bottle of Budweiser. The beer, and the muscle relaxers he had taken earlier, helped to ease the pain in his lower back, but did not entirely eliminate it. Nothing ever stopped the pain. It was with him all the time, twenty-four hours a day, seven days a week, a constant reminder of a fateful moment in time five years earlier.

He had been a carpenter, with a good paying job working for a local construction company. Employed and happy, he owned a nice little condo near the beach; he also owned a beautiful blue Harley Davidson. But everything changed one fateful Friday night when a Cadillac made an illegal left turn in front of him. He tried to avoid hitting the car, but the road was slick from an August thunderstorm, and he smashed into the vehicle at nearly fifty miles an hour. Kevin went airborne over the car, doing a less than graceful half gainer, slamming down on the hard street. He broke his left leg in three places, and crushed several of the vertebrae in his spine.

The driver of the Cadillac was a retired judge, and still had clout in the legal system, so the accident was not charged to either party. Which meant the other guy's insurance company didn't have to pay for the damage to Kevin's bike, or the damage to his body.

He spent nearly a month in the hospital, with an additional six months bedridden at home. Unable to work, he lost his job with the construction company. He also lost his condo when he couldn't keep up with the monthly mortgage payments. He finally healed enough to get out of bed and walk, but there was now a weakness in his back that had never been there before. Going back to his old job was out of the question. No way he could swing a hammer, or carry lumber for a living. He had to settle for the small amount of money he received every month from social security.

In addition to the weakness, there was also a great deal of pain in his back. Pain that always seemed to be with him, morning, noon, and night. Pain that took the beauty from his life, and made him see things with tired, bitter eyes. The bitterness had taken over his life, causing his girlfriend of three years to finally give up on him and move in with somebody else.

Kevin drank his beer, and then ordered another. He wasn't worried about getting drunk because he wasn't driving. Not that he owned a car, or even a motorcycle. Such things were luxuries of the past. He had just enough money for beer, and to pay the rent on the decrepit, one-room apartment he now called his home. He wouldn't even have enough money for that if his older sister didn't help him out from time to time.

"Thank God for big sisters," he said, lifting the new bottle of beer the waitress had brought him. The waitress just frowned and walked away.

The employees of the bar didn't really like him hanging out in their establishment several nights a week, but they tolerated his presence. He always sat alone at a corner table, listening to what the other customers had to say but never attempting to join in on the conversation.

The bar had already announced last call for the evening, and most of the customers had gone home, when he finally decided to call it a night. Finishing the last of his beer, he laid a dollar on the table, grabbed his walking cane, and slowly stood up. The beer and medication had gone to his head, giving him a pleasant buzz that was almost pain free. Almost, for as soon as he stood up, a fiery twinge shot up his back, letting him know that things had not changed.

Using the cane to help support a leg that would never be completely healed, he hobbled out the front door and down the wooden steps to the street. He lived six blocks north of the bar, and it usually took him close to an hour to walk home, depending on how much booze and how many pills he had consumed during the evening. Pausing to light an unfiltered cigarette, he started down the street, his body quickly falling into a rhythmic gate that was part hobble and part drunken stagger.

He turned right on Cordova Street, passing several Victorian homes that had been converted into bed and breakfasts. Though lights burned in the ornate, two-story buildings, it was doubtful if anyone was still up at such a late hour. The temporary residents were probably sound asleep on antique beds, and feather pillows, dreaming of stock trades, bank mergers, and what flavor jam they would put on their croissants in the morning.

"Fuck them," he whispered under his breath. "Fuck them all."

Hobbling past the bed and breakfasts, he came to the Tolomato Cemetery. The cemetery stood empty and dark, a place of dense shadows and eerie silence. Kevin paused for a moment in front of the cemetery's front gates, wondering about the people who were buried inside. He wondered if being dead was any easier than being alive, a thought that often crossed his mind when passing the old cemetery. He had pondered the same question on nights when the pain got too bad for him to sleep, during the hours of endless darkness when he would sit in his tiny living room with a loaded pistol in his hand. One night, maybe soon, he would learn the answer to his question.

"You guys are the lucky ones," he said out loud, his words slurring slightly. "All you have to do is lay there and sleep. No more pain. You ought to come out here, in the real world, and put up with the things I have to put up with."

He smiled, swaying slightly on his feet. Finally, here were some people who would listen to what he had to say.

"That's right. You've got it easy. All of you. Why don't you come on out and join me? Come out and see what the real world is like. Come on. I dare you. I double dare you."

From somewhere in the distance a dog suddenly howled, its cry carried like ghostly music on the wind. Hushing his drunken banter, Kevin paused to listen. The dog howled twice more, then grew quiet, probably shushed by its owner.

Turning his attention back to the cemetery, he studied the row of graves closest to the front wall. The graves were quiet and undisturbed; no one had accepted his invitation to join him in the real world.

"Cowards."

Disappointed, he turned and started down the street, weaving a little more than he had earlier as the beers and muscle relaxers started to catch up with him. He wished he had a car to drive, but he didn't. Maybe he should call his sister and ask for a ride. She wouldn't be too happy to receive a phone call at two in the morning, but he was family. She would come to get him, even if it meant he had to listen to a lecture all the way home.

Deciding he would indeed call his sister, if he could find a pay phone, Kevin continued walking in the direction of his apartment. He had just reached the Old Drugstore when he heard a strange sound coming from behind him.

It was an odd clanging noise, metal on metal, like a mechanic beating a wrench against an old car engine. Thinking that someone might be having trouble, he stopped and turned around. But the street was empty of people and cars, deserted except for the drunken cripple who stood listening in the darkness. Curious about the noise, he started retracing his steps.

He had only gone about half a block, however, when he located the source of the metallic clanging. The sound was caused by the front gates of the Tolomato Cemetery, and the metal chain that held them closed. The gates were jerking back and forth, as if being blown by a strong wind, straining at the heavy chain. But no wind blew; the night air was heavy and still.

The metal gates moved almost a foot one way, then slammed back in the opposite direction. Back and forth they went, slamming against the chain, looking as if someone was jerking the gates in an attempt to break free from the cemetery.

"What the hell?"

He stepped off the sidewalk and moved out into the street, wanting to get a better view of what was happening. Even in the middle of the street there was no breeze to be felt, so it could not be the wind that moved the gates. Nor was anyone trapped inside of the cemetery, trying desperately to get out. He could see through the metal gates into the graveyard, and there was no one there. Still, the gates continued to bang back and forth, their motion growing more frenzied by the moment.

A sudden thought came to him, causing his alcoholic buzz to depart and sending a chill dancing down his spine. A few moments ago, he had dared the dead to join him in the real world, and now it looked like someone was trying to take him up on the offer.

"Shit," he whispered, his mouth going dry. "Shit. Shit. Shit."

Then, as he stood there watching, the gates stopped their frantic movement. The night again grew quiet.

Kevin laughed nervously. "They must have given up."

His laugher quickly died, however, as a horrible odor rolled over him. It was the smell of old roadkill, of something lying dead and rotten in the hot Florida sunshine, the stench of a swollen opossum on a back country road. The smell came from inside the Tolomato Cemetery, rolling thick and pungent out into the street, causing him to gag.

With the odor came something else, a sight much too terrifying to describe. He thought at first his eyes must be playing tricks on him, but it was no trick that he saw. Nor was it a result of too many Budweisers, and too many pills. Something large and black was moving across the grounds of the cemetery, making its way from the back of the graveyard to the front gates. A nearly shapeless mass of infinite darkness that seemed to swallow up everything in its path.

"Dear Jesus, what in the hell is that?"

It was like a low-lying cloud, a patch of fog hugging the ground as it rolled toward the front of the cemetery. Churning, billowing, expanding outward, only to shrink back on itself, it seemed to shimmer and change shape as it moved. As the rolling cloud of blackness drew nearer, it reached out to him with ebony tentacles.

Kevin blinked and shook his head, trying to comprehend what he was seeing. The patch of darkness grew more solid the closer it got to him, took on definition in the night. It looked like a giant black octopus, or maybe a spider.

That was it. The thing moving through the Tolomato Cemetery looked like a giant spider, a nightmarish, mutant spider that continually changed its shape and definition. One moment it was large and round, the next it was thin and narrow.

Suddenly, the thing changed shapes again, transforming into a figure that was almost human. Almost, for the apparition had the body and head of a man, bearded and dressed in a flowing dark robe, but it had long black tentacles for arms. The tentacles stretched out toward the front of the cemetery, reaching for the frightened crippled man who stood in the middle of the street.

It was the thing's almost-human appearance that terrified him most of all, and he damn sure didn't trust the locked gates to keep it inside the cemetery. Instinct told him bars and chains could not stop such a thing. Hell, guns and tanks probably couldn't stop it.

Deciding a hasty retreat was the best plan of action, he stifled a cry and turned away from the Tolomato. He tried to put as much distance between himself and the nightmarish creature as he possibly could, but he could only hobble so fast. Even the added adrenaline rush of fear could not make his body move any quicker.

He had just reached the Old Drugstore when the thing reached the front of the cemetery, nearly ripping the metal gates off their hinges. Flowing out into the street, the multilegged beast of darkness scurried after its prey, its movements silent except for a muffled hooting sound.

Kevin turned and looked behind him, watching in horror as the monster moved out into the street, his bladder silently relieving itself of a night's worth of good beer. He prayed that the thing would go the other direction, but God must not have heard his prayer, for it came after him.

"Shit. Shit. Shit," he said, urging his body to even greater speed.

He turned right on Orange Street, hoping to make it to Avenida Menendez. There was usually traffic on the Avenida, no matter what time of night it was. He would be able to flag someone down and get help.

But he had only made it a block when the thing caught him, a thin black tentacle wrapping around his right ankle. Kevin screamed, a fiery pain ripping up his leg. He turned to see the monster, and wished to God he hadn't. It was better not to see his attacker, for in its true form it was sheer madness to look upon. Such a thing had not been seen in the world of mankind for a long, long time.

His cane slipped out of limp fingers and fell clattering to the street. Kevin made no attempt to pick it back up, for he knew the slender wooden shaft would not protect him. Nor did he attempt to cry for help, for fear had stolen his voice like a thief in the night. He could only stand and stare as the creature before him did a hypnotic little dance, slowly weaving from side to side as it studied him.

Another tentacle wrapped around his waist, slipping beneath the fabric of his jeans. Tiny teeth sliced like razor blades as the tentacle moved down his left leg, touching, tasting, feeding. Pieces of flesh were cut from the bone and swallowed by a hungry mouth.

A single tear ran down his left cheek as Kevin lowered his head and closed his eyes. More tentacles wrapped around his body, snatching his legs out from under him. There was a moment of sheer weightlessness as he was lifted into the air, followed by the indescribable sensation of having the flesh ripped from his bones. Darkness followed.

THE GILDA STORIES

(Excerpt)
by Jewelle Gomez

Caramelle 1864
for Sheridan LeFanu

Looking back it all seems so natural and perhaps it was.
I watched my father, Solomon scan the road outside of
our small house for a sign. It was always uncertain whether
he was more relieved when he discovered one or when he did not.
He often invoked the name of the Lord either way but he sometimes
appeared too exhausted to remember further prayers. He was a tall,
dark man, thinly built, who looked as if he had important jobs to
do. Watching for the sign was one of them.

Now, when I think of my father, it is those fleeting moments
that bring his face to my mind most precisely. His determination
was a force of nature. And freedom was always his goal. He spoke
of it to me and everyone who would listen so often that freedom
became a tangible thing, a thing to taste like berry pie. And it
became our name—Freeman—when we escaped slavery and
settled in Charlmont.

We'd lived on a small New England back road for some years before I understood—our farm was a depot. A place where those, like my father and me, stopped on their way to freedom. No one ever actually said these words, but the succession of 'cousins' who stayed with us in the years before I turned 14 were innumerable. Each would be called by the same name depending on the age. Men were called Cousin Simon, women were Cousin Delia and children were Cousins Henrietta and John. I think Father decided to use the same names so as not to tax my child's memory.

Sometimes it became a source of a smile for Father and me. He'd look up say "Wonder if we'll have a Cousin for dinner tonight?" And I'd say, "Yes, please. May we have them with jam?" It was the purest joy to hear my father laugh out loud.

Later I heard stories of the life of slavery he'd left behind on the plantation. Mostly from the Cousins who 'visited.' One who's skin was drawn so tight by the scars of the lash he could hardly bend over; a ten-year old who, at the sound of the dogs, remembered to cross water so she'd swum downstream with her injured mother clinging to her back. The distance from the world of slavery to our farm was much greater than the sum of the miles.

By the time I was fourteen it ceased feeling like a secret game and I understood the stark terror the 'Cousins' had endured to make the journey north.

"We've got cousins tonight."

"With jam?"

"No, sugar pie. Cousin Delia and Cousin Henrietta be in tonight."

"Oh!"

With that I went to the room where I slept to be certain I'd not left a terrible mess.

I heard the buckboard on the road before Father did. His hearing was getting thinner each year, which he would never admit, of course. Mr. Leavitt, pale in the dim light thrown by the lantern at his side, helped Cousin Delia down first. She was tall and fair-skinned, almost as pale as Mr. Leavitt. She wore her head wrap drawn tightly down across her brow, shadowing her eyes. She was very thin, not unexpected given the journey they'd taken. Fleeing from the south to the north was hardly a nutritious journey.

Delia reached up to lift her daughter down before Mr. Leavitt could and the sinewy strength of her arms and back were barely concealed by the dark cloak she wore. Cousin Henrietta was almost as tall as her mother and just as pale. She could have been 11 or 16 it was difficult to tell in the dim light. Mr. Leavitt, handed my father a small satchel, turned away looking exhausted as if he'd not slept in days, and barely said good night before climbing back up on the seat of his buckboard.

We turned to our charges and offered a small snack.

"We kinda tired suh. If you don't mind we'd like to...."

"I understand, Cousin. No tea?"

"Nawsuh."

I couldn't see her eyes well, but they didn't look tired at all. Her voice didn't seem as weak as her words but I couldn't tell. So I turned to her daughter. She stared back at me with coal black eyes that were full of fear. That made more sense than the sound of her mother's voice so I took her hand, which was exceptionally cool, and led her to the room she'd occupy until it was time for them to move north.

Once they were settled in the room Father rolled back his blanket so I could sleep in his bed. He pulled the curtain across the alcove where I slept while we had cousins; then he lay on a pallet by the stove. And then it was morning.

Father said Cousin Delia had asked they not be disturbed, they might sleep through the day. I put a piece of ham bone in a pot at the back of the stove then worked outside doing my regular chores; chickens and cows and fences don't take care of themselves. Father took the horse over to the Fahey farm to help with their tilling and I tried not to listen at the door. I wanted to really meet Cousin Henrietta.

Near dusk, almost done with my chores around the farm, I ran water over my head like Father always did. When I looked up Cousin Delia stood in the doorway. I felt she towered over me although she wasn't really taller. I'd seen many different colors of colored people since we'd had the visiting cousins but something about this Delia was unlike anyone I'd ever met. Coolness rolled off of her like fog rising from the cranberry bog. I smiled, though and asked if she wanted to go to the barn with me.

"Yes, that be nice…uh…?"

"Elizabeth," I provided.

Delia said, "How fortunate."

I thought that was an interesting response but people on the railroad often had an odd relationship to words, to space, to everything."

"Yes, please, my name is Caramelle."

"You mustn't say that."

"Well it is and I don't like being called something else."

Once we were inside I shut the barn door like always and she looked startled.

"Why'd you do that?"

"You're supposed to shut the barn door so there's no coming and going."

Something about that made her laugh and laugh and then me too. We laughed until we fell down into the pile of hay and the chickens cackled outside in the yard as if they were laughing too. We lay there smiling at the wood beams and the tackle hanging above us. It was the same peacefulness that I enjoyed but it was made richer by Caramelle being here.

"I remember this place."

"How can you remember a place you've never been?" I asked a little uneasy.

"Through dreams, silly!" Caramelle laughed again which took the edge off of her words.

"Do you want to see the secret place?" I asked. She nodded.

"See here."

I opened to gate to the stall and dug the pitch fork around under the hay until I found the seam in the wood floor. I pried until the hatch opened revealing the trough we'd dug into the ground below. It was lined with hay and a blanket but was still not the most inviting accommodations. We'd only used it once when a relentless bounty hunter had followed some cousins almost to our door. But that had been more than a year ago and the news was that the war was almost over.

"Let's get in!" Caramelle said with excitement.

I tipped the hatch back and Caramelle dropped in like she'd been invited in to eat tea cakes. I looked at the closed barn door then slid down beside her in the hole. It could not have been more than four feet by six feet and was about four feet deep. I closed the hatch over us and felt a few sprigs of hay drift through the cracks into the mostly dark.

Caramelle started to giggle and put her arm around me, wriggled in close and whispered in my ear: "Can I tell you the story?"

I could hardly say 'no' in such close quarters and with my curiosity nipping so closely beside me.

"A man who used to visit the plantation pretty regular was determined to buy me and mama. He kept coming back and Massa Harriwell finally give us up; not for cheap though!"

"Once we was on the road...that man he turned us into something."

"What does that mean: 'something?'"

"Mama too."

"But what..."

Her breathing almost stopped so I did too.

"There was so much blood everywhere and I got sick. Mama tried to stop him but he made her bleed too."

I was not able to hold a clear picture in my head. The way she described the profusion of blood made me wonder at their survival.

"From then on we was different."

"Different like what?" I pressed.

"Just different…like…on the plantation we was always hungry. Now I'm never hungry…except…" She stopped again. "And I'm strong now. You saw my hands?"

I had, indeed, seen her hands.

"And we learn how to do things…some of 'em not nice…but we strong."

"What things?"

"Well, I can strike down a buck and drink his blood without spilling nary a drop," Caramelle said with an undercurrent of pride.

That image was clear enough although the idea Caramelle drinking blood made me a bit ill at first.

"Really, it's not such a awful thing," she said as if she could read my mind. "You eat their meat don't ya?"

She was right and I'd seen enough game caught and prepared to sink her extraordinary statements into a recognizable context.

"One night he tried to mess with me and I guess he forgot… about changing us I mean…and mama got mad and killed him."

"Killed him!?" I nearly screeched the words. It wasn't from any judgment about killing someone who thought it proper to buy human beings; it was simply that Caramelle said it so easily; as easily as the killing apparently had occurred.

"Yeah. She took out the small hatchet she keep hid in her cloak and took off his head. She said that was the only thing to do. We really had to run now. She said his people wasn't regular and they was gonna be mad and we had to get north."

The chill that surrounded her mother now also emanated from Caramelle. I hadn't noticed that before. Or maybe remembering the death of her tormentor had dropped her temperature in a fit of emotion.

"We been traveling ever since, trying to figure out how to live since he used to take care of that."

"Take care of what?"

"We better go, ain't your papa coming home soon?" Caramelle said abruptly.

I couldn't convince Caramelle to go on with her story no matter how hard I prodded or what I promised. Finally she relented just a little.

"We met a woman on the road, Gilda."

"Who was she?"

"I ain't never seen nobody strong as her! She say she gonna help me and mama. You'll want to hear about her." Caramelle said this with the first childlike smile I'd seen her convey.

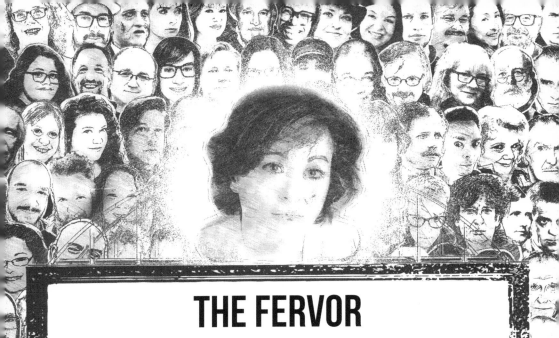

THE FERVOR

(Excerpt)
by Alma Katsu

Bly, Oregon
November 19, 1944

He parked as far off the trail as he could, but the Nash took up most of the road. There was no way around it. The trail was too narrow.

He opened the trunk and was enveloped by the aroma of chocolate. Elsie had decided that, if they were going on a picnic, they needed a chocolate cake. She baked the layers yesterday, setting them out on racks to cool last night. She'd made the frosting this morning, beating the butter and sugar by hand with a big wooden spoon. Elsie only baked chocolate cake once or twice a year, and the thought of it made his mouth water. He lifted the cake carrier and slung the wooden handles over one forearm, then hefted the picnic basket with the other. Inside were turkey sandwiches. A thermos of coffee for the adults and a jug of cider for the kids.

He put the basket on the ground and was closing the trunk when another tiny white seedling, no bigger than a snowflake, landed near his nose. He brushed it away, oddly unnerved by it. That feeling again: a wind surging right through him. He shivered and slammed the trunk.

A woman stood in front of him.

He jumped in surprise, but she remained perfectly still, observing him. She was a young woman and beautiful. She was dressed in a kimono, a nice one from what he could tell, but she was disheveled. Her shiny black hair was falling down in wisps, the ends of her obi fluttering in the breeze.

Where had she come from? There hadn't been anyone on the trail or in the woods—Archie was positive. He'd been paying extra close attention as he navigated the mud.

Funny for someone to be roaming around the mountain in such fancy dress. Though Archie had seen Japanese wearing traditional garb in Bly—years ago.

No Japanese left in town anymore.

The strangest part was the look on her face, the way she smiled at him. Cunning. Sly. It stopped the questions forming in his throat. Kept him from doing anything except stare.

More of the white seedlings drifted between them, swirling playfully. She lifted a finger and gestured toward them. *"Kumo,"* she in a voice barely above a whisper. Archie didn't know the word but he was pretty sure that was what she'd said. *Kumo.*

The sound of children yelling broke his concentration, and Archie looked away. Little Edward—or was it Sherman?—was shouting something in the distance. Had to be sure Elsie was okay, that the kids hadn't gotten up to some mischief…

And when he turned back, the woman in the kimono was gone.

For a moment, he paused, confused. He looked down at the spot where she had stood, and there were no footprints. The mud was untrampled.

A chill ran down his spine, followed by a tremor of guilt.

But then the boys yelled again, in high-pitched, excited little voices, and Archie was forced to let it go.

"What's going on?" Archie called out, picking up the food items again and beginning his trudge toward the tree line. He got closer, and the voices became louder.

"Whoa!" That was Joan's voice.

"Honey?" That was Elsie now. "We've found something. Come look!"

He could see their forms now, through the trees. The creek in the distance, black and twisty as a snake. Something light and large in a clearing, covering the ground like alien moss.

"What is it?" Archie called out, hurrying.

He wasn't at all sure what to make of the shape in the distance: it could be a piece of a banner come loose from a building or warehouse, or even a bedsheet escaped from a clothesline. It was weathered, grayish, and sprawling—unnatural in all this wilderness.

"Some kind of parachute?" Elsie shouted over her shoulder.

A knife of panic. He dropped the basket and the cake. "Don't touch anything!" There'd been a news story a few months back. Something about a parachute falling out of the sky and catching fire on the power lines at a power plant near Spokane. Whole plant could've gone up in smoke but for the generator cutting off. The newspaper had called it a parachute, but onlookers didn't agree. Some feared it was an unmarked weapon of war.

He ran toward them now. "Did you hear me?" His voice came out ragged, breathless. "I said be careful and don't—"

Archie choked and stopped running. Something drifting on the wind caught in his throat. It looked like snow, but it couldn't be. Too early for snow, though not unheard of this time of year. Another seedling—or maybe something else. Maybe it was ash. He saw loads of it in the air now: bits of white fluff, like dandelion seeds but smaller. *No dandelion seeds in November*. He froze, momentarily mesmerized. He lifted a hand to catch one but the wind carried it away.

His hand was still suspended in the air when another bit of white caught on his eyelashes. It was so close to his eye that at first, it was just a semitransparent orb. A mote.

But then, as his eye attempted to focus on it, it moved.

It moved strangely, like it had arms. The arms wove left and right, up and down. With cold clarity, he knew what it was.

A tiny translucent spider.

His shock was cut through with a thundering boom.

And then: he was blown backward, as if from cannon fire.

ROTTERS

(Excerpt)
by Daniel Kraus

An even smaller Antiochus Boggs happening upon those strange and secretive old men—it was hard to imagine their acceptance of him until I remembered how I first came upon Ken Harnett, hostile and uncommunicative in a darkened cabin.

"The point is," he continued, "I've never fit in. Just like you. And I don't mean any offense by that. Not fitting in? In my book, that's a good thing. You can't make a mark on the world if you just vote the party line. So can you see it? How we're the same? Am I making any sense? My brain isn't exactly right."

He looked aggrieved. I felt a need to reassure him. "I guess it makes sense."

"Lord, that's sweet music." His rotund cheeks quivered. His lips made inchworm shrugs. He shut his eyes and I pictured the pure and exquisite ocean that might flow from such resplendent irises. When he regained control over himself he peeked up at me shyly. "Guys like you and me, we're special. We have talents others don't have, won't ever have. Then why aren't we happier? You ever ask yourself that?"

"Yes." If there was one undeniable truth, this was it.

"Me too. Took me a lifetime to figure it out, but I won't make you wait that long. You just have to ask yourself one question: What do we take from the rotters? Aside from trinkets and trifles, what possession of genuine worth do we win for our efforts? The answer ought to depress you, son. The answer is *nothing*. Deep down, that bothers you. Doesn't it? Sure as hell bothers me. And those old men you met, they're satisfied with nothing. With all their gifts—and I won't bullshit you, they have gifts—at the end of the day, they're satisfied with making circles. Over and over. Over and over."

With that, he tucked his small hand inside his coat, eased unseen buckles, and withdrew a large black book.

"I've taken more," he said.

A fist snared Boggs's collar and shoved. He struck the counter, rebounded, lost his balance, and tumbled from his seat. His impact sounded like a gray sack dropped to cabin cement. The vacated stool made merry-go-round circuits. A few feet away, the book slapped down and Boggs lunged for it. The rest was blocked out— Harnett was in my face, haul- ing me to my feet and squeezing me with one hand while he dug for a ten-dollar bill and left it wadded on top of the check.

His face was bloodless. " Your schoolwork."

Numbly I picked up my biology book and Harnett steered us away. Already Boggs was up and blocking our path, over a foot shorter than my father but, due to his fantastic breadth and the startling incongruity of his three-piece suit, just as imposing. Harnett pulled back, holding me in check with an elbow. Boggs's pink face broke into a heedless grin.

"Kenny," he said. "Lord, it's good to see you."

"Step aside."

Boggs shook his head as if there had been some terrible misunderstanding.

"This is silly. We shouldn't fight. If you could just give me a minute I'd be—"

"Get out of my face."

A burly man in chef's whites was leaning over the counter. "There some problem here, folks?"

Oldies still blared from speakers, but beneath the music the dissonance of the diner was smoothing as families broke off their conversations and began to take note. Boggs straightened his vest and adjusted his rumpled tie. He gestured apologetically at a vacated corner booth. If there was anything a Digger feared it was attention, and the longer we stood there the more we got. With a single flex of his jaw, Harnett forced a tight smile at the cook, took three giant steps, and landed on the far bench of the booth. I wandered after and he tugged me down next to him.

Coattails rippling, Boggs slid onto the opposite bench. He pushed aside the uncleared plates and dirty utensils and smacked the book down before him. It was large and non- descript and bulged with its untitled contents. Boggs's little hands stroked the faux-leather cover.

"Two minutes." Harnett flicked his eyes at a nearby clock, where a second hand lazed past bad caricatures of Marlon Brando, Marilyn Monroe, and James Dean. "Time enough for these people to get back to their business."

"You're getting bent out of shape," Boggs said. "There's no reason. It's just me, Baby. Do you know how far I came to see you? Two thousand five hundred seventy-five—"

"Tick tock." Harnett kept his eyes on Marlon, Marilyn, and James.

Boggs sat back and frowned. "Right. Down to business. That's how it always is with you. I guess I'd forgotten. Well, fine. We can make this a business meeting if you want. I do have some business to transact."

"That's up to you," Harnett said. "One minute."

Boggs spoke faster. "You're going to be glad we had this conversation. You're going to see that this is exactly where you belong. Right at this table with me. With me and Joey. The three of us—you remember how it used to be? With me and you and Valerie? We were family then, and the three of us here now, we can be—"

"Don't talk about her. Don't talk. I've got nothing to say to you." But Harnett couldn't resist. "Go back to your hell- hole. Your ditch. Wherever you're squatting now."

The words were like bullets. Boggs flinched at each one. He hid his face, turning to the dirty dishes for guidance. When at last he spoke, the syllables were tentative and imploring. "She's gone now. I know it, I heard. And I'm so sorry, Kenny. You don't know how sorry. But you don't need to be like this. I've done nothing to deserve it. I'm trying to make things better with us. You're my brother and nothing can change that."

"We were never brothers."

Boggs's voice shattered. "How can you *say* that? Of course we are! All those years growing up—what was that? Did that not happen? You need to remember it, Kenny. One of us has to, and my brain is falling out my head. Did I tell you that? It's true. You're probably glad. But you shouldn't be. No one should feel that way about his brother."

"Don't worry. I don't feel anything at all." He glanced at the clock. "Time's up."

"Wait. Now you just wait. I know you like I know me. We think the same. You may not want to admit that, but it's true. We both know, for instance, that when a rotter dies, that's it. There's no fantasy land of heaven or hell. It's like that old say- ing we used to say: *You can't take it with you.* Except here's the thing. You ready? You ready for our business transaction? Turns out they *do* get away with something. Don't they?" He shifted his despairing gaze to me. "Don't they, son?"

"Do not address him," Harnett said. I barely heard. I could not take my eyes from the unnatural thickness of the book.

"What the rotters get away with is dignity. *Dignity*. And that's wrong. And you know it. They had their time. They had their degrees and careers and portfolios. All so they could buy themselves a diamond ring and die with it on, all so they could get themselves buried wearing it—and what's the point, Kenny, seriously now, of a diamond, which is designed to reflect light, what's the point if there ain't no light to reflect? You and me can steal that ring, sure, but that doesn't get down to the real issue, now, does it? Brother— you know I know you know it."

Boggs sank his fingers into the soft flesh of the book and with deliberation slid it across the table. It made the sound of ice being shaved. Boggs twisted his wrists clockwise and the book was suddenly facing my father and me with all the malice of a darkened cellar.

I stared at it. Harnett did, too.

"This is a gift. If you want it. I began it when I heard about our son."

I found myself drawing back the front cover.

"I started it alone but we can finish it together."

When I saw the first Polaroid it was as if I had known all along. My heart did not accelerate; rather it seemed to slow and slug thickly against either lung. I turned pages. More.

"I call it the Rotters Book, Kenny." More. More.

"My Rotters Book. *Our* Rotters Book." More. More. More.

"A bunch of filthy stinking rotters."

On each wrinkled page, nestled between the claws of scrapbook photo corners, were four instant photographs, each one of a corpse smashed flat by the unkind swat of a cheap flashbulb and slathered a garish green by the yellow snot of developing liquid. They were old men, their translucent skin stretched and pocked like moth-eaten fabric. They were little girls, their lips strung with purple pearls of rot, their cheeks appled with rupture. They were genderless skulls, a thousand years old, the dried jelly of what used to be flesh crusted to gray bone. Caught in explosions of white light, once-severe brows were erased, once-regal cheekbones whittled to kernels; they were pink, white, blue; they were the color and texture of afterbirth. And there were hundreds of them, these cold and bent photos, each one stamped with Boggs's muddy fingerprints—the autograph of this intruder who had come at them with chisel and shovel, smashing first their caskets and then their sanctuary. It was sickening and dazzling, this litany of trespass.

I could feel the heat of Harnett's armpits, see the sweat spreading from his hands.

"No one's ever seen anything like it, Kenny. I can promise you that. You know what this is? It's a *communication*. It's going to tell the whole wide world that we're watching. There's not going to be any more creeping around like cock- roaches. No one anywhere is going to even think about dying without having to go through us first."

Page after page—it was as if someone had done my specifying for me.

Boggs's voice was bursting with joy. "I still haven't told you the best part."

Together my father and I looked up.

"Two pictures," Boggs said. "I take two. One goes in the Rotters Book. The other I leave down there with them." He beamed proudly. "Pinned right to their chests."

Harnett went over the table. Condiment bottles spun and clattered; I saw a white line of salt and felt a familiar urge except this time didn't know in which direction to throw. Harnett's hands squeezed at Boggs's throat. The smaller man gurgled in surprise and cranked his foreshortened arms as if he were drowning. His frenzied feet nailed me under the table—my foot, my shin, my thigh—and for a flash I was back within the Congress of Freaks, not son of the mighty Resurrectionist, just Crotch, and these kicks were what I deserved.

I rolled from the booth and hit the floor. Above, Boggs pushed at my father's eyes with his thumbs. Harnett twisted and tried to toss him away, but Boggs had already taken firm hold of my father's coat and they both went crashing. Harnett's head struck the hanging lamp and it whirled.

Knees knocked me; normal people were closing in. Their hovering presence yanked me back to a world I had some- how forgotten. From my sunken vantage I saw beer bellies and holstered cell phones and practical purses, and I wanted it back, all of it. *Take me,* I begged of them, but to their eyes I had long since become oblivion. They only saw strange, face- less men wrestling on top of cheap tableware. Reluctantly I returned to my newer world and within the bedlam saw my father attempt to grab the steak knife still spinning upon the unbused table.

Blood was streaking down his forehead—the lamp had slashed him good. He tried to wipe away an eyeful and Boggs, his compact torso contracting ferociously, took the opportunity to slam him to the table. Plates vibrated and silverware floated in midair; the steak knife twirled and Harnett's hand pinned it to the wall. One second later it was clutched in his fist, the blade flashing.

Finally there were arms everywhere, pulling the two fighters apart, and in the tangle of bodies I saw faces that triggered recognition: here was Brownie, lifting Boggs in a back- ward bear hug; here was Under-the-Mud, prying Boggs's fingers from a bloodied neck; here was Screw, restraining Boggs's thrashing legs; here was Fisher, doing the same to Harnett; here was Crying John, already hoisting Harnett by the coat collar; and here, like a ghost, was the Apologist, gently coaxing the knife from Harnett's fingers.

Through it, the two men roared.

"Kenny! Kenny!" Boggs cried. "What did I do?"

"We should've taken care of you years ago!"

"Was it my brain?" Boggs clawed desperately at the sides of his head. "Did my brain do something wrong?"

"You're no brother to me and no son to Lionel."

"I am! I am!" Boggs shook free from his captors and snatched up the Rotters Book. Panting, he regarded each old man in turn. The pale grief drained from his face and replaced itself with a florid loathing. "Why are all of you looking at me? I don't exist to you, remember? Don't any of you remember? You banished me. All of you agreed to it. That's how much you all loved your Baby. You banished me and you want to pretend that you're blameless. Well, go ahead. Pre- tend. Act like I don't exist. Pretty soon you'll change your mind. I swear it. You see this book?"

"Get out!" Harnett boomed. Crying John took handfuls of his clothes to keep him at bay.

"Yes, brother—oh, sorry, Mr. Resurrectionist, sir. Any- thing you say. Resurrectionist tells Baby what to do and Baby does it. Those are the rules, right?" He futzed with his suit until he recognized its hopeless condition. The tie slopped in an inebriated loop; the vest was missing buttons; the shirt was bedecked with food. The violation of this façade of respectability infuriated him. He grated his tiny teeth and glared at Harnett. "You're no different than the rest of these rot- ters."

"You stay in your territory," Harnett said. "You remember Monro-Barclay and stay the hell away."

"The pact?" Boggs laughed and a mist of blood painted his ruffles. "If I'm not your brother and I'm not Lionel's son, then guess what? I'm an orphan again! I'm an orphan and I belong to nobody. Any pact you rotters have ain't my concern. I plan to finish my book on schedule. And if that takes me into enemy territory, I don't know what to say. I have no enemies. I love all of you. You know that. It's you who don't love me."

Boggs limped in the direction of the door. He muttered as he passed me.

"Ask Daddy about the Rat King," he said. "Ask Daddy about the Gatlins." He turned up the volume so that everyone— Diggers, diners, cooks, everyone—could hear. "The Rat King? The Gatlins? Your memory, old men, is selective!"

At the mention of these curious oaths, Harnett pulled against Crying John's embrace.

Boggs ducked and crabbed sideways. After his stubby fingers hooked the handle of the front door, he scanned the crowd until his eyes found mine. " Your first hole, son. Remember the feeling? Now imagine it times a hundred. Times a thousand. Imagine how a gentle- man of breeding raises his little Digger."

Boggs slipped the Rotters Book inside his coat and I felt a stab of loss. He pushed open the door and a sparkling cone of snow turned him into some dizzying dream. A jingle of door bells, a flare of coattails, and he was gone.

Already the Diggers were threading into the crowd and loosening from my memory. The worst possible thing had happened. They had been seen, addressed in public, and now, thanks to my father's rash behavior, would have to disperse far sooner than they had hoped. As the interlopers withdrew, the surrounding gawkers took on even finer dimension. I wanted so badly to run into their arms and join their routines of afternoon casseroles, evening board games, school-night early bedtimes. Any quiet mundanity—I'd take it and love it and never want anything else, I'd swear to it.

But even these people were scattering, half grinning with the anticipation of the stories they'd tell about the outrageous dispute they'd seen at lunch. Only Crying John remained at my father's side. He took a clean towel from a cook and placed it in Harnett's hand, then lifted that hand so that it ap- plied pressure to the wound. Harnett shook off the man's grip and looked away in shame. With nothing but a lugubrious frown, Crying John slipped through shoulders and became just another plaid shirt receding from spilled food and broken dishes. I thought, but wasn't sure, that I heard a distant muttering: "C'mon, Foulie."

Braver legs approached. " You okay, mister?"

Harnett checked the towel. It was deep red. At his feet, blood made moth blots across the tile. He wiped his slick face and neck and tossed the towel onto the destroyed table.

"The truck," he told me.

"Good," I said, tearing my eyes from the gore and scoop- ing up my biology text. "Let's go home."

We pushed through the crowd and were outside. Boggs was nowhere.

"We're not going home," Harnett said as we carved the cold morning air. The sidewalk behind him was spattered with red.

"What? But school. My test."

"Lionel." For once he ignored the caskets tasting fresh air across the street. "We talk to Lionel."

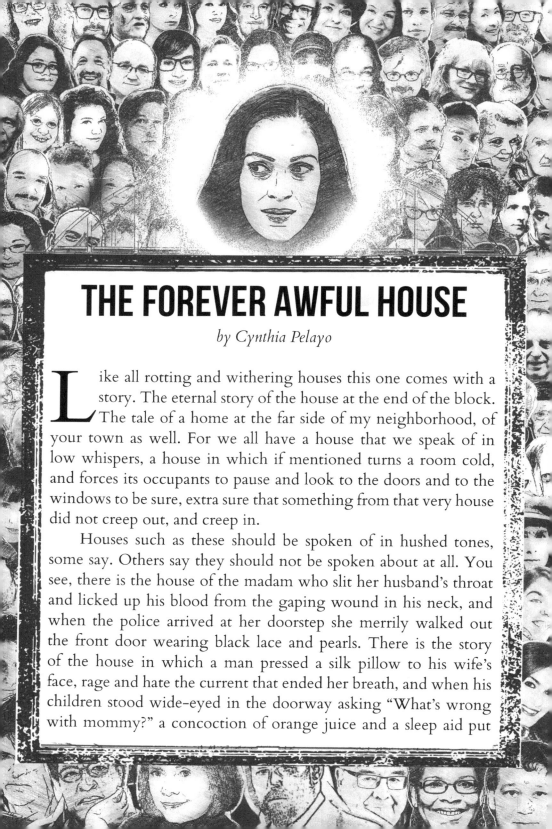

THE FOREVER AWFUL HOUSE

by Cynthia Pelayo

Like all rotting and withering houses this one comes with a story. The eternal story of the house at the end of the block. The tale of a home at the far side of my neighborhood, of your town as well. For we all have a house that we speak of in low whispers, a house in which if mentioned turns a room cold, and forces its occupants to pause and look to the doors and to the windows to be sure, extra sure that something from that very house did not creep out, and creep in.

Houses such as these should be spoken of in hushed tones, some say. Others say they should not be spoken about at all. You see, there is the house of the madam who slit her husband's throat and licked up his blood from the gaping wound in his neck, and when the police arrived at her doorstep she merrily walked out the front door wearing black lace and pearls. There is the story of the house in which a man pressed a silk pillow to his wife's face, rage and hate the current that ended her breath, and when his children stood wide-eyed in the doorway asking "What's wrong with mommy?" a concoction of orange juice and a sleep aid put them all to sleep. There is then the house of the mother who saw a lumbering, black mass looming over her, and so she committed herself to a full bathtub with her newborn nestled on her chest, submerged in warm water so the awful thing could no longer find them.

You see however, they all became the awful things, things of story and whispers, town and city scandals, ghosts that peer out windows and wave hello to little girls and little boys as they ride their bicycle past on Halloween night. They are houses that smell of smoke and iron, where the disembodied scream to the living to *Help Me*, but their screams are forever trapped within mold covered crumbling walls. These houses remain standing, wooden corpses, rarely if ever demolished, for we fear the dust and the rubble from their remains will infect our very selves if we were to tear them down. And so, they stand and we watch, we whisper and we wait.

Haunted houses are meant to lure, are meant to fall on the lips of those around campfires. And as you speak of another house with gunshot blasts in the walls, dried and caked blood between the floorboards, of forever slumbering children once packed in closets, of lovers decapitated and buried beneath basement floors, and of a mistress who murdered them all with glee and laughed, know that your words are power. For each time you speak of a house like this, of death and decay, another awful house emerges in a new town or city somewhere, everywhere.

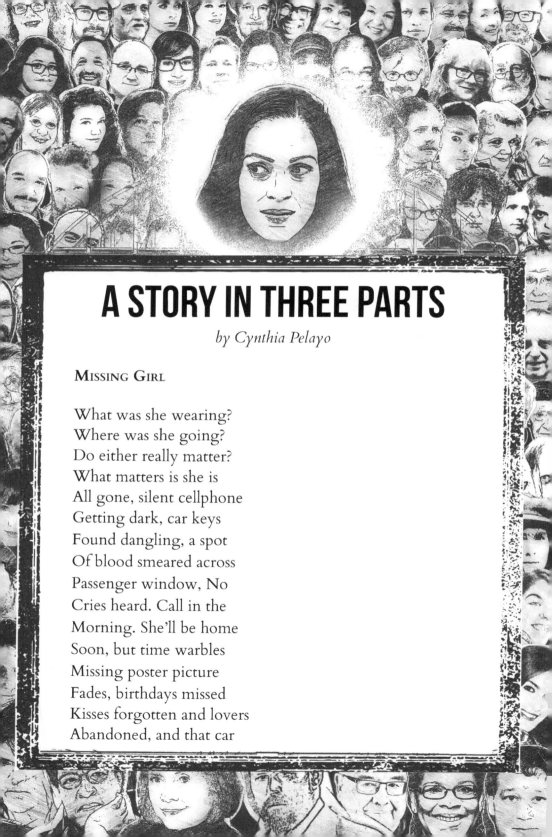

A STORY IN THREE PARTS

by Cynthia Pelayo

MISSING GIRL

What was she wearing?
Where was she going?
Do either really matter?
What matters is she is
All gone, silent cellphone
Getting dark, car keys
Found dangling, a spot
Of blood smeared across
Passenger window, No
Cries heard. Call in the
Morning. She'll be home
Soon, but time warbles
Missing poster picture
Fades, birthdays missed
Kisses forgotten and lovers
Abandoned, and that car

Sits rusted and weightless
Clutching onto her secrets
A seashell playing back
Recorded screams of terror
Lost hope, lost life, lost

DETECTIVE STORY

The detective story is an intellectual game
Of things once there and things rearranged
Water, books, letters, keys, a herring so red
Give the reader ample opportunity to solve
The mystery, no willful tricks, do not play
Deceptions, but let's play with the detective
Rules: No love interest. Never the perpetrator
The detective must be continually turning,
Making calculations, as Dupin says ratiocination
The crime must be solved by natural means
And there must always, always be a body

SKULL BEHIND A WALL

Sometimes you know no one is ever going to find you and sometimes you relinquish your grasp, your hold on this world. You close your eyes and you allow those silent, anguished, warm tears to roll down your cheeks because they are real and they are yours and no one and nothing can rip them away from you as you were ripped away from this world and your screams your screams are yours, and your memories are yours and you wish you wish you had one more time to tell them all you loved them you wish you wish you had one more time to kiss the noon day sun and you wish you wish the last scent that you smelled was not the ogre above you and you wish you wish this was not the place you would haunt for years and years before they found you, covered in burlap and no way to find you and no way to find you and you will never go home because home was years ago and home was them and all of them have died and your memory fades as they faded and you are released to your second death all because an ogre stole you away.

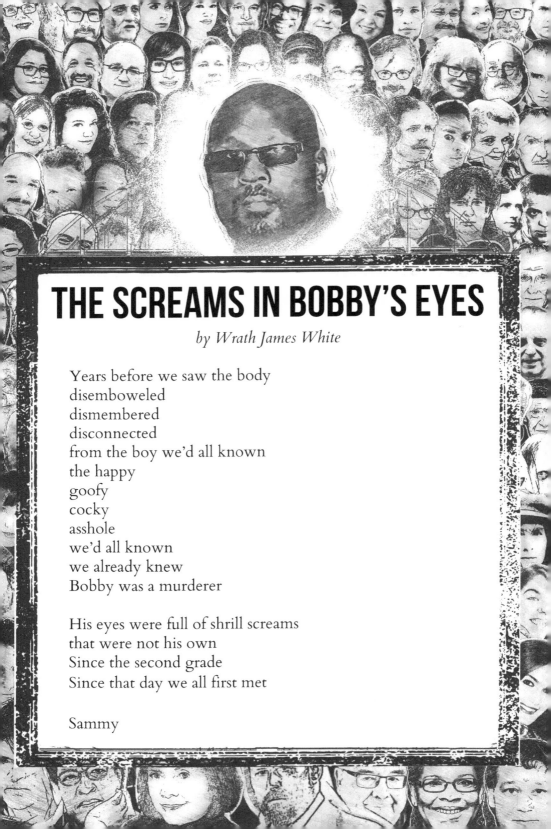

THE SCREAMS IN BOBBY'S EYES

by Wrath James White

Years before we saw the body
disemboweled
dismembered
disconnected
from the boy we'd all known
the happy
goofy
cocky
asshole
we'd all known
we already knew
Bobby was a murderer

His eyes were full of shrill screams
that were not his own
Since the second grade
Since that day we all first met

Sammy

Rick
Tyrone
Trisha
Latonya
Bobby
and me

We met on the playground swings
On a day so hot
the sun blazed off the sidewalk
A blistering white
like we were walking on sunlight

Shimmering waves of June heat
rose from the metal slide
And there sat Bobby
with a magnifying glass
immolating ants

Sammy threw a ball to Rick
Tyrone threw a frisbee
to Latonya and Trisha
And I sat watching Bobby
Murdering ants in dozens

He'd always been sadistic
We knew
We knew
Since he showed us the dead birds
All of those dead birds
Burned
Stabbed
Strangled

Impaled
Bludgeoned
And dismembered
disemboweled
disconnected from the skies
With tools from his dad's toolbox

Just like that Prince song
Bobby made the doves cry
And scream
And bleed

Bobby's father left long ago
Left him with a scar
Like a river on a map
That wound down his forehead

He left him with many wounds
So many wounds
And painful memories
And terrors
And tears
And screams
And desires
And a toolbox
Full of tools
He never taught Bobby to use
But Bobby was creative
So very
very
creative

He couldn't fix his bike chain

Or replace the tire
when the wheels went flat
Or put the limbs back
on his sister's broken dolls
Or repair the computer
where his dad kept the photos
The ones Bobby told us about
After he showed us the birds

The ones of all those children
who looked like Bobby
who died just like those birds
in Bobby's secret treehouse

There were so many feathers
Feathers everywhere
Plastered to the floor
Drifting in the air
Sticking to the walls
White
Gray
Brown
wet
red
feathers
And severed wings
like an abattoir
of slaughtered angels

Bobby told us all about
those bloody photos
on his father's computer
Pointed to each bird

carefully posed
just like the photos
And described each child
with a smile on his face
but not in his eyes
but not in his voice
Chilly as an autumn wind

We already knew
Bobby was a murderer
But he was our friend

The other kids at our school
were all afraid of Bobby
The other kids at our school
should be afraid of Bobby

Bobby was our attack dog
He kept us all safe
safe from all the bullies
He would whisper in their ears
Tell them about his toolbox
Tell them about the birds
And he would smile
But not his eyes
Eyes full of shrill screams
that were not his own
Eyes full of shrill screams
that might be there's
if they persisted

When Trisha's father hurt her
her wicked stepdad

who did wicked things to her
hurt her in the night
when her mother was asleep

She came to Bobby and us
She came to Bobby
because she knew
she knew
we knew
what Bobby would do

When her stepdad disappeared
we all smiled
with our eyes
full of shrill screams
that were not our own
We knew what Bobby had done
We knew what we had all done
Even if we didn't "know"
We knew
We knew

What we didn't know back then
What we would all learn later
Was that this was Bobby's first
Trisha's stepfather
Bobby's first without feathers
First that screamed words
That begged for his life
That made Bobby feel something

We made him a murderer
We made him our murderer

And
Bobby
Could
Not
Stop
Bobby never stopped

When we all began high school
When we all drifted apart
We still thought about Bobby
When kids
Or parents
Or teachers
went missing
We all thought about Bobby

When Sammy became a jock
became a bully
became an asshole
began to harass us
began to terrorize us
we all thought about Bobby
Everyone except Sammy

Sammy must have forgotten
the blood and feathers
the slaughtered angels
Trisha's stepfather
the eyes that never smiled
Eyes full of shrill screams
that were not his own

Sammy must have forgotten
Sammy must have forgotten

Sammy must have remembered
When the hammer struck his hands
When the hammer struck his shins
When the hammer struck his knees
When the hammer struck his elbows
When the white of splintered bone
erupted through red meat
and yellow fat
and tanned skin

When his shrill screams
filled Bobby's ears

Sammy must have remembered
When the screwdriver pierced his hands
When the screwdriver pierced his feet
When the screwdriver pierced his testicles
When the screwdriver pierced his eardrums
When the screwdriver pierced his eyeballs

Sammy must have remembered
When the saw cut off his hands
When the saw cut off his feet

Cut off his calves
Cut of his biceps
Cut off his pectorals
his buttocks
his cock
his head

When his silence
filled Bobby's eyes

When his silence echoed
like a whisper in a tomb
through Bobby's treehouse

It was the first time in years
that we were all together
in Bobby's treehouse

Sammy
Rick
Tyrone
Trisha
Latonya
Bobby
and me

Except Sammy wasn't together
Sammy was everywhere
His skin
His bones
His organs
His muscles
His popcorn-colored fat
was everywhere
plastered to the walls
sticking to the floor
like an abattoir
of slaughtered teenagers
slaughtered classmates
slaughtered assholes
who used to be our friend

Years before
we saw Sammy's body
we already knew
Bobby was a murderer
But Bobby was our friend
But Bobby killed our friend
For us
For himself
For his father

Years before
we saw Sammy's body
we saw all those bodies
pieces of pieces
of pieces of bodies
we already knew
that Bobby had to die

Bobby smiled at us
but not his eyes
His eyes were full of shrill screams
that were not his own

We smiled back at him
But not our eyes
We already knew
that Bobby had to die

We each removed a tool
from Bobby's father's toolbox
Rick took a hacksaw
Tyrone a claw hammer
Trisha found a keyhole saw

Latonya a pry bar
And I picked up a mallet
And Bobby took it all

And our eyes all filled
with Bobby's shrill screams.

DRACULA

"There are bad dreams for those who sleep unwisely."

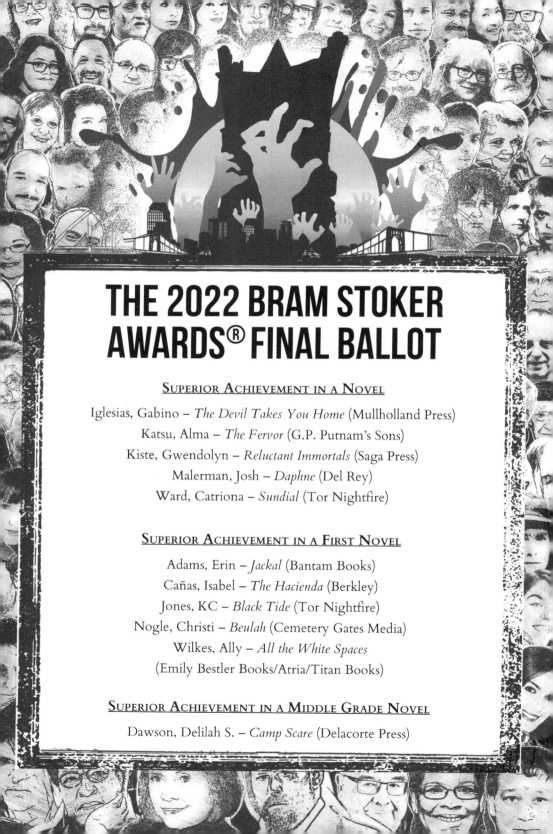

THE 2022 BRAM STOKER AWARDS® FINAL BALLOT

SUPERIOR ACHIEVEMENT IN A NOVEL

Iglesias, Gabino – *The Devil Takes You Home* (Mullholland Press)

Katsu, Alma – *The Fervor* (G.P. Putnam's Sons)

Kiste, Gwendolyn – *Reluctant Immortals* (Saga Press)

Malerman, Josh – *Daphne* (Del Rey)

Ward, Catriona – *Sundial* (Tor Nightfire)

SUPERIOR ACHIEVEMENT IN A FIRST NOVEL

Adams, Erin – *Jackal* (Bantam Books)

Cañas, Isabel – *The Hacienda* (Berkley)

Jones, KC – *Black Tide* (Tor Nightfire)

Nogle, Christi – *Beulah* (Cemetery Gates Media)

Wilkes, Ally – *All the White Spaces*
(Emily Bestler Books/Atria/Titan Books)

SUPERIOR ACHIEVEMENT IN A MIDDLE GRADE NOVEL

Dawson, Delilah S. – *Camp Scare* (Delacorte Press)

Kraus, Daniel – *They Stole Our Hearts* (Henry Holt and Co.)

Malinenko, Ally – *This Appearing House* (Katherine Tegen Books)

Senf, Lora – *The Clackity* (Atheneum Books for Young Readers)

Stringfellow, Lisa – *A Comb of Wishes* (Quill Tree Books)

SUPERIOR ACHIEVEMENT IN A GRAPHIC NOVEL

Aquilone, James (editor) – *Kolchak: The Night Stalker:*
50th Anniversary (Moonstone Books)

Gailey, Sarah (author) and Bak, Pius (artist) – *Eat the Rich* (Boom! Studios)

Manzetti, Alessandro (author) and Cardoselli, Stefano (artist/author) – *Kraken*
Inferno: The Last Hunt (Independent Legions Publishing)

Tynion IV, James (author) and Dell'Edera, Werther (artist) –
Something is Killing the Children, Vol. 4 (Boom! Studios)

Young, Skottie (author) and Corona, Jorge (artist) –
The Me You Love in the Dark (Image Comics)

SUPERIOR ACHIEVEMENT IN A YOUNG ADULT NOVEL

Fraistat, Ann – *What We Harvest* (Delacorte Press)

Jackson, Tiffany D. – *The Weight of Blood* (Katherine Tegen Books)

Marshall, Kate Alice – *These Fleeting Shadows* (Viking)

Ottone, Robert P. – *The Triangle* (Raven Tale Publishing)

Schwab, V.E. – *Gallant* (Greenwillow Books)

Tirado, Vincent – *Burn Down, Rise Up* (Sourcebooks Fire)

SUPERIOR ACHIEVEMENT IN LONG FICTION

Allred, Rebecca J. and White, Gordon B. – *And in Her Smile, the World*
(Trepidatio Publishing)

Carmen, Christa – "Through the Looking Glass and Straight into Hell"
(*Orphans of Bliss: Tales of Addiction Horror*) (Wicked Run Press)

Hightower, Laurel – *Below* (Ghoulish Books)

Katsu, Alma – *The Wehrwolf* (Amazon Original Stories)

Knight, EV – *Three Days in the Pink Tower* (Creature Publishing)

SUPERIOR ACHIEVEMENT IN SHORT FICTION

Dries, Aaron – "Nona Doesn't Dance"
(*Cut to Care: A Collection of Little Hurts*) (IFWG Australia, IFWG International)
Gwilym, Douglas – "Poppy's Poppy"
(*Penumbric Speculative Fiction Magazine,* Vol. V, No. 6)
McCarthy, J.A.W. – "The Only Thing Different Will Be the Body"
(*A Woman Built by Man*) (Cemetery Gates Media)
Taborska, Anna – "A Song for Barnaby Jones" (Zagava)
Taborska, Anna – "The Star"
(*Great British Horror 7: Major Arcane*) (Black Shuck Books)
Yardley, Mercedes M. – "Fracture"
(*Mother: Tales of Love and Terror*) (Weird Little Worlds)

SUPERIOR ACHIEVEMENT IN A FICTION COLLECTION

Ashe, Paula D. – *We Are Here to Hurt Each Other* (Nictitating Books)
Joseph, RJ – *Hell Hath No Sorrow Like a Woman Haunted* (The Seventh Terrace)
Khaw, Cassandra – *Breakable Things* (Undertow Publications)
Thomas, Richard – *Spontaneous Human Combustion* (Keylight Books)
Veres, Attila – *The Black Maybe* (Valancourt Books)

SUPERIOR ACHIEVEMENT IN A SCREENPLAY

Cooper, Scott – *The Pale Blue Eye*
(Cross Creek Pictures, Grisbi Productions, Streamline Global Group)
Derrickson, Scott and Cargill, C. Robert – *The Black Phone*
(Blumhouse Productions, Crooked Highway, Universal Pictures)
Duffer Brothers, The – *Stranger Things*: Episode 04.01 "Chapter One: The Hellfire Club" (21 Laps Entertainment, Monkey Massacre, Netflix, Upside Down Pictures)
Garland, Alex – *Men* (DNA Films)
Goth, Mia and West, Ti – *Pearl*
(A24, Bron Creative, Little Lamb, New Zealand Film Commission)

SUPERIOR ACHIEVEMENT IN A POETRY COLLECTION

Bailey, Michael and Simon, Marge – *Sifting the Ashes*
(Crystal Lake Publishing)
Lynch, Donna – *Girls from the County*
(Raw Dog Screaming Press)
Pelayo, Cynthia – *Crime Scene* (Raw Dog Screaming Press)
Saulson, Sumiko – *The Rat King: A Book of Dark Poetry* (Dooky Zines)
Sng, Christina – *The Gravity of Existence* (Interstellar Flight Press)

SUPERIOR ACHIEVEMENT IN AN ANTHOLOGY

Datlow, Ellen – *Screams from the Dark: 29 Tales of Monsters and the Monstrous*
(Tor Nightfire)
Hartmann, Sadie and Saywers, Ashley – *Human Monsters: A Horror Anthology*
(Dark Matter Ink)
Nogle, Christi and Becker, Willow – *Mother: Tales of Love and Terror*
(Weird Little Worlds)
Ryan, Lindy – *Into the Forest: Tales of the Baba Yaga* (Black Spot Books)
Tantlinger, Sara – *Chromophobia: A Strangehouse Anthology by Women in Horror* (Strangehouse Books)

SUPERIOR ACHIEVEMENT IN NON-FICTION

Cisco, Michael – *Weird Fiction: A Genre Study* (Palgrave Macmillan)
Hieber, Leanna Renee and Janes, Andrea – *A Haunted History of Invisible Women: True Stories of America's Ghosts* (Citadel Press)
Kröger, Lisa and Anderson, Melanie R. – *Toil and Trouble: A Women's History of the Occult* (Quirk Books)
Waggoner, Tim – *Writing in the Dark: The Workbook* (Guide Dog Books)
Wytovich, Stephanie M. – *Writing Poetry in the Dark* (Raw Dog Screaming Press)

SUPERIOR ACHIEVEMENT IN SHORT NON-FICTION

Murray, Lee – "I Don't Read Horror (& Other Weird Tales)"
(*Interstellar Flight Magazine*) (Interstellar Flight Press)

Pelayo, Cynthia – "This is Not a Poem"
(*Writing Poetry in the Dark*) (Raw Dog Screaming Press)
Wetmore, Jr., Kevin J. – "A Clown in the Living Room: The Sinister Clown
on Television" (*The Many Lives of Scary Clowns: Essays on Pennywise, Twisty, the
Joker, Krusty and More*) (McFarland and Company)
Wood, L. Marie – "African American Horror Authors and Their Craft: The
Evolution of Horror Fiction from African Folklore" (*Conjuring Worlds: An
Afrofuturist Textbook for Middle and High School Students*) (Conjure World)
Wood, L. Marie, "The H Word: The Horror of Hair"
(*Nightmare Magazine*, No. 118) (Adamant Press)

ABOUT THE
BRAM STOKER AWARDS®

E ach year, the Horror Writer's Association presents the Bram Stoker Awards® for Superior Achievement, named in honor of Bram Stoker, author of the seminal horror work, Dracula. The Bram Stoker Awards® were instituted immediately after the organization's incorporation in 1987.

To ameliorate the competitive nature of any award system, the Bram Stoker Awards® are given "for superior achievement," not for "best of the year," and the rules are deliberately designed to make ties possible. The first awards were presented in 1988 (for works published in 1987) and they have been presented every year since. The award itself is an eight-inch replica of a fanciful haunted house, designed specifically for HWA by sculptor Steven Kirk. The door of the house opens to reveal a brass plaque engraved with the name of the winning work and its author.

Any work of Horror first published in the English language may be considered for an award during the year of its publication. The categories for which a Bram Stoker Award® may be presented have varied over the years, reflecting the state of the publishing industry and the horror genre.

From 2011 the eleven Bram Stoker Award® categories are: Novel, First Novel, Short Fiction, Long Fiction, Young Adult, Fiction Collection, Poetry Collection, Anthology, Screenplay, Graphic Novel and Non-Fiction.

There are two paths to a work becoming a Nominee for the Bram Stoker Award®. In one, the HWA membership at large recommends worthy works for consideration. A preliminary ballot for each category is compiled using a formula based on these recommendations. In the second, a Jury for each category also compiles a preliminary ballot. Two rounds of voting by our Active members then determine first the Final Ballot (all those appearing on the Final Ballot are "Bram Stoker Nominees"), and then the Bram Stoker Award® Winners. The Winners are announced and the Bram Stoker Awards® presented at a gala banquet, normally during the period between March and June.

In addition, Lifetime Achievement Awards are occasionally presented to individuals whose entire body of work has substantially influenced Horror.

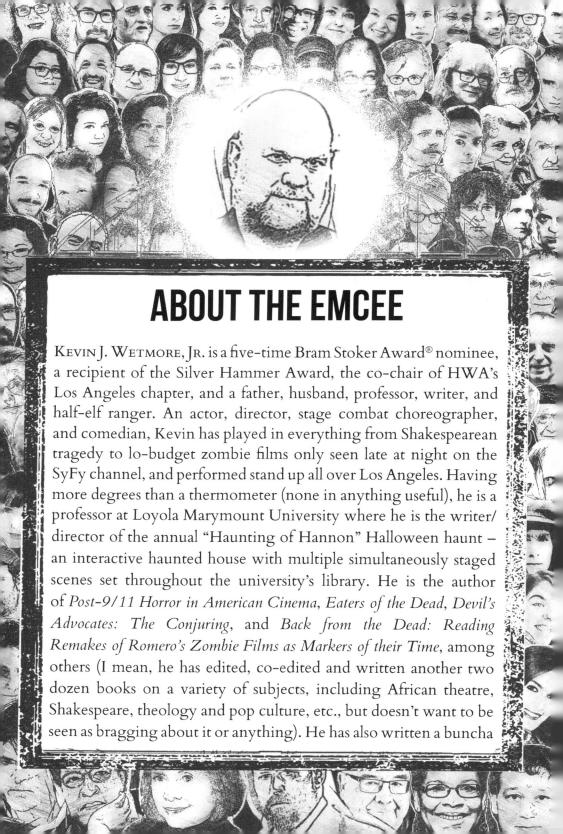

ABOUT THE EMCEE

KEVIN J. WETMORE, JR. is a five-time Bram Stoker Award® nominee, a recipient of the Silver Hammer Award, the co-chair of HWA's Los Angeles chapter, and a father, husband, professor, writer, and half-elf ranger. An actor, director, stage combat choreographer, and comedian, Kevin has played in everything from Shakespearean tragedy to lo-budget zombie films only seen late at night on the SyFy channel, and performed stand up all over Los Angeles. Having more degrees than a thermometer (none in anything useful), he is a professor at Loyola Marymount University where he is the writer/director of the annual "Haunting of Hannon" Halloween haunt – an interactive haunted house with multiple simultaneously staged scenes set throughout the university's library. He is the author of *Post-9/11 Horror in American Cinema*, *Eaters of the Dead*, *Devil's Advocates: The Conjuring*, and *Back from the Dead: Reading Remakes of Romero's Zombie Films as Markers of their Time*, among others (I mean, he has edited, co-edited and written another two dozen books on a variety of subjects, including African theatre, Shakespeare, theology and pop culture, etc., but doesn't want to be seen as bragging about it or anything). He has also written a buncha short stories, perhaps the best known of which are his mashups of Lovecraft and Judy Blume, "Tales of a Fourth Grade Shoggoth" and "Are You There, Azathoth? It's Me, Margaret" as well as dozens of others for a variety of magazines, quarterlies, and anthologies. He lives in Los Angeles with his wife and children, all of which has earned him the privilege of writing short autobiographies in the third person.

ABOUT THE KEYNOTE SPEAKER

Lisa Morton is a screenwriter, author of non-fiction books, and prose writer whose work was described by the *American Library Association's Readers' Advisory Guide to Horror* as "consistently dark, unsettling, and frightening." She is a six-time winner of the Bram Stoker Award®, the author of four novels and over 150 short stories, and a world-class Halloween and paranormal expert. Her recent releases include the *Calling the Spirits: A History of Seances;* forthcoming in October 2023 from Applause Books is *The Art of the Zombie Movie.* Lisa lives in Los Angeles and online at www. lisamorton.com.

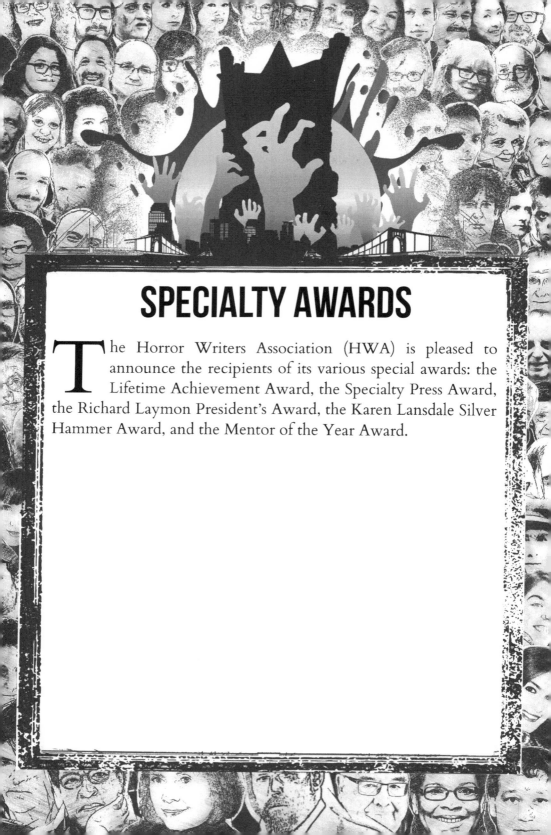

SPECIALTY AWARDS

The Horror Writers Association (HWA) is pleased to announce the recipients of its various special awards: the Lifetime Achievement Award, the Specialty Press Award, the Richard Laymon President's Award, the Karen Lansdale Silver Hammer Award, and the Mentor of the Year Award.

LIFETIME ACHIEVEMENT AWARDS

The HWA is proud to announce our Lifetime Achievement Award recipients: Elizabeth Massie, Nuzo Onoh, and John Saul.

The Lifetime Achievement Award is presented periodically to an individual whose work has substantially influenced the horror genre. While this award is often presented to a writer, it may also be given for influential accomplishments in other creative fields.

The Lifetime Achievement Award is the most prestigious of all awards presented by HWA. It does not merely honor the superior achievement embodied in a single work. Instead, it is an acknowledgement of superior achievement in an entire career.

Congratulations to this year's recipients!

Elizabeth Massie
Nuzo Onoh
John Saul

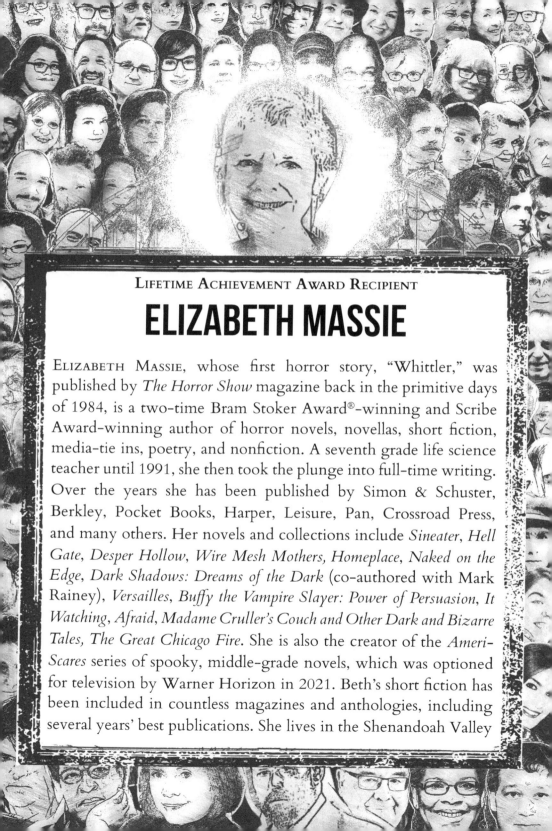

LIFETIME ACHIEVEMENT AWARD RECIPIENT

ELIZABETH MASSIE

ELIZABETH MASSIE, whose first horror story, "Whittler," was published by *The Horror Show* magazine back in the primitive days of 1984, is a two-time Bram Stoker Award®-winning and Scribe Award-winning author of horror novels, novellas, short fiction, media-tie ins, poetry, and nonfiction. A seventh grade life science teacher until 1991, she then took the plunge into full-time writing. Over the years she has been published by Simon & Schuster, Berkley, Pocket Books, Harper, Leisure, Pan, Crossroad Press, and many others. Her novels and collections include *Sineater, Hell Gate, Desper Hollow, Wire Mesh Mothers, Homeplace, Naked on the Edge, Dark Shadows: Dreams of the Dark* (co-authored with Mark Rainey), *Versailles, Buffy the Vampire Slayer: Power of Persuasion, It Watching, Afraid, Madame Cruller's Couch and Other Dark and Bizarre Tales, The Great Chicago Fire.* She is also the creator of the *Ameri-Scares* series of spooky, middle-grade novels, which was optioned for television by Warner Horizon in 2021. Beth's short fiction has been included in countless magazines and anthologies, including several years' best publications. She lives in the Shenandoah Valley

of Virginia with her husband, artist/illustrator and Theremin-player Cortney Skinner. When not writing she knits, goes geocaching, spends time chilling at Starbucks, and seeks out locations she's never visited before. If she can find the remains of a crumbling, abandoned amusement park, all the better.

NUZO ONOH

NUZO ONOH is a Nigerian-British writer of Igbo descent. She is a pioneer of the African horror literary genre. Hailed as the "Queen of African Horror," Nuzo's writing showcases both the beautiful and horrific in the African culture within fictitious narratives.

Nuzo's works have been featured in numerous magazines and anthologies. She has given talks and lectures about African Horror, including at the prestigious *Miskatonic Institute of Horror Studies, London*. Her works have appeared in academic studies and been longlisted and shortlisted.

Nuzo holds a Law degree and a Master's degree in Writing, both from Warwick University, England. She is a certified Civil Funeral Celebrant, licensed to conduct non-religious burial services. An avid musician with an addiction to Jungyup and K-indie, Nuzo plays both the guitar and piano, and holds an NVQ in Digital Music Production. She resides in the West Midlands, United Kingdom.

JOHN SAUL

JOHN SAUL was born in 1942 in Southern California and grew up in Whittier, California. Jack and Betty Saul were his parents, and he had a sister, Helen, who was two years older. He was in Seventh Grade when his English teacher told him he should consider writing as a career. John attended four colleges, studying Theater and Anthropology. He wrote plays, short stories, poetry and eventually novels. Though he enjoyed writing humor, John's first novel was purchased by Dell Publishing to compete in the rapidly expanding thriller market of the late 1970s. With the immediate success of *Suffer The Children,* he was off and running. John's partner (now husband) of 47 years, Mike Sack, helped with book ideas and plotting. When they first met, Mike was a clinical psychologist at a state hospital and shared his experiences with John. Both Mike and John helped organize and taught at the Maui Writers Conference and School. His third novel, *Cry For The Strangers*, was made into a TV movie, and all of John's books have been published in over 35 countries worldwide and millions have been sold.

SPECIALTY PRESS AWARD

The HWA is pleased to present the Specialty Press Award to Undertow Publications.

The HWA Specialty Press Award is presented periodically to a specialty publisher whose work has substantially contributed to the horror genre, whose publications display general excellence, and whose dealings with writers have been fair and exemplary.

The award was instituted in 1997, largely due to the efforts of long-time HWA member and specialty press aficionado Peter Crowther.

Congratulations to Undertow Publications!

UNDERTOW PUBLICATIONS

"I am extremely grateful to be receiving the H.W.A. Specialty Press Award. To be honored and recognized by my peers in this way is truly unexpected. I am pleased beyond words, and giddy with joy. Thank you! The warmth and support from the horror community has been overwhelming. I am indebted to you all."

- Michael Kelly, Founder/Editor-in-Chief

UNDERTOW PUBLICATIONS began in 2009 with the goal of proving that speculative and literary fiction could coexist in the same strata, and that modes of writing shouldn't be judged by their genre but by their literary aesthetic. Literary spec-fic is what we aspire to. Our first publication, "Apparitions," an anthology of literary ghost stories, garnered a Shirley Jackson Award nomination. Since then we've won 2 Shirley Jackson Awards; a British Fantasy Award, and are 5-time World Fantasy Award finalists. We have been profiled in the Globe and Mail, the Toronto Star, and Wall Street Journal.

We crave stories of human relationships. The stories we publish explore human identity and the global, cultural, and natural influences that connect and shape us. No matter the setting, it's vital to us to publish real stories of real people - their struggles; their triumphs. Fiction holds a mirror to the common world and helps us understand. It makes us feel. And it entertains. Often, that's enough.

Undertow Publications continues to push against genre prejudice; publishing a diverse cross-section of authors, and continues to prove that horror and speculative fiction is not a pejorative.

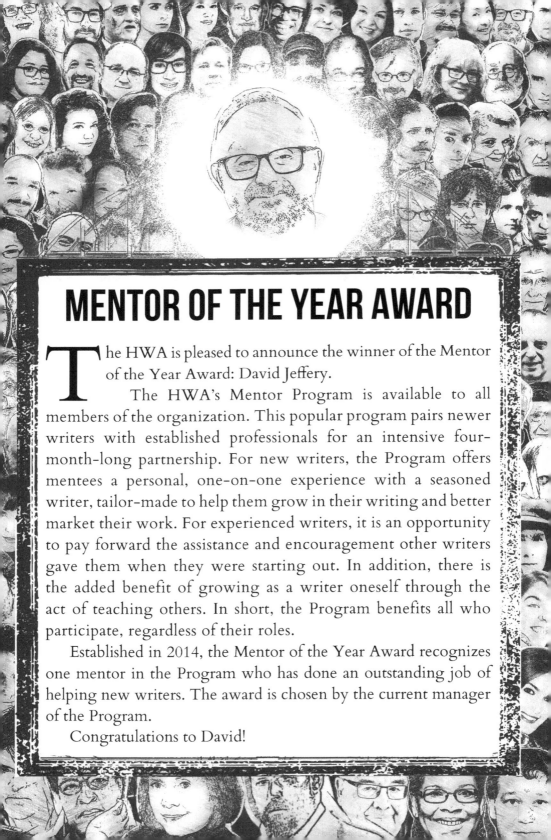

MENTOR OF THE YEAR AWARD

The HWA is pleased to announce the winner of the Mentor of the Year Award: David Jeffery.

The HWA's Mentor Program is available to all members of the organization. This popular program pairs newer writers with established professionals for an intensive four-month-long partnership. For new writers, the Program offers mentees a personal, one-on-one experience with a seasoned writer, tailor-made to help them grow in their writing and better market their work. For experienced writers, it is an opportunity to pay forward the assistance and encouragement other writers gave them when they were starting out. In addition, there is the added benefit of growing as a writer oneself through the act of teaching others. In short, the Program benefits all who participate, regardless of their roles.

Established in 2014, the Mentor of the Year Award recognizes one mentor in the Program who has done an outstanding job of helping new writers. The award is chosen by the current manager of the Program.

Congratulations to David!

DAVID JEFFERY

DAVID JEFFERY epitomizes what a mentor should be. He is dedicated to helping other writers improve their craft and always eager to participate in the Program each semester. The writers he's worked with have nothing but great things to say about him, as evidenced by this quote from one of his recent mentees:

> "Dave deserves praise and was everything one could ask for as a mentor. He was kind, he offered his expertise in a way that I could apply to my work, he made himself readily available, and he tailored his feedback and suggestions to my aspirations as a writer. In short, Dave was an excellent ambassador for the HWA and writers in general."

> "It's been a pleasure for me to work with Dave these past several years, and I would like to point out that he also helps writers in other ways, as he is the co-chair of the HWA's Wellness Committee. Without members like David, the Mentor Program would not exist."
>
> –JG Faherty, HWA Mentorship Program Manager

David is the author of 18 novels, two collections, and numerous short stories, and he's also an accomplished screenwriter. Many of his novels have been featured on Amazon #1 bestseller lists, including his Necropolis Rising series. David has been a mentor for the HWA for several years now, and he consistently receives outstanding praise from his mentees. In addition to being a member of the Horror Writers Association, David also belongs to the Society of Authors and British Fantasy Society. A former registered mental health professional, David is currently the co-chair of the HWA's Wellness Committee and has written several books, academic papers, and research articles relating to the field of mental health.

KAREN LANSDALE
SILVER HAMMER AWARD

The HWA is pleased to announce the winner of the Karen Lansdale Silver Hammer Award: Karen Lansdale.

In 2022, the Horror Writers Association renamed the Silver Hammer Award to the Karen Lansdale Silver Hammer Award in honor of the tremendous amount of work Karen did starting the HWA.

Our physical award has also been updated. Instead of a hammer, a new stylized sculpture has been designed and cast by the same company that mints our Bram Stoker Award® statues. We look forward to sharing the new design at StokerCon2023.

The HWA periodically gives the Karen Lansdale Silver Hammer Award to an HWA volunteer who has done a truly massive amount of work for the organization, often unsung and behind the scenes. It was instituted in 1996, and is decided by a vote of HWA's Board of Trustees.

The award is so named because it represents the careful,

steady, continuous work of building HWA's "house" — the many institutional systems that keep the organization functioning on a day-to-day basis.

Congratulations to Karen!

EXCERPT FROM JOE R. LANSDALE'S
"HOW THE HORROR WRITERS' ASSOCIATION CAME TO BE"

Once upon a time dear hearts, there wasn't a Horror Writers Association, and the writers who specialized in horror fiction existed random of one another, like stars, and they were lost in a dark void.

And then Karen Lansdale came along, and the void was filled.

Let me explain how that happened. Let me try and put a continuous misunderstanding aside so that it might die in a field alone, and let true credit be given where credit is due.

Robert R. McCammon, who was very much involved in the horror field back when it was in its boom, along with his then wife, Sally, met Karen and me in an elevator at a World Fantasy Convention. Hearing me speak to Karen, Rick said, "I bet you're Joe R. Lansdale. I can tell by the accent."

Took one Southerner to recognize another. The elevator was slow, but the McCammons and Lansdales hit up an immediate friendship, right then and there.

The elevator stopped, and we sat and visited, and Rick, as McCammon preferred to be called, said he had an idea that since horror was growing, and had become a recognized commercial genre, it should have an organization. He called the idea HOWL. Horror Occult Writer's League, which to this day I prefer to the soberer Horror Writers Association. He was talking about something along the lines of The Mystery Writers of America, Science Fiction Writers of America, Western Writers of America, and so on.

But there was a problem. He didn't have the time.

Karen immediately said, "I'll do it."

It would be easy to say the rest was history, but it didn't quite work out that way.

It went like this.

Karen, at that convention, began to make a list of names and addresses of writers who might be interested in such an organization. Rick had come up with the idea, but was too busy to pursue. He had the seed, but Karen planted and water and fertilized it until it grew into a tree.

THE RICHARD LAYMON PRESIDENT'S AWARD

The HWA is pleased to announce the winner of the Richard Laymon President's Award for Service: Meghan Arcuri.

The Richard Laymon President's Award for Service was instituted in 2001 and is named in honor of Richard Laymon, who died in 2001 while serving as HWA's President. As its name implies, it is given by HWA's sitting President.

The award is presented to a volunteer who has served the HWA in an especially exemplary manner and has shown extraordinary dedication to the organization.

Congratulations to Meghan!

MEGHAN ARCURI

MEGHAN ARCURI is a Bram Stoker Award®-nominated author. Her work can be found in various anthologies, including *Borderlands 7* (Borderlands Press), *Madhouse* (Dark Regions Press), *Chiral Mad,* and *Chiral Mad 3* (Written Backwards). She is currently the Vice President of the Horror Writers Association.

Prior to writing, she taught high school math, having earned her B.A. from Colgate University—with a double major in mathematics and English—and her masters from Rensselaer Polytechnic Institute.

She lives with her family in New York's Hudson Valley.

WHY THE BRAM STOKER AWARD® MATTERS

by Michael A. Arnzen

Who among us does not recognize and covet the Bram Stoker Award® — the hallmark trophy of horror literature? For one thing, the Horror Writers Association has the coolest and perhaps heftiest statue ever created for writers, molded in the form of a haunted house complete with giant insects crawling out from the window shutters and a working front door that reveals the bronze etching of the winner's name and title. The only thing missing is a creaking sound effect when you open it up. If you get a chance at the Stoker banquet, gaze upon this fine sculpture, which truly is a work of art. To most people, it would make an awesome Halloween decoration — but for those of us who own one, we'd would rather keep it away from sugar-fingered children and secure it as safely as gold, perhaps tucked away someplace near our books or our computer, for inspiration and affirmation.

The thing is freaking awesome. The designer, Brian Kirk,

deserves to have a real life Stoker house built just for him, bugs and all, for what he has gifted us with, and which we have been handing out to swooning, gushing scary writers for decades.

In 1988, the first Stokers were awarded, and smart alecs ever since ever since have been asking – "If it's named after Bram Stoker, who wrote *Dracula*, why is the statue a haunted house?" Harlan Ellison famously quipped that he thought it should be called the Usher, not the Stoker, because it does resemble Edgar Allan Poe's infamous House. There is no straight answer to this question, but why not memorialize our annual selections for "Superior Achievement" in novels, stories, anthologies, poetry collections and virtually all literary expressions of terror in a nod to both writers? Like any haunted house — it's only symbolic, and it contains many secret rooms. Bram might be the dark landlord of this Usher house, but there's plenty of vacancy to hold those we deem to be the Stokers and Poes of today.

One might ask: *But are they really?* No award list is perfect, but ours is quite solid. Over the years I've heard many bitter voices scoff at the winner's list, yet many of those skeptics are now long gone, nursing their ulcers, while so many of our past winners continue to write and succeed in longstanding careers. Trends in publishing come and go, the membership ebbs and flows and sometimes the final ballot looks like a popularity contest…but don't be fooled by all the hullabaloo. It's not. Those who vote for the winner must earn the right, by achieving "Active" status in the organization, which is only met by publishing professionally and getting paid for it. Maybe this is why, compared to other speculative fiction writing awards, ours remains consistently solid, without all the politics and failures of other genre contests. Because it isn't really a contest. The Stoker has remained a rock steady meter for the understanding our amazing genre, because even if horror isn't booming, the award persistently reflects our community's understanding of itself as a collection of *writers who read each other*, and it stands at the center of the HWA and StokerCon as a testament to our stability.

It's easy to become jaded and think the Stoker is the only reason some writers participate in the HWA, or that the trophy is a pointless prize given to the same old veterans and that it gets too much attention. That isn't true; we are a thriving living community — the worms who writhe inside the haunted house of our genre — and it brings us together in a kind of pro writer's book club. I'm not just talking about gatherings at StokerCon or any of the previous Bram Stoker Award® Weekends from days of yore. Because the membership can recommend, nominate and ultimately vote for the award, the Stoker process is founded on the presumption that we all actively read each other's work, and while some of us might feel inundated by all the offerings for free copies that crowd our email accounts and mailboxes, I find it enlivening and educational. I never hesitate to renew my HWA dues each year, because I get more than my membership fees back in free reading all year long and I love to see what everyone is up to.

I am not alone in this regard. The Stoker ballot shows the world what we think we are "up to" in our dark circles. We shape our own legacy as an organization and a genre when we grant this award, because the finalists and winner's lists become "reading lists" for others — from librarians looking for something new to add to their collection to a teacher compiling titles for a class syllabus to a new horror fan surfing the net to see what she should read next. Perhaps most of all, the awards signal to new and upcoming writers what our genre feels are models of contemporary horror fiction, and everyone getting started in this business should be reading the shortlist and learning whatever they can from it. The Stoker serves an educational function, and this is yet another reason why it matters so much.

As an author, I want to be proud of my work, and also proudly share the work of my peers, and the HWA has never let me down. I won the first of my four Stokers back in 1994, in the "First Novel" category, for my book, *Grave Markings*. Winning didn't make me more money, but it truly made my career, because it opened many creaky doors for me. As a mass market paperback original, the book had a relatively short shelf life and though its first run sold well, winning the award did not send my royalty statements off the charts, nor did the award instantly turn me into some celebrity author with a status like Stephen King. Only newbies and strangers think awards translate into fame and fortune. It *does* help, naturally, because it adds a little clout to your byline and you might get a better reception from editors – or even a few direct invitations to write for them – but there are no guarantees of publication with your new work. The award is ultimately not for the person, but for something they produced in the past year, earning the appellation of a "Superior Achievement."

What does a writer get out of that? Well, there's quite literally that "winning" sense of achievement — but what you get out of a Stoker foremost is a kind of confidence that shapes your sense of self as an author. You worry less about whether you've really got what it takes. You've been told you have artistic, literary value that transcends the merely monetary "award" you get for your creative talents and dark vision. You know that others believe in you, and that's a priceless thing. You can look at that creepy statue on your shelf when you're feeling glum and realize that while you're not the next Stephen King, the man does have the same exact trophy on his shelf, too. He's in one of the rooms, as is Robert Bloch, Clive Barker, Joyce Carol Oates, Peter Straub, JK Rowling, Ray Bradbury, Ramsey Campbell, Thomas Ligotti… and dozens upon dozens of great authors you recognize, living and dead, right alongside old Bram and Edgar.

So when you win this award, you proudly add the accomplishment to your resume, your CV, your bio... perhaps even your business card or even your tombstone. One is all you need to proclaim to the world you're a genuine "award-winning author" and actually have earned the rank. But perhaps you're the ambitious type and see it as a way to keep score: Once you get one, you aim to get another and another and another. You want bookends, perhaps. I've won four of them and you'd think that would be enough, but I want to win one in every category so that someday I can make a gigantic Monopoly set and use them for hotels. But in all seriousness, the award is not really a competition, and while it might feel like one when you're sitting at the Stoker Banquet, the truth is that — as with all writing activities — you are really only competing with yourself to do your best and perhaps "beat" your past achievements. That's another reason the Stoker matters: it encourages us to do our best, and to grow. This is why, for instance, we give a "First Novel" award—one of the rarest, because it can only be won once. It says: keep going and maybe you'll win the most-prestigious "Novel" award for your second if you're on your game. All the categories are like incentives for us to read widely, to think of the genre as more than just one "thing." I once won a Stoker in the now defunct "Alternative Forms" category for my author's newsletter, for crying out loud. And you know what? It made me try harder to make it more than just a promotional newsletter, and I've kept it going for many years now. Winning the Stoker for my other titles in fiction and poetry has helped me continue to believe in myself over my 30+ yearlong career.

It's like a college diploma—a superior achievement in learning. My parents once told me getting a college degree was worth the money because it was something "no one can ever take away from you." They were right. I had my diplomas in a dusty frame on a wall, yet I *never* looked at them with a swoon of nostalgia or pride. But I *do* look at my Stokers still, and grin. Sometimes I even make creaky noises when I open the doors and cackle with glee. And sometimes, just sometimes, I hold it up to my ear and imagine I hear all those horror author voices trapped inside there, laughing along with me, then saying, in unison: *stop being goofy, nothing really matters but the writing itself – so shut the door now, and go play on the page. Just go write.*

MICHAEL ARNZEN holds four Bram Stoker Awards® and an International Horror Guild Award for his disturbing (and often funny) fiction, poetry and literary experiments. He has been teaching as a Professor of English in the MFA program in Writing Popular Fiction at Seton Hill University since 1999. See what he's up to now at gorelets.com

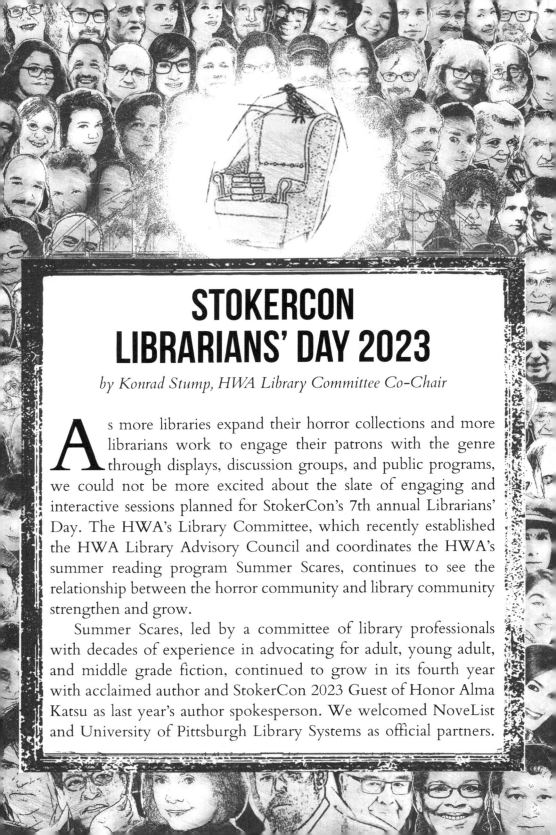

STOKERCON LIBRARIANS' DAY 2023

by Konrad Stump, HWA Library Committee Co-Chair

As more libraries expand their horror collections and more librarians work to engage their patrons with the genre through displays, discussion groups, and public programs, we could not be more excited about the slate of engaging and interactive sessions planned for StokerCon's 7th annual Librarians' Day. The HWA's Library Committee, which recently established the HWA Library Advisory Council and coordinates the HWA's summer reading program Summer Scares, continues to see the relationship between the horror community and library community strengthen and grow.

Summer Scares, led by a committee of library professionals with decades of experience in advocating for adult, young adult, and middle grade fiction, continued to grow in its fourth year with acclaimed author and StokerCon 2023 Guest of Honor Alma Katsu as last year's author spokesperson. We welcomed NoveList and University of Pittsburgh Library Systems as official partners.

The Summer Scares Programming Guide, provided by the Springfield-Greene County [MO] Library, incorporated sample program ideas in each age group to help libraries engage their communities with materials from the Horror Studies Archive, as well as sample program ideas to connect libraries with area HWA chapters and local authors. The guide also featured an article by Yaika Sabat, Manager of Reader Services at NoveList, about her love of the horror genre and how librarians and library patrons can use NoveList to find Summer Scares related content and to find print, ebook, and audio titles inspired by their interests and reading preferences. And, at the back of the guide, we debuted a handy guide to new and forthcoming releases by Summer Scares authors and spokespeople.

For anyone who has yet to experience Librarians' Day, here is a rundown of the various programs we were able to offer during and after StokerCon 2022, including in-person and virtual content and incorporating Summer Scares content. We were able to offer three on-demand discussions about the 2022 Summer Scares selections moderated by members of the Summer Scares selection committee, with the Adult panel moderated by Konrad Stump, the YA panel moderated by Becky Spratford, and the Middle Grade panel moderated by Julia Smith. These pre-taped panels debuted at StokerCon 2022, but afterwards were made available on the HWA's YouTube page. Through the YouTube page, you have access to four years worth of Summer Scares content to not only enjoy yourself, but that you can share with friends and that libraries can share with their communities. During Librarians' Day in Denver, we were able to offer the following sessions:

GENRE BLENDING IN HORROR: moderated by librarian and HWA Volunteer Coordinator Lila Denning and featuring Gabino Iglesias, Alma Katsu, Clay McLeod Chapman, and Cynthia Pelayo.

PROMOTING COLLECTIONS THROUGH HORROR PROGRAMMING: moderated by HWA Library Committee Co-Chair Konrad Stump and featuring Ben Rubin from the University of Pittsburgh's Horror Studies Archive; Hillary Dodge, Librarian and HWA Colorado Spring Chapter Co-Chair; Yaika Sabat from NoveList; Michael Allen Rose from the Oak Park Public Library; and Erin Sladen and Nadia Rendon from the Denver Public Library.

MEET THE CURRENT HWA DIVERSITY GRANT SCHOLARSHIP RECIPIENTS: moderated by Diversity Grant selection committee members Larissa Glasser and V. Castro and featuring the 2022 recipients.

HWA CHAPTERS AND YOU: HWA National Chapter Co-Coordinator Shawnna Deresch and local chapter coordinators Carina Bissett and Hillary Dodge explain how library workers can join the HWA and their local chapter.

HORROR PRESS ROUNDTABLE: moderated by Tor Nightfire Blog Coordinator Emily Hughes and featuring representatives from Burial Day Books, Raw Dog Screaming Press, Off Limits Press, and Black Spot Books, among others.

MIDDLE GRADE HORROR: moderated by HWA Library Committee Co-Chair Becky Spratford and featuring Daniel Kraus, Fleur Bradley, and Josh Roberts from Spooky Middle Grade, as well as Cat Scully and more.

DIFFERENT PATHS TO HORROR SUCCESS: Moderated by HWA Trustee and Lifetime Achievement Award Winner Linda Addison and featuring StokerCon 2022 Guests of Honor Brian Keene and John Edward Lawson, as well as Stephen Graham Jones and Lisa Kröger.

We cannot wait for you to join us in person at Librarians' Day during StokerCon 2023 in Pittsburgh, where we will be offering a fun-filled and informative day of programming designed for library workers, graciously sponsored by LibraryReads and NoveList, with lunch included for one price. Anyone who purchased a full StokerCon ticket is welcome to attend Librarians' Day with just an add on payment for lunch.

We'll have an exciting slate of in-person programs. The Librarians' Day team has worked with authors and publishers to arrange some stellar free books and swag for attendees, which our Library Advisory Council will "buzz" about to kick off the day. Librarians from across the country will share how they've featured horror at their libraries, we'll host a roundtable discussion to brainstorm ways to engage patrons with the genre and the horror community, and you'll have the chance to hear Summer Scares authors, spokespeople, and partners discuss their experiences with the program. Also appearing in person will be Guests of Honor Cynthia Pelayo, Alma Katsu, Daniel Kraus, Owl Goingback, Jewelle Gomez and Wrath James White, as well as authors Brian Keene, Eric LaRocca, V. Castro, Hailey Piper, Clay McLeod Chapman, and more.

We love Librarians' Day and the Summer Scares summer reading program because they have both connected numerous libraries and librarians with the horror genre, including helping many librarians see that engaging with the genre is not nearly as scary as they might think it is, and because more horror titles have been incorporated into libraries through collection development, displays, book discussion groups, and public programming. And, more authors and local HWA chapters have been connected to their local libraries, building a robust network of resources to connect communities with meaningful experiences.

So, while you're attending StokerCon, consider adding Librarians' Day to your schedule, and please explore our virtual content. Librarians' Day is a fantastic networking opportunity for authors to connect with library workers from across the country to start building relationships. Join us for a full day of thrilling discussion and frightful fun as we celebrate our love of horror.

Konrad Stump is a Local History Associate for the Springfield-Greene County (MO) Library, where he co-coordinates the library's popular "Oh, the Horror!" series, which attracts hundreds of patrons during October, and created the Donuts & Death horror book group, featured in Book Club Reboot: 71 Creative Twists (ALA). He is the Horror Writers Association Library Committee Co-Chair, and co-coordinates StokerCon's Librarians' Day and the HWA's Summer Scares program.

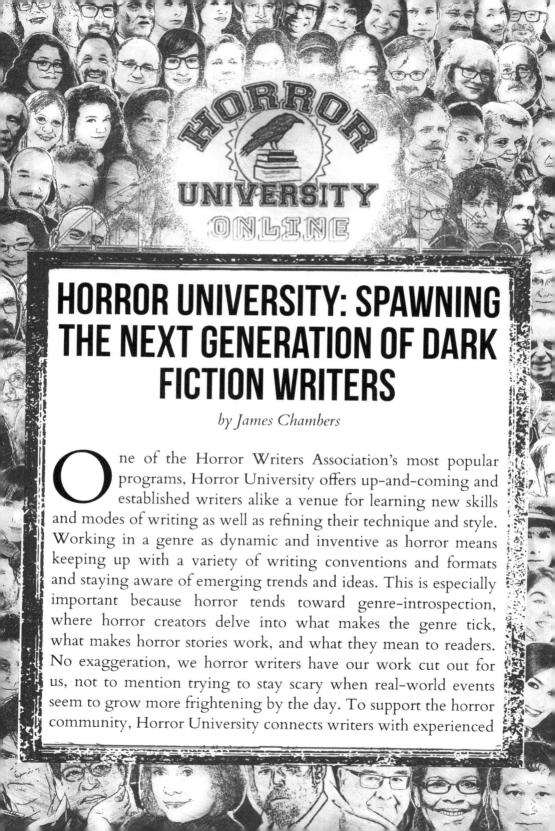

HORROR UNIVERSITY: SPAWNING THE NEXT GENERATION OF DARK FICTION WRITERS

by James Chambers

One of the Horror Writers Association's most popular programs, Horror University offers up-and-coming and established writers alike a venue for learning new skills and modes of writing as well as refining their technique and style. Working in a genre as dynamic and inventive as horror means keeping up with a variety of writing conventions and formats and staying aware of emerging trends and ideas. This is especially important because horror tends toward genre-introspection, where horror creators delve into what makes the genre tick, what makes horror stories work, and what they mean to readers. No exaggeration, we horror writers have our work cut out for us, not to mention trying to stay scary when real-world events seem to grow more frightening by the day. To support the horror community, Horror University connects writers with experienced instructors who bring insight and expertise from their careers to each workshop. Each year, the recipient of the HWA's Scholarship from Hell attends StokerCon with the opportunity to take each and every workshop offered that year—part of the HWA's ongoing efforts to spawn the next generation of dark fiction writers.

As a co-coordinator for Horror University for the past several years, I've assembled HU programming for five StokerCons, including one virtual, and three online sessions, a digital expansion of Horror University through the HWA's school on the Teachable platform. I've had the pleasure of working with many talented instructors, even attending some of their workshops, and hearing feedback from HU students, whose enthusiasm for all things horror inspires my work on the program. Co-coordinator Kevin Wetmore lends his unique insight and academic experience to the program too. Kevin has supported our in-person and online sessions, helping the HWA raise the bar for HU and expand its programming. As I write this, we are in the midst of the eight-workshop Winter 2023 session, the largest yet HU online program and compiling the workshop roster for Pittsburgh.

I always keep in mind two things when assembling Horror University line-ups. One, does a workshop bring something new to the program or the genre, such as a new writing more or format or a new approach to novels, short stories, screenplays, and so on? Two, does the roster reflect the variety of interests and voices of the horror community? Of course, many other factors go into choosing the workshops for any session, but those considerations help keep Horror University focused on expanding and enlivening the horror writing community and delving into all its shadowy corners. It's not always easy. Not every workshop choice connects as well as others. Some topics find perennial interest among writers. The basics are always a good bet. People love a workshop that tackles a new angle for making their stories more disturbing, more unsettling—and just plain scarier!

I don't know right now what the final lineup for Pittsburgh

will be, but it's taking shape, and I'm already eager to roll it out to StokerCon attendees. About half the workshops are set as of this writing, and some exciting prospects are percolating for the rest of the spaces. Horror University offers writers a chance to delve into new areas of writing, tackle difficult subjects, and improve their craft. All of these items are essential to the mission of the HWA and StokerCon to build up the community and share knowledge and ideas. They're part of what makes StokerCon an essential professional conference for horror writers.

Horror University Online has enabled the HWA to pursue those goals beyond StokerCon and around the world. Our instructors and students have signed on from many parts of the globe, often at odd hours due to time differences. As a bonus, recordings of those workshops make them available to anyone to view them anytime at their convenience. Slowly, but surely, the HWA is building a fantastic online library of institutional, genre knowledge to support horror writers for years to come. I encourage you to check it out if you haven't already (at https://horror-university.teachable.com/). And while the online world has opened many doors for Horror University, there are few better experiences than sitting in person with a master of the genre to learn.

JAMES CHAMBERS is a Bram Stoker Award®-winning author of horror, crime, fantasy, and science fiction stories. He wrote the Bram Stoker Award®-winning graphic novel, *Kolchak the Night Stalker: The Forgotten Lore of Edgar Allan Poe*. He is the author of seven short story collections, including *The Engines of Sacrifice*, a collection of four Lovecraftian-inspired novellas published by Dark Regions Press. He lives in New York.

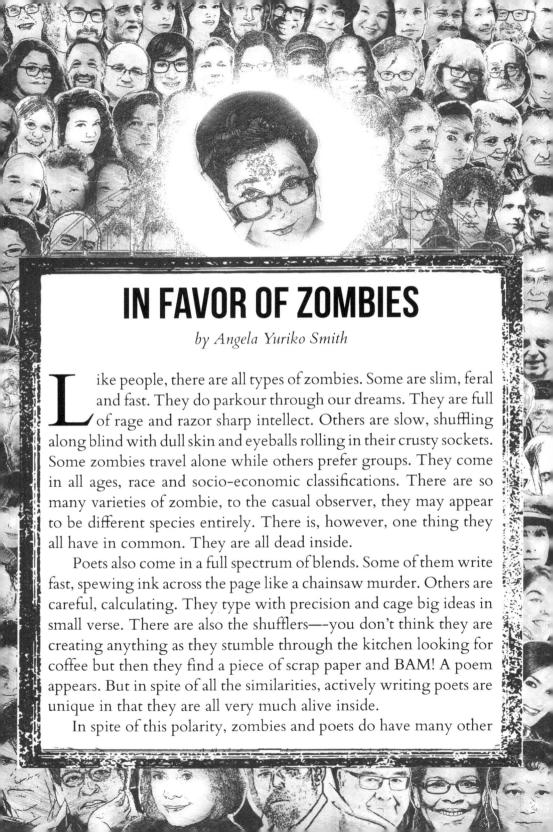

IN FAVOR OF ZOMBIES

by Angela Yuriko Smith

Like people, there are all types of zombies. Some are slim, feral and fast. They do parkour through our dreams. They are full of rage and razor sharp intellect. Others are slow, shuffling along blind with dull skin and eyeballs rolling in their crusty sockets. Some zombies travel alone while others prefer groups. They come in all ages, race and socio-economic classifications. There are so many varieties of zombie, to the casual observer, they may appear to be different species entirely. There is, however, one thing they all have in common. They are all dead inside.

Poets also come in a full spectrum of blends. Some of them write fast, spewing ink across the page like a chainsaw murder. Others are careful, calculating. They type with precision and cage big ideas in small verse. There are also the shufflers—-you don't think they are creating anything as they stumble through the kitchen looking for coffee but then they find a piece of scrap paper and BAM! A poem appears. But in spite of all the similarities, actively writing poets are unique in that they are all very much alive inside.

In spite of this polarity, zombies and poets do have many other common traits. They can both be found staring into space at inconvenient moments. Often their speech will come out slurred and incoherent. Their appearance can be startlingly disheveled. They can lose track of time and go missing for hours only to be found sitting in the driver's seat of a car staring at nothing. One of the most fascinating areas of commonality, however, would be both species' fascination with brains.

Both zombies and poets seem to have this insatiable hunger for active minds. While their preferred manner of intake varies, the two species seem to activate from a near inert state to frenzied consciousness when there is a brain in their vicinity. In a very similar fashion, zombies and poets will become animated in the presence of gray matter, and will go to great lengths to consume it.

Because of the similarities, some researchers have posed that perhaps zombies and poets are actually the same creature in different states of development. There is a theory, not widely subscribed to, that poets are actually the evolved form of zombies. Researchers that follow this line of thinking suggest that the zombie is a sort of poet larvae, an immature, juvenile form of poet that develops from the husk of zombie. They theorize that a corporeal zombie could act as an animated chrysalis housing the embryonic poet until it is strong enough to emerge on its own.

Ethically speaking, if this were true it would necessarily change the way we both view and work with zombies. To dispatch a zombie in the current fashion could be in actuality dispatching a Walt Whitman, or a Poe. This researcher believes that accurate and open minded research is essential to uncovering the zombie-poet connection if there is even the slightest possibility it could be true.

Indeed, there seems to be a correlation between lack of poets and an increased number of zombies, suggesting that perhaps the presence of poets in an area actually stimulates the process of metamorphosis, allowing the zombie population to self-regulate independent of current attempts to mitigate the zombie impact. This has the potential to be an equitable solution for a situation that, until now, had none.

I call for an immediate end to all zombie eradication while we study the ecological and literary implications this new research calls into question. If an end to zombies means an end to poets, I will personally offer my own brains on a silver platter in the quest for conclusive proof of the zombie-poet relationship. I write this in the hopes that, through our poets, we can find a way to connect with the zombies and learn to coexist. I believe, from the bottom of my actively beating heart, this is possible.

All we need are brains.

ANGELA YURIKO SMITH is a third-generation Uchinanchu-American and an award-winning poet, author, and publisher with over 20 years of experience in newspaper journalism. Publisher of Space & Time magazine (est. 1966), a three-time Bram Stoker Awards® Finalist and HWA Mentor of the Year for 2020, she offers free classes for writers at angelaysmith.com.

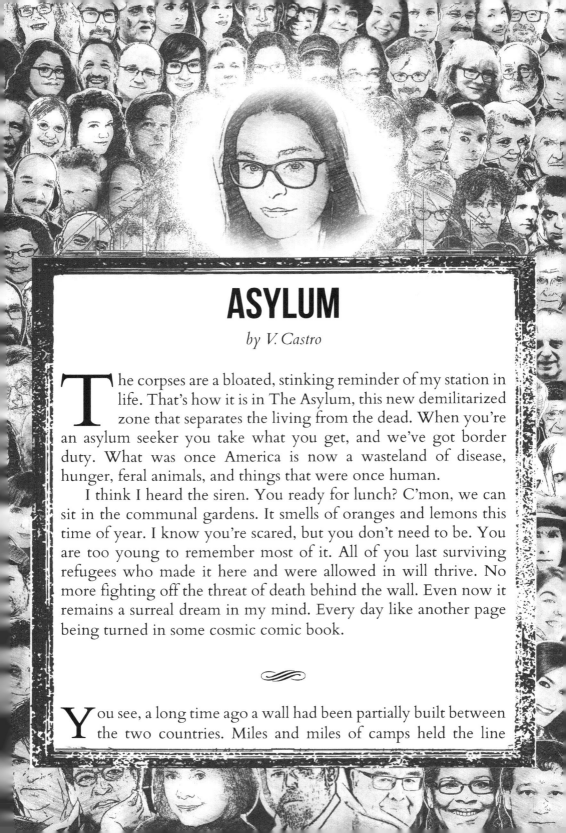

ASYLUM

by V. Castro

The corpses are a bloated, stinking reminder of my station in life. That's how it is in The Asylum, this new demilitarized zone that separates the living from the dead. When you're an asylum seeker you take what you get, and we've got border duty. What was once America is now a wasteland of disease, hunger, feral animals, and things that were once human.

I think I heard the siren. You ready for lunch? C'mon, we can sit in the communal gardens. It smells of oranges and lemons this time of year. I know you're scared, but you don't need to be. You are too young to remember most of it. All of you last surviving refugees who made it here and were allowed in will thrive. No more fighting off the threat of death behind the wall. Even now it remains a surreal dream in my mind. Every day like another page being turned in some cosmic comic book.

❧

You see, a long time ago a wall had been partially built between the two countries. Miles and miles of camps held the line between us and them. Once the amoeba mutated, the cartels threw all their resources into finishing the wall to keep the Americans out. You weren't let in unless you possessed a useful skill, had enough melanin in your skin to take the harsh sun increasing in intensity year after year, or were a citizen from any country south of the border. When the time came for Mexico and the Cartel of Central and South American Countries to decide which asylum seekers they would allow in, all the built-up resentment and frustration between the divided countries foamed like poison from a dying man's mouth.

As you have seen, when the mutants clamor for a way in, they eventually die. Oof, it's fucking gross up close. The smell is worse with that first blast from a flame thrower. Both with the power to knock you off your feet. The stink rises with the smoke, sticks to your hair like cooking fat. Mexico remained unscathed from that damn wall and the heat. We owe our gratitude to the blistering sun.

By the time most of the amoeba-infected bodies made it to the border, they shuffled half-decomposed and slow as hell. The mutants are only as strong as the sloughing muscle left clinging to their bones. An armadillo could outrun them. Those things weren't the threat; it was the tiny creature that could not be seen until it was too late. Entire reservoirs of water left polluted from decomposing flesh seeping into the ground.

To stave off the amoeba infection, the cartel ordered the bodies to be collected and burned before the animals—at least what is left of the stray animals—had a chance to feast on the decaying flesh and make their way into Mexico. There are men whose sole duty is to shoot down buzzards. The crack of high-powered rifles is almost like a call to prayer here. Animal traps lay in wait like IEDs. The rat poison so strong it stings your nostrils when the wind kicks up. That's why we all wear bandanas over our noses and mouths. I already know I'm probably in for an early death. Same for you.

Thank Dios for Felicia Garcia, narco queen turned leader of

a Mexico that has never done better for this part of the world. When the Mexican government couldn't pull enough resources together, they reached out to the cartels for help enforcing the closed border. Felicia took this opportunity to strong arm her way into government with the finesse and sense only a woman could bring to a situation teetering towards disaster. Like an amoeba, she took control when the elected officials failed in their political cowardice to make big decisions. Didn't even see her coming as they squabbled over petty shit to stroke their male egos. It was a bloodless coup that happened before anyone could stop it. With a swift declaration of power, she separated Mexico before the infection had a chance to take root like it had in America. Locked and loaded, she ordered a complete lockdown.

I made it just in time. The day I left, I took only what I could carry on my back. I knew my car would eventually have to be sold, or I'd have to sell the remaining gas in my tank. I needed to be light and swift on my feet so I could hide or run at a moment's notice. The cartels took control of the camps at the border because the Americans were losing control everywhere else. Focus shifted to closing the cities. The cartels patrolled the area; those things were on the loose, infected animals ran wild, also biting and infecting. People took whatever had value as rationing became difficult to enforce. Half the rich fucks fled to Europe, but many didn't make it out before the rest of the world closed their borders. Even private planes had to turn back or be shot down before reaching foreign airspace. When I reached Mexico, I gave up my car, what little jewelry I had on me, and showed a guard my family photo album to prove my ancestry, plus a print-out of my DNA that was popular at that time. Second generation on my pop's side and fourth on my mom's side. After all this, I was free to cross into Mexico. They processed me and gave me the job of drone lookout. Mexican American by birth raised in a country that never made me forget I was Mexican first. My skin just a shade too dark to pass for anything but an invader, an inconvenience like a cold sore even though I was born there. Felicia welcomed me like a prodigal daughter.

Maybe I should rewind a bit. I think I'm making it sound too simple. Before you even reached the border a line of military trucks and SUVs with armed soldiers waited for you to pull some shit so they could shoot. If you looked healthy enough to get past the men in tanks, you would be directed to the doctors in hazmat suits. A simple jab to your palm alerted them to foreign bodies in your system. Any traces in your blood, and you were taken to the far side of the desert to be put to sleep on the spot. No questions, no tears. Nada. To be fair, many people accepted this. Nobody wanted to wander around in a stupor covered in black spots with little things swimming beneath their skin, crushing their veins. The mutants embodied the merciless rot the world had become.

The infection begins like a cluster of blackheads on your face. This is amoeba waste. It then painfully pushes through the pores and spreads, like mold. The waste contains spores that cling to their host and travel through coughs, sneezes, bodily fluids, or touch. Eventually the creature takes over the brain and gives only one directive to the body: infect others, spread. Within a few weeks, the body decomposes as the amoeba eats you from the inside out. After a while, you are walking around with half your skin hanging off and insides oozing from your ass. You are a walking amoeba, a mutant.

Mutant bodies and infected animals burn day and night in an area called The Pits. The flames and smoke remind us of the light Felicia has returned to our great nation. Don't look at me like that. The tales are true. Seen it with my own eyes, with goggles of course. Not even the scavengers, human or animal, dare to go to The Pits. You have to piss someone off real bad to be assigned there. A great number of politicians who didn't leave the U.S. in time or make it as far as Canada tried to bribe their way into Mexico. Felicia was having none of it. But like a glamorous telenovela villain, she had a plan. Make no mistake, she is no villain; she is a savior queen. These enemies sauntered in and then were sent to The Pits to work as payback. Those who opposed her, dictators south of Mexico who refused to cooperate because they cared more for their own pockets instead of their people—they were pobrecitos in The Pits. Video from the drone over The Pits illuminated every football stadium for us to watch the worst of the worst get marched to hell. People need entertainment. And the Gods need their sacrifices.

In The Pits there is a pocket of water in an old quarry filled with decaying bodies. The flesh decomposes to create a skin of blood and algae on the surface. Seagulls with yellow and red eyes pull and pick at this. There will be a human eyeball in a beak, maybe a finger. They sit, feast, and lay eggs. Around the water there are nests made from hair, torn clothing, and plastic. Little eggs nestle inside. As long as the gulls remain in their little world they are not shot down. Those sent to The Pits are not executed. No, they must sit by the flesh water until death comes for them. The gulls are aggressive and will pick and peck at them.

Felicia didn't make many announced appearances because she wanted to see how the new nation operated without her watchful eye; however, she always made time to address the people every Friday night. Her speeches were recorded and would be sent all over the world for everyone to see what was occurring here.

She walked up on stage in heels and a bright red suit tailored to her curvy frame. On other nights she wore boots and jeans. Her makeup was impeccable with the blackest eyeliner winged from the corner of each eye, some lip gloss and maybe foundation. It could have just been the sun giving her that glow.

"My people, my friends. From what I hear and see, you are all doing a wonderful job considering the circumstances. You should be cheering for yourselves. All I am doing is ensuring that we all survive and make this a better place. I've read from other parts of the world that I am ruthless or unqualified. This makes me laugh, considering who is writing these things. It is the very people who exploited us and took advantage. They are angry they no longer hold us on a leash. So I say to you: Keep working together. Let's make this the best nation we can together. I am in service to you because you are in service of each other. Everyone will get what they deserve in the end. Just look at The Pits."

It was then the crowd went wild, her wicked smile a dark gaze straight into the camera. Then she went back to work protecting us.

My job today is to stand in a turret along the wall looking at far distances with drones. If we spot packs of the mutants or the barely living, we alert guards on the ground who ensure whoever approaches doesn't get too close. If they appear to be living, we meet them and see if they are of any value. You must have value. There are no family names, bank accounts, companies, business cards. There is nothing but what you can do for the survival of the Cartel of South and Central American States and Mexico. The new super power of the world I am proud to call home.

I remember the first time I genuinely felt sorry for some of them. The Others.

As I passed through the safe zone, a family begged the guards to be let in. Their pale white skin blistered from waiting for days to get this far into processing. The asshole guards toyed with them. The family had two small children who looked malnourished and dehydrated. One of the guards I knew, Francisco, called me over and stuck an elbow in my rib, "What you think, mujer? Should we let them in?"

I couldn't look into their pleading blue eyes. Instead, I stared at the scruffy shoes of the children. "Let them in, cabrón. They have kids. You got kids? Plus, it's almost harvest time. We will need more workers." My job wasn't easy standing in the elements all day, but I did not want to get transferred to harvest. He sucked his teeth and narrowed his eyes as he scanned the family. "What do you have to trade?"

The little girl reached beneath her sock to unlatch a watch wrapped around her scrawny ankle. As she did this the family tightened closer around her. The guard bent down to look into her eyes. This child couldn't have been more than five or six. Her father squeezed her bony shoulder. The guard tried to appear friendly, and he mostly is, but I know what sits behind his resentment. He was only a kid when he was separated from his parents. He sat in a camp for weeks watching other kids from all parts of Central and South America die from a flu outbreak. Yeah, the fucking flu. Tax breaks before outbreaks in those days. Anyway, a riot broke out and he escaped. Been with the cartel ever since. Helped me get fluent in Spanish. So, he was still kinda angry.

"Mija, this is all you have for me? Nothing else?"

She began to cry like children do when they have been scolded even though Francisco spoke in a quiet and calm tone. "Yes. I'm hungry." It was the voice of a little mouse.

"You aren't lying to me? I get very angry when people lie."

Her bottom lip quivered. I could tell she was trying to be a big girl. Save her family. It rested on her ability to convince us they are worthy. "No, sir. Nothing."

The guard inspected the watch then faced the parents. "You're lucky this is a Rolex. Follow the signs for water and processing. The cartel is gonna put you all to work. It's harvest time soon. Our great nation needs feeding. ¡Ándale! Before I change my fuckin' mind."

"Ay, be nice Francisco," I scolded him. "Felicia does not approve of children being treated like that."

He shrugged his shoulders. "You are right. But some things I will never forget, and we shouldn't forget them."

I stood there, watching them all wait in line not knowing how to feel. The family scurried past me in a hurry. The woman turned and mouthed "Thank you" to me. I'm not sure I deserved a thanks because getting into Mexico is just the beginning. You must learn to survive living here. Registration begins your journey. You will be assigned work immediately and found refugee accommodation. Felicia cares for all. I'm a single woman so I need very little. I have a comfortable room with a bed and small kitchenette in an apartment complex. The toilets and showers are communal. It isn't Trump Tower, but I'm alive. No rent due, no grocery bills because we are all fed enough, no cost for my education if I decide to start classes again. Felicia is very clear on her protection of women and children. For her, it's personal. The consequences of abuse are fatal. The Pits, in fact.

How did it all start? Might want to take that last bite of flauta. It's going to sound like a cliché, but it all started with the poorest of the poor. Ain't it always the way. You wanna know how to take the temperature of a nation? Check on the ones left at the bottom. They will let you know if you have motherfucking fever or not. That's why no one bothered to notice or act until it was too late. That would never have happened with Felicia. U.S. government-sponsored food was cheap, processed crap that looked barely edible, but governments around the world took the hard line that beggars couldn't be choosers. Same went for healthcare and education available to a majority of the populations. All these kids around the globe fell ill. Most of them died. Protests and outrage dominated the news coverage, and committees looked for the source of the problem. Suits with red ties blamed it on the same reasons there were all those E. coli outbreaks with lettuce and spinach in years past. The world called it a bunch of poor people getting sick and spreading their sickness to others.

All it took was one elite boarding school and a shipment of organic milk and vegan sausages to change the tune of those in charge. Seventy-five kids, all sick, and taken to the best hospitals.

Whatever was in that milk mutated since it killed those on government cheese.

We now know the free-range, super-cared-for, special cows giving the one percent milk were drinking infected water from a pond located on their idyllic home. The same company also ran a beef processing plant with less-than-hygienic practices that hired illegals at an alarming rate. Turns out whatever used to process the beef and their vegan sausages was not fit for human handling. They were bringing in illegal immigrants because the desperate are considered expendable, and the company covered it up. Just like a damn conspiracy film. What did they play last month in the stadium? Some old-time one. Erin Brockovich. Yeah, it was some Erin Brockovich shit going down. I shit you not.

Mija, sometimes when your skin is closer to the color of shadow, that is exactly how you are treated.

For days I lay in bed sweating, scared as hell to eat or drink anything. The situation worsened by the day and my anxiety threatened to take control over my every thought and movement. I didn't want to shower for fear there was something in the water and it would inadvertently splash into my mouth. That is when I decided to get out. Parents passed and no siblings made the choice easy for me. Life inside my home and mind was unbearable. I packed quickly and set off for Mexico because none of this was happening south of the border or in remote places that didn't take part in the food scheme. I'd rather die on a beach in Mexico in a tequila and lime stupor, getting laid every night, or in Guadalajara at the feet of María Natividad Venegas de la Torre, a saint my Catholic father said is related to us. Anything besides a crowd of amoeba-carrying people fighting over a pack of toilet paper. Don't they know that by the time you shit your liver you lose the ability to know how to use it?

After Mexico sealed off its borders, so did everyone else. The Americans left on their own with no allies. If not for Mexico or

Canada, all would be lost on this continent. Without the cartels lead by our narco queen, chaos would rule. She has brought the underworld up to our world, which has made the difference to millions of people. The developing worlds have been given the space to truly develop. All of Felicia's guns, goons, and money created a well-oiled machine made for a part of the world on the brink of collapse.

Mexico and South America on the whole have never been more at peace or successful. Bounty abounds. Fun fact: Central America is home to one of the largest pharmaceutical companies in the world. Production rivals India. They have plants all over. No, not recreational drugs, but shit for the shits, headaches, and antibiotics, to name a few. All in our brown hands, including the priceless drug to kill those silent amoeba motherfuckers in fresh water. Believe that. A teacher from Guatemala sick of seeing her children suffer from waterborne diseases created a test and a cure. Felicia wasted no time bringing this woman to the border and giving her a blank check to recreate her discovery. All the foreign-owned maquiladoras seized and repurposed to bring hope to the world.

Felicia Garcia brokered deals with the rest of the world to maintain the balance between life and death. Sure, it is a ruthless rule of law that will pluck your heart out with bare fingers, but the rules are very clear. You work, you pay your dues, you don't fuck with anyone's shit, you're all good. Stealing, rape, murder (unless sanctioned by a Jefa) is strictly forbidden. When the shortages hit, the cartels set up a food-for-weapons trade. A dead man doesn't need a weapon and a weapon can't grow maize. Hunger won in the end. Felicia has created a space where only she has the firepower. But there is a freedom in this. I feel safe. It's far from perfect, but it's all we have, a dystopian tale of rotting flesh, heat and salvation in an unlikely place. The cartel goes for the better-feared-than-loved philosophy. Snitches don't get stitches, they are rewarded, so keep your eyes open and your hands to yourself. We love Felicia because she has reinvested everything back into the country. Look to the sky, that building over there. A banner with her dark brown eyes looking down upon her flock like the blessed La Virgen. But with gold earrings and red lipstick, hair long and blowing in the wind. One hand carries a torch. Its flames burn bright with small amoebas dying as they touch the flames. In the other a banner with the image of La Virgen de Guadalupe. Thick vertical scars on her exposed wrists show us that she too is a survivor who has bled. She knows sorrow; you can see it in her eyes. She is one of us. If only Diego Rivera was alive to paint a great mural in her honor. She is the Miguel Hidalgo of our time.

North. What about up north? Canada shut their border but had a harder time fighting the mutants without a wall. The cold months kept them somewhat safe as the mutants couldn't withstand the volatile storms of winter. Hell returned with spring. The warmer weather brought animals out to feast on the decomposing bodies until they fell. When the liquid rot seeped into the ground or washed away with the melting snow, who knew where the amoeba would find sanctuary. What is laughable is some of the American politicians actually thought the Canadians would allow them to run the States from within their country, not that there was anything to run. America itself was a living dead thing.

I don't know how many are left in what used to be the United States. The flow of healthy humans has slowed in recent months—lucky for you. I've heard rumors there are some that live in remote areas like the mountains surviving off the land and what healthy animals are left. We had a few enter stating the Native American reservations are bolt-holes that remain safe. Everyone is turned away except for their own. Good for them. Maybe the land will heal itself, and they can reclaim it. I'm not too smart, no fancy degree—yet—but I think it belongs to them anyway.

The amoeba spread exponentially until nothing remained. We

watched from the outside thanking the Gods and Felicia for taking us into their bosom for protection. As the States burned, Felicia built a kingdom. That is why we owe Felicia our loyalty. Respect her claws as sharp as the Eagle perched on a nopal cactus. While we work, we recite her mantra: *Love the Cartel and the Cartel will love you back. ¡Viva La Raza!*

Let's get back to work. We have a world to fix.

V. CASTRO is a two-time Bram Stoker Award® nominated Mexican American writer from San Antonio, Texas now residing in the UK. As a full-time mother she dedicates her time to her family and writing Latinx narratives in horror, erotic horror, and science fiction. Her most recent releases include *Mestiza Blood* and *The Queen of the Cicadas* from Flame Tree Press and *Goddess of Filth* from Creature Publishing.

Her forthcoming novels are *Alien: Vasquez* from Titan Books and *The Haunting of Alejandra* from Del Rey.

Connect with Violet via Instagram and Twitter @vlatinalondon or www.vcastrostories.com. She can also be found on Goodreads and Amazon. TikTok@vcastrobooks

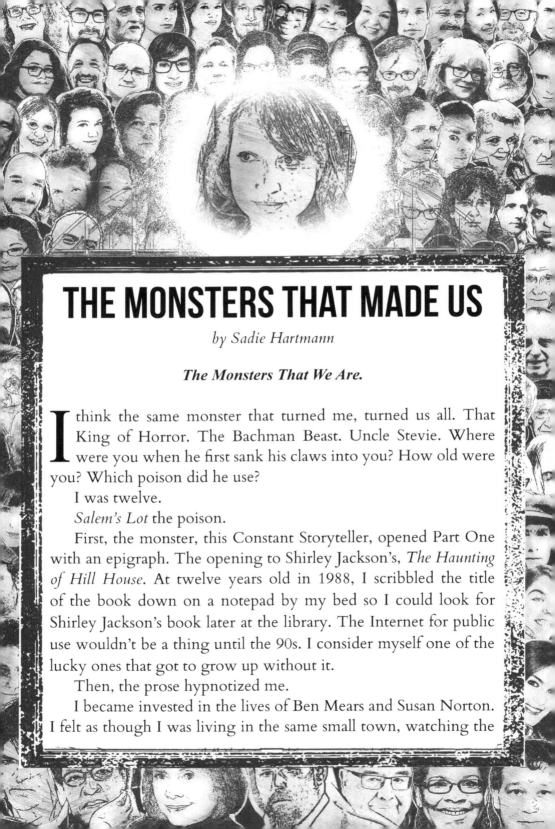

THE MONSTERS THAT MADE US

by Sadie Hartmann

The Monsters That We Are.

I think the same monster that turned me, turned us all. That King of Horror. The Bachman Beast. Uncle Stevie. Where were you when he first sank his claws into you? How old were you? Which poison did he use?

I was twelve.

Salem's Lot the poison.

First, the monster, this Constant Storyteller, opened Part One with an epigraph. The opening to Shirley Jackson's, *The Haunting of Hill House*. At twelve years old in 1988, I scribbled the title of the book down on a notepad by my bed so I could look for Shirley Jackson's book later at the library. The Internet for public use wouldn't be a thing until the 90s. I consider myself one of the lucky ones that got to grow up without it.

Then, the prose hypnotized me.

I became invested in the lives of Ben Mears and Susan Norton. I felt as though I was living in the same small town, watching the leaves turn, getting ice cream at the local parlor, and voyeuristically watching the intimate lives of the townsfolk while they do vile, naughty things.

Immediately, I'm addicted.

The poison ran through my veins. I was already a monster at twelve years old, I just wouldn't fully realize it until much later. The impact this Constant Storyteller would have on my life.

In the book, at 7:30 p.m. Marjorie Glick let her boys Danny and Ralphie leave the house so they could walk to Mark Petrie's house. I wondered why she would let them go out so late and why she waved as they walked out the door saying, *"Be home early."*

They walked through the woods and were followed. They saw eyes tracking them. Ralphie cried out, frozen with fear. The Constant Storyteller writes, *"The darkness enfolded them."*

Inside my chest, I felt my warm heart of flesh and blood that beat true for sweet, magical, fantasy books slowly start to cool as it darkened. I knew I would never crave those stories again.

The darkness enfolded me.

Later, Ralphie is missing and Danny Glick is pronounced dead. His family organizes the funeral.

Mark Petrie, just a boy and an avid reader of comics was shocked by the disappearance of Ralphie Glick and the death of Danny but not frightened. The invincibility of youth shielded him from those thoughts. The Constant Storyteller writes, *"Understand death? Sure. That was when the monsters got you."* But monsters aren't real are they? I would soon find out.

About two-hundred pages in Danny Glick is floating outside Mark Petrie's window.

"Let me in Mark. I want to play with you."

"The pallid face outside the window tried to smile, but it had lain in darkness too long to remember how. What Mark saw was a twitching grimace—a bloody mask of tragedy."

Holy. Fucking. Shit.

That was the moment the monster got me. I have never been the same since. All I want is to read horror books in order to capture a little bit of that same feeling of icy terror in my veins like I felt when Danny Glick tried to lure Mark into death. And who better to lead and guide me on my journey into darkness, the one who turned me; the one who turned us all.

"We all float down here."

And we like it. No, we love it. The monsters that we are.

SADIE HARTMANN, also known as 'Mother Horror' online, is the Bram Stoker Award®-nominated editor of Dark Hart Books and co-owner of the horror fiction subscription company Night Worms. She lives in the Pacific Northwest with her husband, their children, and a Frenchie named Owen.

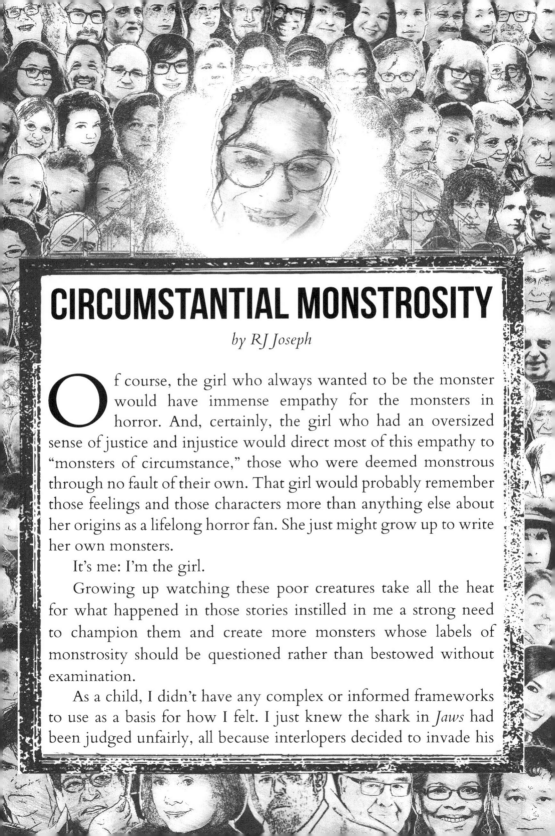

CIRCUMSTANTIAL MONSTROSITY

by RJ Joseph

Of course, the girl who always wanted to be the monster would have immense empathy for the monsters in horror. And, certainly, the girl who had an oversized sense of justice and injustice would direct most of this empathy to "monsters of circumstance," those who were deemed monstrous through no fault of their own. That girl would probably remember those feelings and those characters more than anything else about her origins as a lifelong horror fan. She just might grow up to write her own monsters.

It's me: I'm the girl.

Growing up watching these poor creatures take all the heat for what happened in those stories instilled in me a strong need to champion them and create more monsters whose labels of monstrosity should be questioned rather than bestowed without examination.

As a child, I didn't have any complex or informed frameworks to use as a basis for how I felt. I just knew the shark in *Jaws* had been judged unfairly, all because interlopers decided to invade his natural habitat. Same with Gill-Man from *The Creature from the Black Lagoon.* Carrie White should have destroyed everyone she possibly could because most of the people tasked with caring for her didn't care for her at all. And Blacula—don't get me started on the injustice of his being forced into eternal damnation just because he refused to help Dracula relegate his people to slavery. Frankenstein's monster was the most tragic of all: he had no guidance and no care from his creator, so how was he to know the things he did were socially wrong?

That same type of societal restriction plagued me as a teen. I sometimes felt like the monster I was often called and even wanted to be, but without the dominance I imagined I should have had through that label. I was condemned for going through puberty and for daring to think for myself about things my community and family had decided I shouldn't think about at all. My insatiable curiosity and endless questioning made people in power angry. Yet, I was voiceless in the face of this labeling, despite slowly becoming a feared creature in my own right.

My transformation into full-fledged monster was complete when I became a woman. I, and other Black women like me, were, apparently, the downfall of all civilization. We were loud and vulgar, too smart for our own good. The suitors in our community didn't want us and the ones outside our community didn't want to get to know us. Our experiences had no value and we were ugly, inside and out. We were useless outside of our breeding capabilities. Our needs and safety didn't have to be considered in lawmaking—we were disposable, anyway. Those of us who couldn't be prodded into submission were labeled monstrous and then our erasure began.

But I wouldn't disappear.

Like the shark, Gill-Man, Carrie, Blacula, and Frankenstein's monster before me, I used the power I gained from being a monster. With that control, I create more monsters. I fight invaders who seek to destroy me inside my own home and my community. I set everything on fire and take prisoners, sucking or strangling their life force from them and using it to power my own growth. I tell stories that cannot be erased. I give a voice to "monsters" who react to attacks by others, especially when those attacks come through firmly entrenched, harmful social structures.

I write about unfortunate creatures who simply desire acceptance for who they are and not for the ways they're othered. I create beings who, under different circumstances, might not be monsters, after all. We lean into our monstrosity and use our strength to rectify the power imbalances that plague our existences. Each and every one of us is an homage to our predecessors, the monsters of circumstance from my youth. Here's to all of them, beloved creatures. May they live happily in the monster afterlife knowing they will continuously be avenged through me and my monsters.

RJ JOSEPH is an award winning, Stoker Award® nominated, Texas based academic and creative writer. She has had works published in various venues, including *The Streaming of Hill House: Essays on the Haunting Netflix Series* and the Halloween 2020 issue of *Southwest Review.* When she isn't writing, reading, or teaching, she can usually be found wrangling her huge blended family.

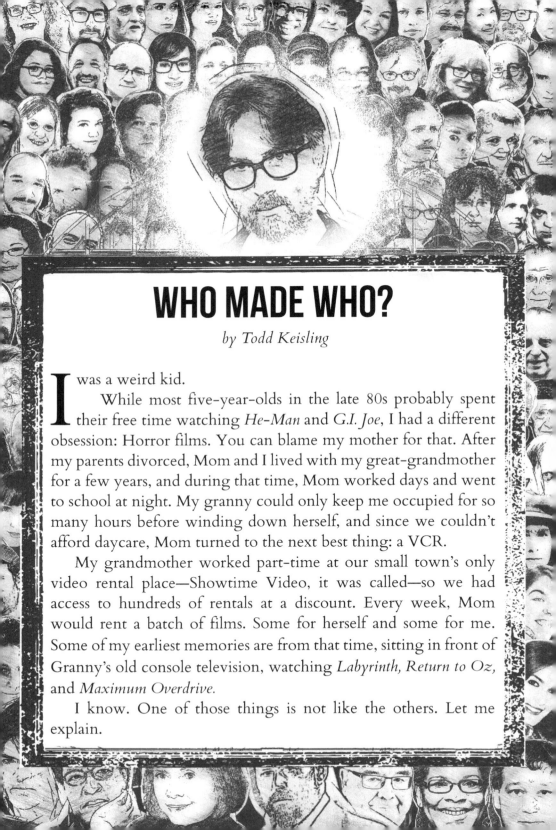

WHO MADE WHO?

by Todd Keisling

I was a weird kid.

While most five-year-olds in the late 80s probably spent their free time watching *He-Man* and *G.I. Joe*, I had a different obsession: Horror films. You can blame my mother for that. After my parents divorced, Mom and I lived with my great-grandmother for a few years, and during that time, Mom worked days and went to school at night. My granny could only keep me occupied for so many hours before winding down herself, and since we couldn't afford daycare, Mom turned to the next best thing: a VCR.

My grandmother worked part-time at our small town's only video rental place—Showtime Video, it was called—so we had access to hundreds of rentals at a discount. Every week, Mom would rent a batch of films. Some for herself and some for me. Some of my earliest memories are from that time, sitting in front of Granny's old console television, watching *Labyrinth*, *Return to Oz*, and *Maximum Overdrive*.

I know. One of those things is not like the others. Let me explain.

In her defense, I'm not sure Mom really expected me to watch all of the movies she rented for me. She probably figured I'd get bored with them or fall asleep before I could finish them. As you might imagine, the exact opposite happened. When I finished my movies, I started watching hers. Films like *The Texas Chainsaw Massacre, Phantasm, A Nightmare on Elm Street,* and *Friday the 13th* were part of my VHS diet. Out of all of them, though, two favorites emerged: *Maximum Overdrive* and *Evil Dead 2: Dead By Dawn.*

I'm not sure what it was about them that captured my imagination so much. *Maximum Overdrive* is a terrible film (what I'd call a good "Bad" movie), but it has that Green Goblin truck, and it has some hilarious moments (the Ice Cream truck, the lawnmower, the vending machine at the baseball park). I say hilarious because, to a five-year-old, those scenes aren't particularly scary. They're inanimate objects coming to life—just like in the cartoons I also watched—but with a lot more bad language and AC/DC providing the soundtrack.

Evil Dead 2: Dead By Dawn is a far better film—one of my all-time favorites, in fact—driven by bizarre effects, over-the-top acting by the amazing Bruce Campbell, and a batshit crazy storyline about the Necronomicon, demon resurrection, MacGyver-like resourcefulness, and time travel. The film also has its own share of (intentional) hilarity and slapstick, from Bruce Campbell getting blasted in the face by a geyser of blood to fighting off his possessed hand. While most kids in elementary school had their heroes like Batman and Superman, I admired the guy who was willing to cut off his own hand and replace it with a chainsaw in order to fight evil. I wanted to be Ash Williams for Halloween; instead, I was a vampire. Years later, I had an opportunity to meet Bruce Campbell when he was on tour for his autobiography, and I told him about this grim origin story of mine. He said he was sorry for "de-enhancing" my life.

But I digress. When I say these films were my favorites, I mean

I was obsessed with them. I watched them every day. Every time Mom went back to Showtime Video, I asked her to rent them again. And again. And again. There was a point where Mom had rented them so many times that it would've been cheaper for her to just buy the movies—which weren't cheap back then. So, she had a friend copy both films onto a blank VHS cassette—along with a film of her choosing, which happened to be *Dirty Dancing*.

That personalized VHS cassette was one of my most prized possessions. I carried it with me everywhere. Whenever I went to my dad's place for the weekend, I brought that cassette with me and subjected him to its insanity. Needless to say, Mom didn't get to watch *Dirty Dancing* very much. In fact, that whole section of the cassette was nearly ruined from my constant fast-forwarding from *Maximum Overdrive* to *Evil Dead 2*.

Naturally, this constant exposure to horror from an early age had an effect on young Todd. My childhood drawings involved monsters and heroes. I made up stories about fighting evil. I tucked my hand into my sleeve and replaced it with a toy weapon which I used to fight off twisted creatures from the abyss. Sometimes I donned an old cape I'd worn at Halloween and hunted these monsters in Granny's backyard. I was cautious of semi-trucks, ice cream trucks, lawnmowers, and chainsaws. And somehow, I had memorized the lyrics to "Hells Bells" before completing elementary school. I knew the word "fuck" was a powerful one, having blurted out "fuck face" in front of Granny one afternoon that earned me both a sore behind and an awkward conversation with my mother later that day.

I'm sure all the parents out there are probably cringing and wagging their fingers, but don't misunderstand my point. I'm not writing this to throw my mom under the bus (or a semi-truck, for that matter). Quite the contrary, in fact. Mom recognized my affinity for these gruesome subjects very early on, and she saw what they did for my creativity. Most parents these days would probably try to curb such influences, but I'm grateful that my mother didn't.

My obsession with horror defined me in a lot of ways, and I have her to thank for that.

Life is kind of funny in the way it sets up so many parallels and intersections. Things you didn't know were related later reveal themselves to be intricately entwined. *Maximum Overdrive* and *Evil Dead 2* are perfect examples, as more astute horror fans have no doubt already noticed.

Several years ago, I learned that *Maximum Overdrive* was Stephen King's directorial debut, based on his short story, "Trucks." Although Mr. King needs no introduction, it's worth mentioning that several years prior to its release, he provided a quote for an upcoming horror film by a bunch of no-name filmmakers from Michigan. That film was the first *Evil Dead,* and the filmmakers were Sam, Ted, and Ivan Raimi. Years later, while directing *Maximum Overdrive,* King would lend some of his crew to those same filmmakers to help out with the filming of *Evil Dead 2.*

Of course, Mom was also an avid reader. She always had novels by King and Koontz and Hautala on her nightstand.

If we're keeping score, that's a lot of Stephen King in my young life. A lot of horror, too. Some might call that kismet. King fans might also call it *ka.*

My point is, when I look back on my early years and try to examine what put me on this path to being a horror writer, I always go back to those days at Granny's house. Those days when I camped out in front of her old console television, watching Emilio Estevez fire a rocket into an oncoming truck while shouting, "Adios, motherfucker!" Those lazy afternoons when I recited the demon resurrection passages along with Professor Raymond Knowby, "Nos-feratos, amantos, kanda."

These days, whenever I hear Brian Johnson sing "Who Made Who?" I have to smile because I know the answer to that question. I mean, isn't it obvious?

TODD KEISLING is a writer and designer of the horrific and strange. His books include *Scanlines*, *The Final Reconciliation*, *The Monochrome Trilogy*, and *Devil's Creek,* a 2020 Bram Stoker Award® finalist for Superior Achievement in a Novel. A pair of his earlier works were recipients of the University of Kentucky's Oswald Research & Creativity Prize for Creative Writing (2002 and 2005), and his second novel, *The Liminal Man*, was an Indie Book Award finalist in Horror & Suspense (2013). He lives in Pennsylvania with his family.

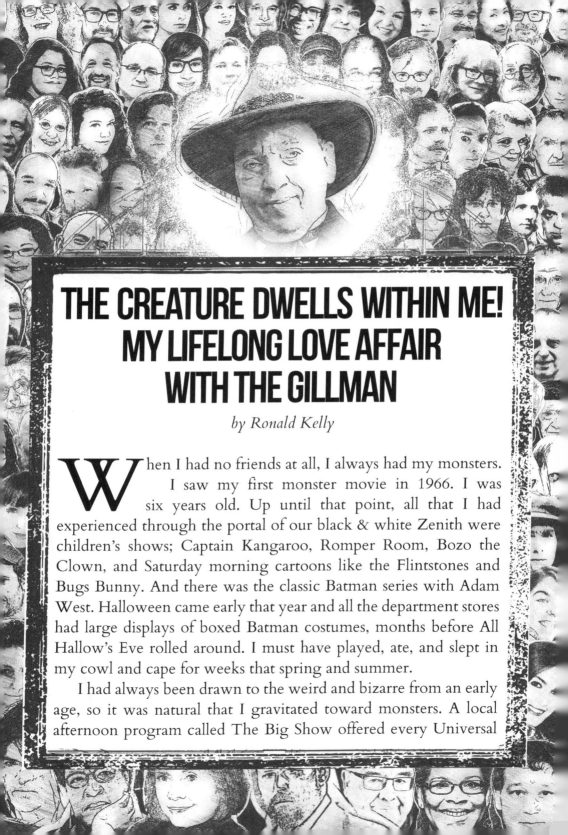

THE CREATURE DWELLS WITHIN ME! MY LIFELONG LOVE AFFAIR WITH THE GILLMAN

by Ronald Kelly

When I had no friends at all, I always had my monsters. I saw my first monster movie in 1966. I was six years old. Up until that point, all that I had experienced through the portal of our black & white Zenith were children's shows; Captain Kangaroo, Romper Room, Bozo the Clown, and Saturday morning cartoons like the Flintstones and Bugs Bunny. And there was the classic Batman series with Adam West. Halloween came early that year and all the department stores had large displays of boxed Batman costumes, months before All Hallow's Eve rolled around. I must have played, ate, and slept in my cowl and cape for weeks that spring and summer.

I had always been drawn to the weird and bizarre from an early age, so it was natural that I gravitated toward monsters. A local afternoon program called The Big Show offered every Universal

Monster movie and 50's sci-fi thriller you could imagine. My mother waited until my sixth birthday approached, then agreed to let me watch one after school. The first one turned out to be *The Creature from the Black Lagoon.*

There's something you must know about me when I was that age. Two years earlier, a coffee percolator (if you've never seen one before, Google it) had toppled off my aunt's stove and doused my left arm with scalding water.

Even with skin grafts, it was horribly scarred on the bicep and forearm, nearly wrapping all the way around. After that, I was a damaged child in the eyes of my peers; someone to be feared and avoided. No kid my age would come near me, afraid that they would 'catch' my scars. Some in Sunday School even believed I had leprosy and, according to biblical terms, I was *unclean.* This had a profound effect on my personality during my formative years. I became quiet and extremely withdrawn, distrustful of those around me, ashamed of my arm and the reactions it drew from children and adults alike. It was something I carried around with me, like a badge of shame, even into my teenage years.

So, when I sat down in front of the TV at age six and saw the Gillman for the very first time, I had two immediate reactions. The first was a sense of delicious fright and a spark of internal excitement I had never experienced until that point. The second was his glistening, fish-scaled flesh. *His skin looks like mine*, I thought in wonder, looking at my own scars with fresh eyes. I told my mother that and said, "Look, Mama, he's a monster, just like *me*!" Afterward, I went back to watching the Gillman wreak havoc on the passengers and crew of the *Rita*. My mother went into the kitchen, sat down at the table, and cried.

After that, monsters became my closest friends; my companions at play, the willing models for my notebook art, my confidants and protectors in the dark hours of night. Dracula, the Frankenstein Monster, the Wolfman, King Kong… all were members of my childhood entourage. But, the Creature… he was the one who held the key to my monster-loving heart. The one who abducted me and hauled me to his watery lair at the bottom of the Black Lagoon, and, in turn, presented possibilities and opened doorways into the imagination that I could never have realized at that early age.

Recently, I've claimed my mother's fondness for reading EC Comics like *Tales from the Crypt* and *Haunt of Fear* during her pregnancy with me as my personal origin story. But the true one took place years later, as I breathlessly watched a webbed hand snake through the open flaps of an archeologist's tent and claw the face off an unsuspecting victim. After that, the Gillman became an important part of me; emerging every so often to flip through the pages of *Famous Monsters of Filmland* magazine, or to glue and paint a glow-in-the-dark model of my favorite movie monster. And, even later, as I struggled as an aspiring writer, he was there behind me, clammy hands on my shoulders, showing me the direction and the genre that suited me best.

You may ask… whatever happened to those ugly scars, both physically and emotionally, that affected me so strongly at an early age? The ones that altered people's first-glance impression back in the 1960s and 70s… and, in turn, my low opinion of myself? They diminished in size and importance in time, as well as the self-criticism and doubt that plagued me doggedly into young adulthood.

The Creature is a tough one. You can shoot him, harpoon him, poison him, douse him in kerosene and set him aflame. But he always comes back… he always survives. The one within me possesses the same stubborn will to live and thrive…and, in my writing, evolve and continue creating at the age of sixty-three.

He's the one who gave me the tough skin and claws. The one who taught me to dive deep and rip the nets apart when times get tough.

Born and bred in Tennessee, RONALD KELLY has been an author of Southern-fried horror fiction for 37 years, with fifteen novels, twelve short story collections, and a Grammy-nominated audio collection to his credit. Influenced by such writers as Stephen King, Robert McCammon, Joe R. Lansdale, and Manly Wade Wellman, Kelly sets his tales of rural darkness in the hills and hollows of his native state and other locales of the American South. During his long career, he has published with Zebra Books, Berkley Books, Pocket Books, Cemetery Dance Publications, and various independent presses. His published works include *Fear*, *Undertaker's Moon*, *Blood Kin*, *Hell Hollow*, *Hindsight*, *The Buzzard Zone*, *Mister Glow-Bones & Other Halloween Tales*, *Season's Creepings: Tales of Holiday Horror*, *The Halloween Store & Other Tales of All Hallows' Eve*, *Irish Gothic*, *After the Burn*, and *The Saga of Dead-Eye* series. His collection of extreme horror tales, *The Essential Sick Stuff*, won the 2021 Splatterpunk Award for Best Collection. He lives in a backwoods hollow in Brush Creek, Tennessee with his wife and young'uns.

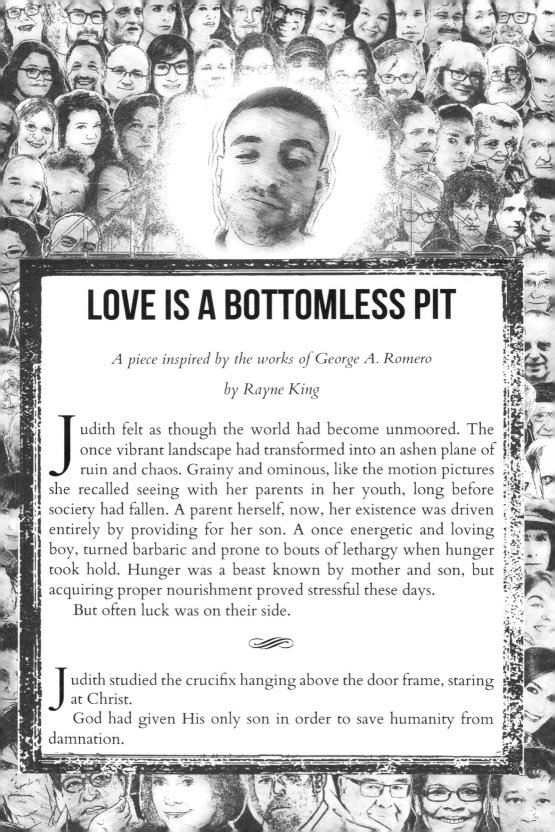

LOVE IS A BOTTOMLESS PIT

A piece inspired by the works of George A. Romero

by Rayne King

Judith felt as though the world had become unmoored. The once vibrant landscape had transformed into an ashen plane of ruin and chaos. Grainy and ominous, like the motion pictures she recalled seeing with her parents in her youth, long before society had fallen. A parent herself, now, her existence was driven entirely by providing for her son. A once energetic and loving boy, turned barbaric and prone to bouts of lethargy when hunger took hold. Hunger was a beast known by mother and son, but acquiring proper nourishment proved stressful these days.

But often luck was on their side.

∽

Judith studied the crucifix hanging above the door frame, staring at Christ.

God had given His only son in order to save humanity from damnation.

Judith had resolved to do the opposite.

She crossed herself out of habit before unlocking the door and entering the room. The kid remained where she had left him, sitting on the chair in the middle of the otherwise barren room. He sat with his hands in his lap, his fingers laced. A pretty boyish face was hidden beneath a layer of dirt and grime. His hair was greasy and matted from not being washed. Eyes that had lost the innocence of childhood too early blinked at her nervously as she entered. "I promise I haven't been bitten," he pleaded. Judith had found the kid while conducting her daily patrol, inspecting the makeshift border she had begun constructing once the news reports had turned utterly bleak. She had started by boarding up the windows, barricading the doors. After that, she had moved on to building a crude perimeter. She aimed to steadily reinforce it each day. Aside from that, the future was an empty promise.

"I believe you," she said.

Worry lifted from the kid's face and his body relaxed visibly as relief washed over him.

He released a heavy sigh, then licked his chapped lips. "Thank you," he said.

She smiled weakly.

His stomach betrayed him, growling loud enough for them both to hear it. "You're hungry," she stated flatly.

He shrugged. "Guess so."

"You guess?"

"I've kind of gotten used to it."

"Where are your parents?"

"They've been gone for a while now."

Silence emerged in the space between them at the kid's answer. Judith turned to leave the room.

"Wait, wait!" the kid called after her, panicking.

She stopped mid-stride, looking over her shoulder. "Yes?"

"Where are you going?"

"To bring you something to eat," she said, shutting the door behind her.

From deep within the depths of the house, the faint sound of moaning could be heard. Or

perhaps it was a variation of a growl in its own right.

The kid pretended he didn't hear it.

Desperation makes us capable of tricking ourselves into believing anything.

J udith returned carrying a tray. On top of the tray was a steaming bowl of pork and beans that had come from a can. Next to the bowl was a chunk of somewhat stale bread. She placed the tray at the kid's feet on the floor, whose nostrils flared at the smell of the food.

"Wait until I back away before you move, please," she instructed. He nodded eagerly in compliance.

She stepped backwards, keeping an eye on him.

"Go ahead," she said once she had reached the door.

Similar to a famished dog, the kid lunged at the tray, shoveling the pork and beans into his mouth, only stopping intermittently to bite off a piece of bread. In a flash, the entire meal was consumed. He sat back, leaning against the chair, and appeared embarrassed. He avoided her stare out of shame, wiping his mouth clean.

"It's okay," she said, reassuring him.

"Thank you," he said again.

"I'll be back."

When she reappeared in the doorway, she had a rolled sleeping bag and pillow tucked

beneath each of her arms. She went about setting up his bedding.

The kid watched on in disbelief, unable to make sense of his sudden good fortune. "You haven't been sleeping." It wasn't a question.

"N–no," he agreed quietly.

"Go ahead, lay down."

She left once more and came back holding a mug of warmed evaporated milk. She

handed the mug to him, and he accepted it with the same reverence of a churchgoer receiving the host. He nursed the drink, savoring it.

She was an angel to him.

In the night, the kid woke to find Judith standing over him. He barely remembered falling asleep at all. His head was heavy and his tongue felt swollen in his mouth. He looked up at her in delayed confusion, her silhouette a contrast against the shrouding darkness.

He didn't get a chance to speak.

Without hesitation, she swung a crowbar downward into his head. A sharp crack as his skull shattered upon impact. His body spasmed within the sleeping bag. Blood flowed from the savage wound, staining the pillow crimson.

She watched his body convulse for a moment before repeating the motion. Harder this time, to be sure.

More blood.

Shards of bone flew across the floor.

The kid stilled.

Judith dragged the sleeping bag containing the kid down into the unfinished cellar. Mildew and damp earth helped mask the rancid smell, but couldn't conceal it entirely. She hauled the bag to the edge of a relatively deep pit burrowed into the ground, and peered into the hole. Below was her rotting son, lurching around mindlessly. She called his name and he looked upwards at her, snarling and moaning. Whether he recognized his name or simply was responding to the sound of her voice, she didn't know.

She unzipped the sleeping bag and rolled the kid into the pit, where he landed with a thud and released a whimper. Barely alive, but that's all that her son required—a pulse, regardless of how weak. Her son tore into the kid, ripping him apart by hand and mouth.

Judith observed her son devouring the kid, eating him raw.

She thought of God again and how He had sacrificed His only son to save humanity. That wasn't the case for her.

On the contrary, she was ready to sacrifice all of humanity to preserve her son.

Her love was a bottomless pit, occupied by nothing except him.

RAYNE KING is an author of horror and dark fiction, with several short stories and the novella, *The Creek*, to his name. As an autodidact, he has learned to write through trial and tribulation. His influences are widespread, ranging from magical realism to cosmic horror. Because of this, his writing borrows elements from a multitude of genres, as he feels comfortable using whatever tools necessary to tell his sinister tales. He resides in the Hudson Valley with his family. Find him on Twitter via @Channel_King.

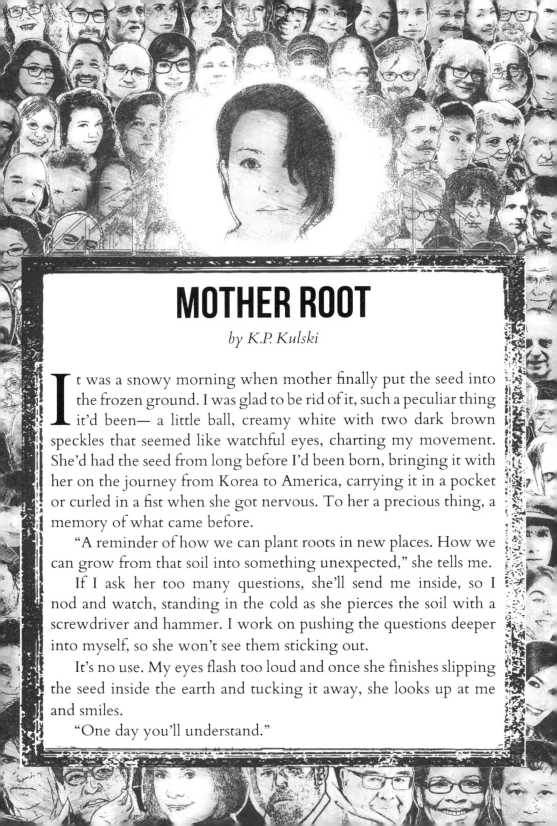

MOTHER ROOT

by K.P. Kulski

It was a snowy morning when mother finally put the seed into the frozen ground. I was glad to be rid of it, such a peculiar thing it'd been— a little ball, creamy white with two dark brown speckles that seemed like watchful eyes, charting my movement. She'd had the seed from long before I'd been born, bringing it with her on the journey from Korea to America, carrying it in a pocket or curled in a fist when she got nervous. To her a precious thing, a memory of what came before.

"A reminder of how we can plant roots in new places. How we can grow from that soil into something unexpected," she tells me.

If I ask her too many questions, she'll send me inside, so I nod and watch, standing in the cold as she pierces the soil with a screwdriver and hammer. I work on pushing the questions deeper into myself, so she won't see them sticking out.

It's no use. My eyes flash too loud and once she finishes slipping the seed inside the earth and tucking it away, she looks up at me and smiles.

"One day you'll understand."

Then she sings to me in a whisper and watches the horizon. Eastward and I realize she's caught between worlds, and I'm forever caught between her and America.

"*Arirang, Arirang, Arariyo, Arirang gogaero neomeoganda, Nareul beorigo gasineun nimeun— Arirang, Arirang, Arariyo. You are going over Arirang Pass. The one who leaves me.*"

It was a sunny morning when she died. Spring. How could the earth dare to bloom? What right did it have to show its colors and sunlight while taking her away from me? There are days, I think I'll hate the sun forever. And the little slip of soil mother had cut and pushed the seed into has filled with grass and dandelions. I hated them most of all.

"Go away little lion. I don't want your sunshine today or any day," I say rushing past on my way to school.

"I look like you," a kid calls to me, pulling at the corners of her eyes. The other children snicker as I walk past, trying to ignore them. It's not the first and it won't be the last. "Wang Chang," they say as I turn the corner into my classroom.

On my ninth birthday, my father takes me to McDonalds. "A party," he tells me but nothing more. When we step into the plastic façade, I see many people, but none are there for me. The only party is the one inside a happy meal though I'm pleased to have the little toy car wrapped in plastic.

My father watches with his blue eyes and I wonder if the world looks like an ocean to him.

That night there's a rustle outside, a pack of coyotes yipping in the distance. I tip-toe from my soft warm bed and peer out the window. Below there are blobs of gray-black shapes, stationary shadow things of remembered daytime things—the garbage can, a shrub, the ornamental tree. One of the stationary things bolts across the yard and I gasp, tumbling back in surprise.

When morning comes, I push the door open and step onto scattered dirt littering the little stone path. Big chunks of it. Where the dandelions bloomed, there's only a hole now, blown open in the soil. Beside it lays the remains of a deer leg, stripped of flesh. The rest of the animal seemingly gone, stolen away to be feasted upon somewhere else. Or perhaps, a three-legged deer continues to bleed in the woods waiting for the inevitable end. Either way, it will be a feast for the wild. As for me, I'm happy to see the dandelions gone.

I grip my bookbag and skip over the chunks of blown apart earth.

"Wang Chang," the school kids call again, and I think about their legs stripped of meat too.

That night, I sit in the window of my room and wait, listening for howls. There are none, perhaps the coyotes have moved on. When the moon pokes full out from the clouds, I push my sleepy feet into the yard and stand in my nightgown. Waiting for something. I am sure it will come if I only call for it. So, I open my mouth and sing.

"*Arirang, Arirang, Arariyo, Arirang gogaero neomeganda, Nareul beorigo gasineun nimeun, Shimnido motgaseo balbyeongnanda— Arirang, Arirang, Arariyo, You are going over Arirang Pass, The one who leaves me. Your feet will be sore before you go ten li.*"

The wounded ground writhes, kicking up more dirt until finally something comes scurrying out. Naked and thin it stretches itself until I can see it standing, like a woman. With a snap, it turns to me. The moonlight touches her face and I realize she's masked, making her take on the features of a fox, the edges of the mask are tendrils, nine smokey arms. The painted-on eyes, I remember them, and a chill goes through me. The same two marks on the seed my mother planted. On the breeze, a gentle bend of song drifts to me, an answer, a continuation of our song.

"*Cheongcheonhaneuren janbyeoldo manko, Urine gaseumen huimangdo manta— Just as there are many stars in the clear sky, There are also many dreams in our heart.*"

The woman beckons me, and I am not afraid. Lifting a graceful arm, she removes the mask and I falter only for a moment. Instead of the face I love so much are nine eyes, some stare, others blink sleepily, still a few are empty, just hungry black nothingness, but all of them are hers, nine replicas of my mother's eyes.

She passes me the mask and when I touch it, the tendrils erupt into nine red angry flames, and I know.

"*Jeogi jeo sani baekdusaniraji— There, over there, that mountain is Baekdu Mountain,*" I whisper.

Tears fall from those eyes and the mask floats from our hands to my face and settles there sinking into my flesh, my bones, my brain.

"*Dongji seotdaredo kkonman pinda— Where even in the middle of winter days, flowers bloom.*"

In the morning, when the sun shines and the dandelions bloom. I greet them and feel my feet take root. This is my home. At school when the kids call out their taunts, my eyes shine, beautiful, sad, but also full of hope—just like my mother's.

K.P. KULSKI is a Korean-American author born in Honolulu, Hawaii. A wanderer by requirement and later by habit, she's lived in many places stateside and internationally. In addition to writing, K.P. has embarked on many career adventures including the U.S. Navy and Air Force, video game design, and history professor.

She's the author of the gothic horror, *Fairest Flesh,* from Strangehouse Books and *House of Pungsu,* from Bizarro Pulp Press. Her short fiction has appeared in various publications including *Fantasy* and *Unnerving Magazines*, and anthologies, *Chromophobia,* from Strangehouse Books, *The Dead Inside,* from Dark Dispatch and *Not All Monsters,* from Strangehouse Books.

She now resides in the woods of Northeast Ohio with her husband and children. At this moment, she's probably doing laundry, eating kimchi chigae and smashing the patriarchy. Find her at garnetonwinter.com and on Twitter @garnetonwinter.

THE BLACK LAGOONS OF OUR EYES

by Hailey Piper

She finds him, like all before her have, along a tributary of the Amazon River.

The guide has warned in both English and Portuguese that none should come to this place. He's right, she knows it, but she's heard the rumors, seen the notes, needs to witness, and she prays her presence won't stain this miracle. She and the guide keep to the shore, where they won't disturb the water. The air clouds with mosquitos, swollen with larvae and disease.

In the past, this voyage has meant death. Mangled and drowned corpses, sinking boats, fiery wreckage charring nearby foliage. This does not stop others now. Upriver, yellow bulldozers await bridge construction in progress that will lead them charging through this lush tropical splendor.

But she spots him surfacing a few yards from the far shore, and the journey has been worth it.

He has wide dark eyes, adapted for the tributary's rich

underwater world. Leaf-green scales coat his hide, except where firm fins jut down his spine and limbs. His hands and feet sport webbing to help propel him through the water, and though he is humanoid in shape, he is not human.

He wears scars, too. Evidence of old battles with torches, machetes, and rifles. He's survived every shot and scalpel, every burn, even attempted metamorphosis, as if manmade hell could produce a once-gilled butterfly.

A hundred theories guess at the creature's origins, his biology. Does he share a common ancestor with humanity? Is he morphological coincidence? Reactionary evolution? Maybe the result of cross-breeding between mankind and a divine piscatory entity, or an interdimensional breach releases energies into the lagoon that grace all they touch with fins, scales, and gills.

They came first to kill him, and when death didn't take, they tried to tame him. Failing that, they made to change him. None of those scalpel-wielders ever set an end game; they cut him because they could. Burned his scales for skin, tore his gills for lungs. Clothed him like a man, and what next—stick him in a cubicle? Teach him to create advertisements and type eighty words per minute?

A pointlessness named progress.

Similar progress rumbles distantly. She watches him glide upriver, chasing echoes of the bridge construction site and its eventual bulldozers. He's familiar with manmade sounds. Boat propellers, gasoline engines. Rifles reloading, cocking, firing.

His innocence is lost. He'll be forever wary of those who mean to dig a knife into nature's beauty.

She wants to tell him she understands, at least a little. First they tried to kill her, too, inside herself. Later, an attempted taming when they misunderstood her shape. Like the creature, she was born with enough similarities to men that they thought to Right and Correct her deviations, the way a vibrant rainforest is Righted into a cornfield, or a flowery meadow is Corrected into a parking garage.

But she's cut off those unneeded similarities, the way the creature has torn off pointless clothing.

Now both are here, in his home. He glides toward the grind of construction, while she watches from the shore. She can feel his wariness even as their distance grows, trickling through the soup-thick air. He might have spotted her, and part of his mind might wonder, *Will she try the same? Does she mean to hurt me, tame me, change me?* Only to be distracted by bigger, louder fish.

She would speak the truth, but he wouldn't understand. Even shouting it across the water would only startle jungle birds, capybaras, and maybe the green creature, too. A verbal hand, grabbing for his attention and polluting his world. She isn't immune to the temptation of influence. If only she and the rest of mankind could collectively let their hands dangle at their sides, quit grasping and taking, and bask in the simple harmony of a miraculous existence.

But pointless progress charges on so that somewhere in the world, a stock market number will count a little higher than a moment earlier. There is no number high enough.

As night falls, she spies orange-yellow flames upriver from hers and the guide's camp, through tent flaps and mosquito nets. An inferno dances atop the running water. Gunshots echo downriver, chased by choked screams.

The trouble with digging a knife into nature's beauty is that it then learns of blades. It begins to wield knives of its own. Teach a creature the power of fire, and you risk suffering its burn.

So goes the night, on a tributary of the Amazon River.

By daybreak, only wreckage remains of a would-be bridge and the men who meant to build it. They will try again, drumming up purposelessness—progress—but they know better than to seek the creature out. To try changing him to their ways.

She helps the guide take down the tents, the mosquito nets, to clean up all evidence of human touch on this shore. She is meticulous. Perhaps stalling.

The guide warns that, had the creature not been distracted with machines last night, he might have come for her, and the guide would have left her. She tells him, in broken Portuguese, that leaving would have been the right call. The guide only nods.

She spots the creature surfacing one last time as they begin the return journey. His black eyes take in the sunlit rainforest, too bright for his underwater senses, and yet she can't help thinking that he's watching her. She won't shout to him; that would disturb his world. Can't make him understand what she wants to say, same as she can't speak across decades, centuries, eons, to whatever link exists between them, whatever catalyst allows them to coexist on this Earth, in this moment.

But she can tell it quietly from the shore, while staring into his eyes. She can hope her intent will trickle across the humid air, and that somehow, he'll know.

"They tried to change me, like you," she whispers. "And like with you, they failed."

HAILEY PIPER is the Bram Stoker Award®-winning author of *Queen of Teeth, No Gods for Drowning, The Worm and His Kings*, and other books of dark fiction.

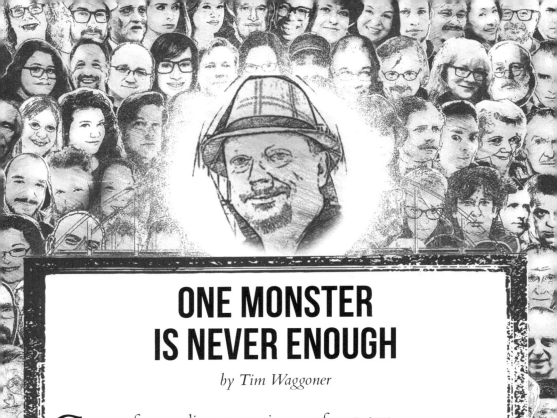

ONE MONSTER IS NEVER ENOUGH

by Tim Waggoner

S ome of my earliest memories are of monsters.

I remember being six months old and my mother taking me around the neighborhood for Halloween. She dressed me in a bunny onesie, complete with rabbit ears, and carried me to her friends' homes so they could exclaim, "Isn't he cute? Isn't he just *darling?*" I had no idea why these people were making such a fuss over me, and I really didn't care. What I was interested in was all the kids running around in costume. I think I recognized them as children wearing outfits, and I definitely remember not being afraid of them. I was, however, very confused and fascinated. I don't recall specific costumes I saw, but I'm sure many kids were dressed as Dracula, Frankenstein, the Wolf-Man, the Mummy, skeletons, devils, witches, ghosts … Perhaps that was the night I became one of the Halloween People myself.

When I was four, my parents let me watch *Frankenstein Meets the Wolf-Man* on television. I sat too close to the screen in a tiny rocking chair I had, and watched the movie – not scared, but enthralled. I was already aware of both monsters, maybe from other TV shows or from older kids in the neighborhood, but it had never occurred to me that these two monsters might actually live in the same world and be able to meet each other and fight. The world of horror became so much larger for me that night.

As I got a little older, I was allowed to read horror comics and magazines – *House of Mystery, House of Secrets, Creepy, Eerie,* and *Vampirella,* and of course the monster kid's most sacred text *Famous Monsters of Filmland.* I also read the gore-filled tales of Eerie Publications' B&W horror magazines such as *Terror Tales, Horror Tales, Tales of Voodoo, Witches' Tales,* and *Weird.*

I loved watching *The Munsters* and *Addams Family* on TV, and I watched the horror and science-fiction movies that played every weekend on *Shock Theater,* with local horror host Dr. Creep. I loved every one of those movies, even the bad ones, and perhaps my favorite of all was *Mad Monster Party?* (the question mark is part of the title), a stop-motion animated comedy featuring all the famous movies of the movies. (The filmmakers couldn't get the rights to King Kong, so the giant ape in the movie is called It, which is a terrible substitute. Why didn't they try Kinga or Kron or something at least close to King Kong?)

Then I fell in love with the legendary horror comics and magazines Marvel put out in the 1970's, such as *Tomb of Dracula, Werewolf by Night, Man-Thing, Tales of the Zombie, Vampire Tales* (featuring Morbius the Living Vampire). And like my beloved *Frankenstein Meets the Wolf-Man,* these characters sometimes met and fought each other—and they met and fought a number of Marvel's superheroes, too.

As I looked back at the monsters that made me the person and writer I am today in preparation for this essay, I realized something that had never occurred to me before. *All* the monsters made me who I am. Not individually, *but together.* Sometimes they literally shared the same world in the movies and comics I loved, but in comics like *House of Mystery,* which contained several stories in the same issue, one supernatural threat followed another. Same with reading *Famous Monsters.* One article might be about a Dracula movie, the next might feature Godzilla, etc. Each issue was a conglomeration of monsters. My absolute favorite TV show when I was a kid? *Kolchak the Night Stalker*, which featured an everyman reporter battling a different monster each week.

My short fiction tends to focus on one main idea/situation—as short stories do—so there isn't a lot of room for multiple monsters. But novels? Plenty of room there, and I fill them with as many monsters as I can. At least half of the over fifty novels I've written have multiple monsters in them. Even my Blade of the Flame fantasy series for Wizards of the Coast had multiple monsters, based on the Universal monsters I love as a kid. And my Nekropolis books are love letters to the horror media of my youth, filled with famous monsters from literature and film as well as ones of my own creation.

And I realized something else when thinking about what I was going to write for this essay. Cramming your fiction full of monsters is a *terrible* way to write horror. Having a solo monster (whether a creature, a human, or a malevolent force) is far more effective than having many different monsters. Even the zombie apocalypse scenario, created by George Romero and John Russo, has only one monster – the flesh-eating zombie. There's just a shit-ton of them. And killer clans in such films as *Texas Chainsaw Massacre*, *The Hills Have Eyes*, and *The Devil's Rejects* are comprised of basically *one* type of killer multiplied within *one* family.

One monster works best in horror because monsters are an intrusion into our reality, a violation of what we believe to be true. One serial killer? Scary. Five of them, each with very different looks, personalities, motivations, and ways of killing can be fun in a film or book, but they aren't scary. We ask readers to suspend their disbelief when they read fiction, and readers will accept one monster (or one type multiplied) in a story. Ask them to accept killer alligators, evil robots, and ghosts of dinosaurs all in the same story, and they won't be able to. It'll seem like a weird mish-mash to them. It may even seem ridiculous, absurd, laughable ... not exactly the effect most horror writers strive to create. I would never advise anyone to write the kind of novels I do. You really limit your potential pool of readers.

So does this mean I don't write horror, at least at novel length? In which case, why the hell did I write two books *about* writing horror—*Writing in the Dark* and *Writing in the Dark: The Workbook*?

When I was in grad school in the late eighties, I began to wonder why fantasy fiction didn't incorporate more horror, and why horror – at least the supernatural kind—didn't incorporate more fantasy. (Clive Barker was just starting to write and publish novels back then, and I hadn't gotten into his work yet. Same with Neil Gaiman.) I thought it would be cool to blend the two genres and see what happened, and as the years went by, I did more and more of this in my fiction. Don D'auria has been my editor at Leisure Books, Samhain Publishing, and Flame Tree Press, and we've put out a lot of books together. Not too long ago, we were talking, and Don said, "Your books are as much fantasy as they are horror." I like to write horror that's nightmarish and surreal, and you can't achieve that effect writing about a bigfoot killing people in a small town. That's still mostly a realistic story (except for the bigfoot, of course). But when you open the gates of the imagination wider, there's a dark universe of wonders waiting for you to play in. I had those gates thrown open for me one Halloween night in 1964 when my mother took me out into the night to experience a world transformed and filled with so many different strange and delightful creatures.

And I suppose I've been writing about that night, one way or another, ever since.

If you want to check out some of my most monster-filled books, I recommend *The Harmony Society*, *Pandora Drive*, the Nekropolis series, *The Forever House*, *The Mouth of the Dark*, and *They Kill*.

TIM WAGGONER's first novel came out in 2001, and since then he's published over fifty novels and seven collections of short stories. He writes original dark fantasy and horror, as well as media tie-ins. He's written tie-in fiction based on *Supernatural, Grimm, The X-Files, Alien, Doctor Who, A Nightmare on Elm Street,* and *Transformers,* among others, and he's written novelizations for films such as *Halloween Kills, Resident Evil: The Final Chapter* and *Kingsman: The Golden Circle.* His articles on writing have appeared in *Writer's Digest, The Writer, The Writer's Chronicle.* He's the author of the acclaimed horror-writing guide *Writing in the Dark,* which won the Bram Stoker Award® in 2021. He won another Bram Stoker Award® in 2021 in the category of short nonfiction for his article "Speaking of Horror," and in 2017 he received the Bram Stoker Award® in Long Fiction for his novella *The Winter Box.* In addition, he's been a multiple finalist for the Shirley Jackson Award and the Scribe Award, and a one-time finalist for the Splatterpunk Award. His fiction has received numerous Honorable Mentions in volumes of *Best Horror of the Year*, and he's had several stories selected for inclusion in volumes of *Year's Best Hardcore Horror.* His work has been translated into Russian, Portuguese, Japanese, Spanish, French, Italian, German, Hungarian, and Turkish. In addition to writing, he's also a full-time tenured professor who teaches creative writing and composition at Sinclair College in Dayton, Ohio.

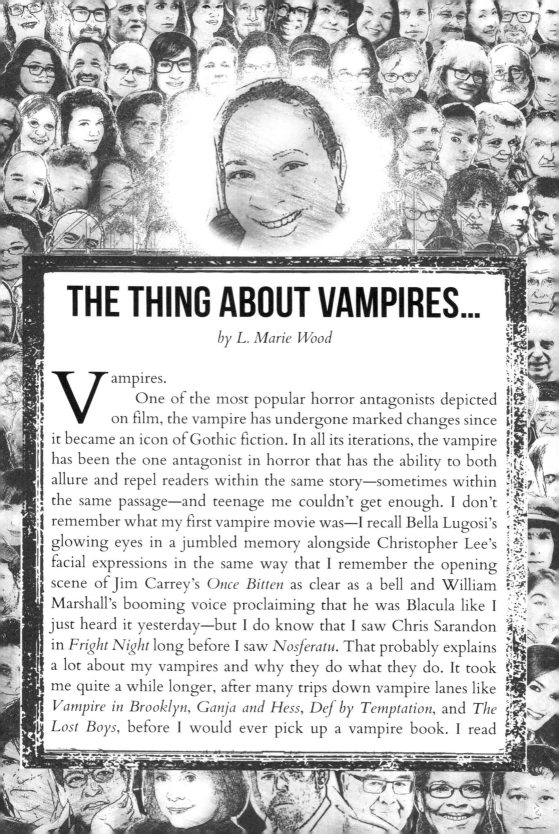

THE THING ABOUT VAMPIRES...

by L. Marie Wood

Vampires.

One of the most popular horror antagonists depicted on film, the vampire has undergone marked changes since it became an icon of Gothic fiction. In all its iterations, the vampire has been the one antagonist in horror that has the ability to both allure and repel readers within the same story—sometimes within the same passage—and teenage me couldn't get enough. I don't remember what my first vampire movie was—I recall Bella Lugosi's glowing eyes in a jumbled memory alongside Christopher Lee's facial expressions in the same way that I remember the opening scene of Jim Carrey's *Once Bitten* as clear as a bell and William Marshall's booming voice proclaiming that he was Blacula like I just heard it yesterday—but I do know that I saw Chris Sarandon in *Fright Night* long before I saw *Nosferatu*. That probably explains a lot about my vampires and why they do what they do. It took me quite a while longer, after many trips down vampire lanes like *Vampire in Brooklyn*, *Ganja and Hess*, *Def by Temptation*, and *The Lost Boys*, before I would ever pick up a vampire book. I read

Interview with a Vampire before reading *Dracula*. Again, this is very telling. I discovered vampires during that tumultuous time in life when our hormones are raging and every emotion is expressed at its most extreme. Vampires were taboo, untouchable, not gone, but definitely dead, beautiful but with flesh as hard as stone... how delicious for a young person with an overactive imagination. Can you guess what my favorite vampire movie is? *Bram Stoker's Dracula*.

Of course it is.

Even before I learned that there was more than one kind of vampire, I was under their spell. Before I read Mary Eleanor Wilkins Freeman's story, "Luella Miller" and understood the power that an emotional vampire wields; before I understood the concept of a psychic vampire at all, to say nothing of lifestyle vampires, auto-vampirism, clinical vampirism, and the sanguinarians of the world, I had fallen hook, line, and sinker for the sentimentalists who pondered the meaning of life, death, and rebirth. I had heart eyes for the ones who used their charms to get what they desired. I wanted to watch Jerry Dandridge dance at the club with Amy. I was mesmerized by Maximillian's stare. I was enthralled by the character development of what should be considered a demon, a devil, something to be feared, but instead, presented as charming, alluring... something to be coveted. I wanted to play in that world, to create vampires who disarmed their prey by enticing them, luring them by a sex appeal that they shouldn't possess, not when we think about what they do in the dark of night, how they drink blood for sustenance because that is all their reanimated corpses can tolerate. I wanted to play with them because I chose to focus on what they *could* be: protective partners, eternal lovers.

Sigh.

When I met Lestat and Louis, Armand and later Queen Akasha between Anne Rice's pages, I was smitten. Many were. This was by design. These were not your bloodthirsty beasts skulking around in the shadows; these vampires were not of Nosferatu's ilk... at least that's what we told ourselves. They were the beautiful ones, turned in their prime, cultured, desirable, oh so enchanting. Add in a smidge of compassion, a little restraint, and some feelings of love à la Bill Compton and Edward Cullen and you've spoken to the teenager inside me who still thinks of her vampires as tortured, poetic souls rather than hardened beasts of the *30 Days of Night* variety, out for a midnight snack.

Still, vampires are dangerous.

Unfathomably dangerous.

They are *I Am Legend* type of dangerous. They all are. One false move and they will rip your throat open, being sure to drink their fill before your heart stops beating and they throw your drained carcass to the floor. For me, the moment of revelation that the vampires I'm enamored with are, indeed, one and the same as the beasts that haunt the night bloody-fanged and crazed, when the blood they hunger for comes from an unsuspecting neck much like my own – that's the stuff of nightmares... and the story of my dreams.

So, I write about vampires because the greats showed me how to.

I write vampires you wish would love you the way you love them... until they do.

L. Marie Wood is a two-time Bram Stoker Award® and Rhysling nominated author, screenwriter, essayist, and poet. She writes high concept fiction that includes elements of psychological horror, mystery, dark fantasy, and romance. She won the Golden Stake Award for her novel *The Promise Keeper*. She is a recipient of the MICO Award and has won Best Horror, Best Action, Best

Afrofuturism/Horror/Sci-Fi, and Best Short Screenplay awards in both national and international film festivals. She is also part of the 2022 Bookfest Book Award winning poetry anthology, *Under Her Skin*. Wood has penned short fiction that has been published in groundbreaking works, including the anthologies like *Sycorax's Daughters* and *Slay: Stories of the Vampire Noire*. Her academic writing has been published by Nightmare Magazine and the cross-curricular text, *Conjuring Worlds: An Afrofuturist Textbook.* She is the founder of the Speculative Fiction Academy, an English and Creative Writing professor, a horror scholar, and a frequent speaker in the genre convention space. Learn more about L. Marie Wood at www.lmariewood.com.

HWA COMMITTEES

We want to send a note of appreciation to the members of all of the HWA Committees and for the wonderful work that you do. Following are a few messages from some of our committees.

BRAM STOKER AWARDS® COMMITTEE
BRAM STOKER AWARDS® JURY CHAIRS
CHAPTER PROGRAM MANAGERS
DIVERSE WORKS INCLUSION COMMITTEE
ELECTIONS COMMITTEE
GRIEVANCE COMMITTEE
HORROR UNIVERSITY TEAM
iMAILER COORDINATOR
LIBRARY COMMITTEE
LIFETIME ACHIEVEMENT AWARD COMMITTEE
LOCAL CHAPTER CHAIRS
MEMBERSHIP COMMITTEE
MENTOR PROGRAM
NEWSLETTER

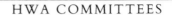

POETRY BLOG
PUBLICATIONS COMMITTEE
SCHOLARSHIP SUB-COMMITTEE
SOCIAL MEDIA TEAM
VETERANS COMMITTEE
VOLUNTEER COORDINATOR
WELLNESS COMMITTEE

VETERAN'S COMMITTEE

by David Rose

The veterans committee launched in 2022 with the intent to showcase military vets within the HWA. Through the *Veterans in Horror Spotlight* and the monthly *Unquiet Front* column, writers who served (or who are still serving) are given opportunities to promote their work and talk a bit about how their experiences within their nation's military may have influenced their writing.

One of the newest committees within the HWA, we have high hopes: workshops, scholarships, anthologies. Stay tuned.

DAVID ROSE is the author of *Amden Bog, The Scrolls of Sin,* and *Lovecraft's Iraq.* That last one was included in the 2022 HWA Bram Stoker Award® Reading List. He lives in Orlando, Florida.

CHANCE FORTUNE is an American Dark Fantasy and Horror author based out of Eugene, Oregon. Chance graduated from the University of Wisconsin with a degree in writing and a minor in media communication. He is the author of *In the Web of the Spider Queen* now available on Amazon and KDP. Chance served ten years with the Minnesota Army National Guard and is a veteran of the global war on terror.

HWA DIVERSE WORKS INCLUSION COMMITTEE

The Seers Table

by Linda D. Addison

The Mission Statement for the committee begins:

"To ensure the Horror Writers Association (HWA) includes the widest possible representation of those working in the horror/dark fantasy genre, the HWA has formed the Diverse Works Inclusion Committee (DWIC). This committee is tasked with actively seeking underrepresented demographic writers and editors. The committee has adopted the broadest definition of the word diversity to include, but not limited to, gender, gender identity, race, ethnicity, sexual orientation, disabled and neurodiverse."

You can read the full mission statement on the HWA site under the Diverse Works menu, along with the latest month's column.

The point of the DWIC committee is not to influence the Bram Stoker Award® juries, scholarship opportunities, etc. Its only purpose is to expand membership's awareness of individuals whose work they might not know. The committee was created by Lisa Morton in 2016, then HWA President, from concern about the lack of diversity recognized by the membership and separate conversations with Rena Mason and Tom Calen.

Each month, since March 2016, the committee presents write-ups of writers and editors for the monthly HWA newsletter in a column called *The Seers Table*. For each person highlighted we include a short bio, excerpt of their work and ways to find them online (website, etc.). *The Seers Table* column is on the HWA site and available for public viewing, not just for members of the organization.

As of April 2023 we have introduced over 370 creators since the committee began *The Seers Table* column. The current members of the committee are Linda D. Addison, Tish Booker, Rob Costello, Theresa Derwin, Ace Antonio Hall, Janet Holden, Kate Jonez, Kate Maruyama, Lauren Salerno, Mireya S. Vela, and Tawana K Watson. Previous members are Tom Calen, Ari Drew, Michael Paul Gonzales, and Andrew Wolter.

Linda D. Addison grew up in Philadelphia and began weaving stories at an early age. Ms Addison is the first African-American recipient of the world renowned HWA Bram Stoker Award® and has received five awards for collections: *The Place of Broken Things* written with Alessandro Manzetti; *Four Elements* written with Charlee Jacob, Marge Simon and Rain Graves; *How To Recognize A Demon Has Become Your Friend* short stories and poetry; *Being Full of Light, Insubstantial; Consumed, Reduced to Beautiful Grey Ashes*. In 2018, she received the HWA Lifetime Achievement Award. In 2020,

Addison was designated SFPA Grand Master of Fantastic Poetry. She co-edited *Sycorax's Daughters* anthology of horror fiction & poetry by African-American women with Kinitra Brooks PhD and Susana Morris PhD, which was a HWA Bram Stoker finalist in the Anthology category. She currently lives in Arizona and has published over 400 poems, stories and articles. Look for her story in the *Black Panther: Tales of Wakanda* anthology (Titan/Marvel).

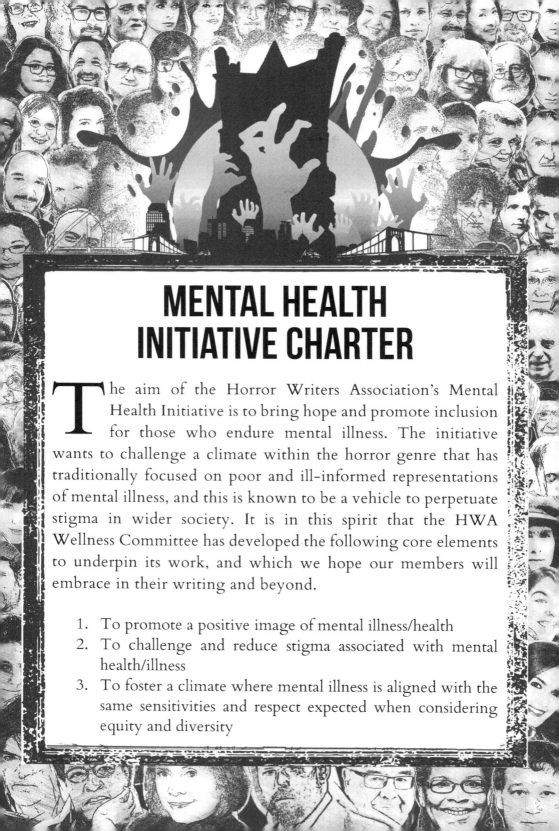

MENTAL HEALTH INITIATIVE CHARTER

The aim of the Horror Writers Association's Mental Health Initiative is to bring hope and promote inclusion for those who endure mental illness. The initiative wants to challenge a climate within the horror genre that has traditionally focused on poor and ill-informed representations of mental illness, and this is known to be a vehicle to perpetuate stigma in wider society. It is in this spirit that the HWA Wellness Committee has developed the following core elements to underpin its work, and which we hope our members will embrace in their writing and beyond.

1. To promote a positive image of mental illness/health
2. To challenge and reduce stigma associated with mental health/illness
3. To foster a climate where mental illness is aligned with the same sensitivities and respect expected when considering equity and diversity

4. To advocate that the HWA membership conducts sound research in the development of mental health related themes in horror genre literature
5. To be sensitive to the fact that HWA members themselves have experienced social exclusion and societal stigma
6. To strive for a climate of hope and recovery through creativity
7. To disseminate mental health materials and statements that are supported with a robust evidence base and/or an emphasis on the lived experience of mental health and illness
8. To develop over time a 'Notable Works' list of publications as good practice examples when writing about mental illness in the horror genre.

Lee Murray & Dave Jeffery
Co-Chairs HWA Wellness Committee

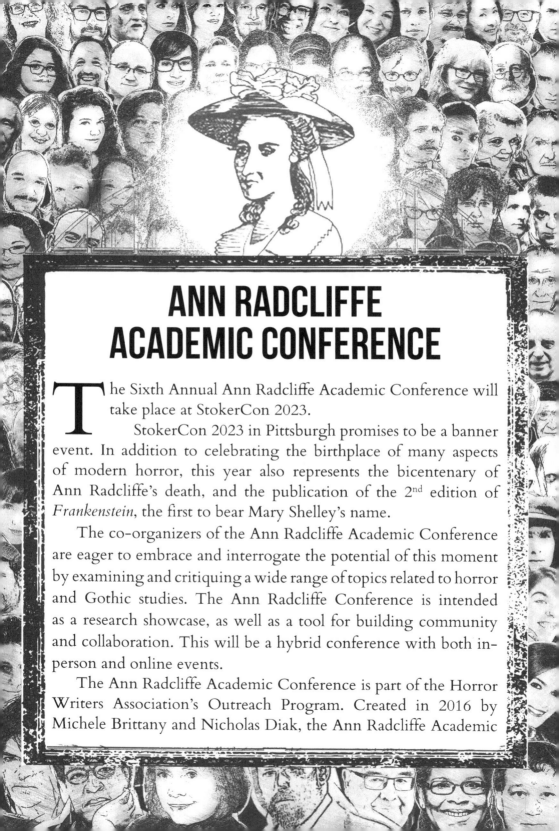

ANN RADCLIFFE ACADEMIC CONFERENCE

The Sixth Annual Ann Radcliffe Academic Conference will take place at StokerCon 2023.

StokerCon 2023 in Pittsburgh promises to be a banner event. In addition to celebrating the birthplace of many aspects of modern horror, this year also represents the bicentenary of Ann Radcliffe's death, and the publication of the 2nd edition of *Frankenstein*, the first to bear Mary Shelley's name.

The co-organizers of the Ann Radcliffe Academic Conference are eager to embrace and interrogate the potential of this moment by examining and critiquing a wide range of topics related to horror and Gothic studies. The Ann Radcliffe Conference is intended as a research showcase, as well as a tool for building community and collaboration. This will be a hybrid conference with both in-person and online events.

The Ann Radcliffe Academic Conference is part of the Horror Writers Association's Outreach Program. Created in 2016 by Michele Brittany and Nicholas Diak, the Ann Radcliffe Academic

Conference has been a venue for horror scholars to present their work alongside professional writers and editors in the publishing industry. The conference has also been the genesis of the Horror Writer Association's first academic release, *Horror Literature from Gothic to Post-Modern: Critical Essays,* composed entirely of Ann Radcliffe Conference presenters, published by McFarland in February 2020.

The conference is now lead by Bridget Keown and Rhonda Jackson Garcia. There is no additional registration or fees for the Ann Radcliffe Academic Conference outside StokerCon registration.

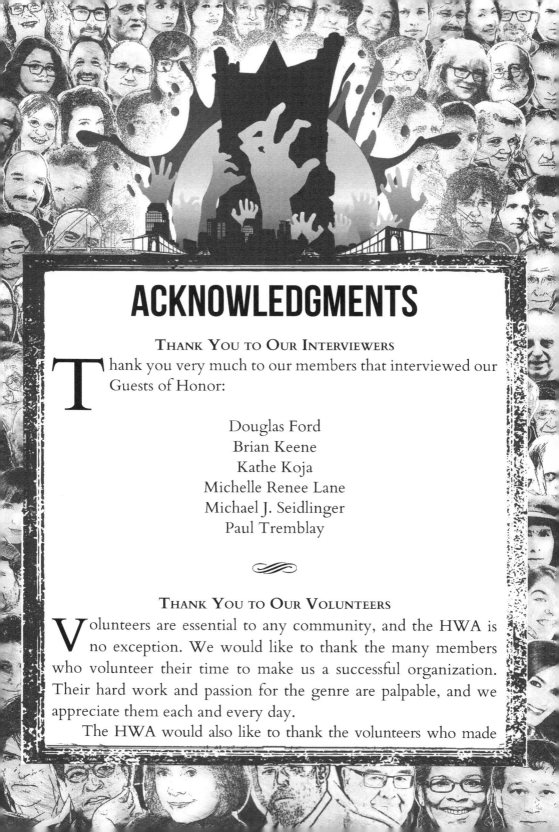

ACKNOWLEDGMENTS

THANK YOU TO OUR INTERVIEWERS

Thank you very much to our members that interviewed our Guests of Honor:

Douglas Ford
Brian Keene
Kathe Koja
Michelle Renee Lane
Michael J. Seidlinger
Paul Tremblay

THANK YOU TO OUR VOLUNTEERS

Volunteers are essential to any community, and the HWA is no exception. We would like to thank the many members who volunteer their time to make us a successful organization. Their hard work and passion for the genre are palpable, and we appreciate them each and every day.

The HWA would also like to thank the volunteers who made

StokerCon® 2023 possible. We appreciate your commitment and dedication to the convention.

Special thank you to StokerCon® 2023 Co-Coordinators, Michael A. Arnzen, Ben Rubin, and Sara Tantlinger. We appreciate all they have done to make StokerCon® 2023 a success.

Thank you to all the people who signed up to volunteer after the printing of this book, as well.

ABOUT THE ILLUSTRATORS

GEMMA AMOR is a Bram Stoker Award® nominated author, voice actor, illustrator, and budding screenwriter based in Bristol, in the UK.

She has published eleven novels, and is the co-creator of horror-comedy podcast *Calling Darkness*, starring Kate Siegel. Her stories have been featured many times on hugely popular horror anthology shows like *The NoSleep Podcast*, *Shadows at the Door*, *Creepy*, and more. She has also been featured in a number of print anthologies. The short Gothic horror film she co-wrote, *Hidden Mother*, is currently showing in festivals. Gemma illustrates her own works, hand-paints book cover artwork, and narrates audiobooks.

LYNNE HANSEN is a horror artist who specializes in book covers. She loves creating art that tells a story and that helps connect publishers, authors and readers. Her art has appeared on the cover of the legendary *Weird Tales Magazine,* and she was selected by Bram Stoker's great-grandnephew to create the cover for the 125th Anniversary Edition of *Dracula.* Her clients include Valancourt Books, Cemetery Dance Publications, Thunderstorm Books and Raw Dog creaming Press. She has illustrated works by *New York Times* bestselling authors including Jonathan Maberry, Brian Keene, and Christopher Golden. Her art has been commissioned and collected throughout the United States and overseas. For more information, visit LynneHansenArt.com.

CHAD LUTZKE lives in Battle Creek, MI. with his wife and children. For over two decades, he has been a contributor to several different outlets in the independent music and film scene, offering articles, reviews, and artwork. He's had several dozen short stories published and is known for his heartfelt approach to the dark side of humanity with books such as *Of Foster Homes & Flies, Wallflower, Stirring The Sheets, Skullface Boy, The Pale White, Three-Smile Mile,*

and *The Neon Owl*. Lutzke's work has been praised by Jack Ketchum, Richard Chizmar, Joe R. Lansdale, Stephen Graham Jones, and his own mother.

RYAN MILLS is an illustrator, cover designer, and avid reader of horror, including the collection *Burn the Plans* by Tyler Jones, and the *My Dark Library* novella series curated by Sadie Hartmann and Cemetery Gates Media. You can see more at ryanmills.art.

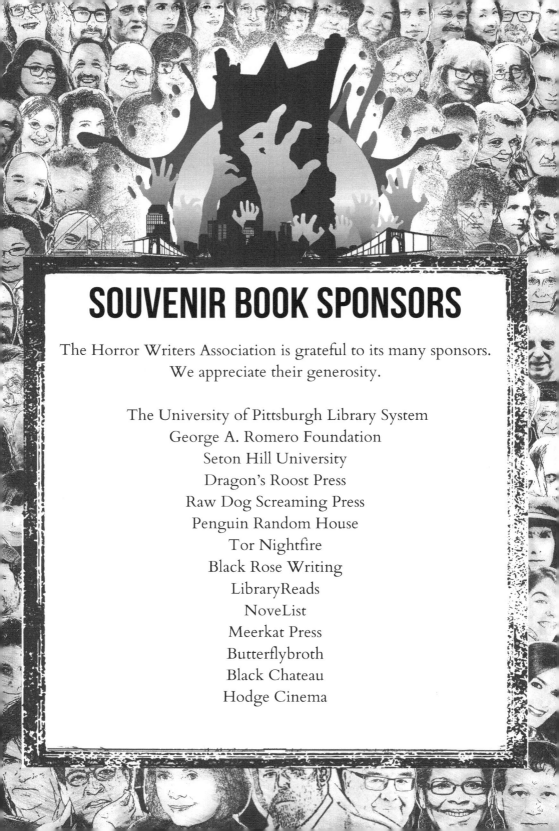

SOUVENIR BOOK SPONSORS

The Horror Writers Association is grateful to its many sponsors.
We appreciate their generosity.

The University of Pittsburgh Library System
George A. Romero Foundation
Seton Hill University
Dragon's Roost Press
Raw Dog Screaming Press
Penguin Random House
Tor Nightfire
Black Rose Writing
LibraryReads
NoveList
Meerkat Press
Butterflybroth
Black Chateau
Hodge Cinema

CONGRATULATIONS
TO OUR NOMINEES

KATE ALICE MARSHALL

Finalist for Superior Achievement in a Young Adult Novel for *These Fleeting Shadows*

ALMA KATSU

Guest of Honor and Finalist for Superior Achievement in a Novel for *The Fervor*

ISABEL CAÑAS

Finalist for Superior Achievement in a First Novel for *The Hacienda*

PUTNAM

Dragon's Roost Press

Bringing You the Best
Dark Speculative Fiction,
Poetry, and
Horror Related Analysis

NIGHTFIRE
CONGRATULATES OUR 2022
BRAM STOKER AWARD® FINALISTS!

CATRIONA WARD
Superior Achievement in a Novel

Photo credit: Robert Holdsworth

KC JONES
Superior Achievement in a First Novel

Photo courtesy of the author

ELLEN DATLOW
Superior Achievement in an Anthology

Photo credit: Gregory Frost

And a Special Thanks to
StokerCon 2023 Guest of Honor
DANIEL KRAUS

Photo credit: Suzanne Plunkett

 @tornightfire   @tornightfire tornightfire.com

Public Library Staff:

Interested in FREE advance copies of
top adult titles for pre-pub promotion?
Want to help library staff across the
country create the monthly Top Ten list
of recommended adult reads?

LibraryReads is a monthly "staff picks"
list for adult titles. Our goal is to
connect readers to books, drawing
upon the power that library staff have
in building word-of-mouth for new
books and a variety of authors.

Learn more about us at:
www.LibraryReads.org

RAW DOG SCREAMING PRESS

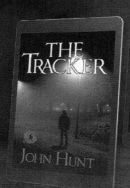

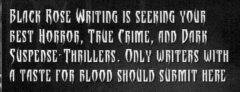

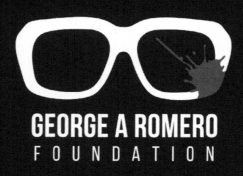

GEORGE A ROMERO
F O U N D A T I O N

The University of Pittsburgh Library System, home of the Horror Studies Collection, is proud to support StokerCon!

University of Pittsburgh | Library System

HORROR STUDIES

library.pitt.edu

SIGNATURES

SIGNATURES

SIGNATURES

SIGNATURES

SIGNATURES

SIGNATURES